THE DOCTOR OF THE GREAT NORTH WOODS

Sawyer Hall

For Dr. B, who gave me a chance

ONE

My residency began with Eleanor Hodges, a ninety-two-year-old spitfire who cooked her own bratwurst and dominated the pinochle club.

It ended with my father, dead at sixty-two.

The overhead page came as I was finishing lunch in the hospital cafeteria: *Aubrey Lane, please call 4588...Aubrey Lane, please call 4588...*

Just minutes earlier, I'd turned in my pager—along with my ID badge, scrubs, and prescription pad. My co-resident plucked an M&M off my tray and joked, "Guess they decided not to parole you after all."

I took the call from the cafeteria phone, dubiously placed between the trash cans and soda machines. The operator delivered her standard line. "Dr. Lane, go ahead please."

"Hello?"

Static blared in my ear. After ten seconds of meaningless noise, a burst of clarity delivered two words. The first was "father." The second was "dead."

"Hello." I pressed the phone against my skull. "Hello? I can't hear you—"

The line cut out.

I dialed the operator—once, twice, five times. As she tried to restore the connection, I scanned the sea of zombie-like faces in front of me, all scarred by whatever illness or tragedy had brought them here. Despite my many hours in this cafeteria, I had never appreciated its collective consciousness. I had seen it only as a place to satisfy a basic need, and the food was so terrible that it barely accomplished that.

I focused on one face: a little girl, maybe four-years-old, with blond pigtails and pink ribbons, flanked by a woman who could only be her mother. They sat together at a table that had no real room for them, their trays angled vertically and chairs pushed together so they would fit. The girl never met my gaze, but her mother did. Her eyes seemed to say, *Now you know.*

While people swarmed my exposed little corner, I listened to the dial tone until it turned, finally, to silence. For years, I'd raced to answer all kinds of pages—some important, most not—and abandoned hot lunches and much-needed breaks to get the job done. Now, there was nowhere to get to; no task to complete before the nurse paged me again. There was nothing to do but sit and stare and wish it all away.

I was one of them now.

***

I went out to the ambulance bay to make a call on my cell phone. A rare California rain had sent the paramedics inside, along with everyone else who retreated here for a break from the crazy. When the sound of sirens finally died down, I called my father's office number in the Great North Woods of Maine, realizing on the third ring that he would never answer again.

My mother might pick up at the house, but we hadn't spoken in five years, and I couldn't bring myself to dial the number. After all, *she* hadn't called *me.* That task had fallen to Jim Ranson, the town sheriff, whose voice I still recognized even though it had been over a decade since we'd exchanged a single word.

So I dialed his number, my childhood version of 9-1-1. Like his voice—and so much else about my hometown, I hadn't forgotten it.

Jim Ranson picked up before the first ring ended. "Aubrey?" The connection was poor, the voice distant. "Aubrey, that you?"

"It's me," I said.

"Thank God. Jim Ranson here. I'm not sure how much you heard, the connection was a goddamn horror—"

"My father died." I let those words—those awful, familiar words—earn their place in the silence. "Is that it?"

"Yes." With an appropriately somber pause, he added, "I'm sorry, Aubrey."

"Where's my mother?"

"Oh, she's here. Just, you know, pretty upset."

Bullshit. My mother hadn't shed a tear since 9/11. "How did he die?"

"It, ah, looks like a heart attack."

I couldn't say what I was hoping to hear: freak accident? Stroke? I supposed heart attack was as tragic and wrong and deadly as any. In the end, none of us really had a choice.

"You're sure?"

"Yep."

"When?" I asked.

"This morning. He was in with a patient."

"Who was the patient?"

Another pause. Admittedly, this question broke the most basic of confidentiality laws, but Jim Ranson didn't play by the rules. As sheriff of Callihax, Maine, population 431, he didn't have to. I was surprised he hadn't come right out and told me.

"I think it might be best if we, ah, talk in person."

Across the street, a city bus lurched to a noisy stop. Harried people piled off; others climbed on. Los Angeles was not for everyone, but I loved it. This city had so much *life*, its oversized heart beating in tune with the millions who called it home. Callihax, in contrast, was a ghost—black, dead, inert. The Great North Woods was its corpse.

"Aubrey?"

I watched the last little girl climb on while her mother fumbled with a stroller. The bus driver helped them on despite rain, and wind, and the blistering impatience of two-dozen passengers anxious to get on with it.

"Aubrey? You there?"

"I, um…I need to make travel arrangements."

"Sooner is better. If you fly into Clayton Lake—"

"I know."

"Right. Well, if you need anything, just give a holler."

"Just tell my mother I'm on my way, would you, please?"

"Of course. And Aubrey, I'm so damn sorry about your father."

He wasn't sorry—not as people said they were, nor as the grieving wanted them to be. I knew. I knew because I had uttered those same words to someone else hours ago; had uttered them for years. *I'm sorry about your mother. Your grandfather. Your son.*

For a resident, it inevitably become routine. Part of the work-day. A check-box on a list of tasks that had to get done, no matter how personal or tragic.

Now you know.

***

My destination was a spit of civilization near the Maine-Canadian border, some 170 crooked miles northwest of Bangor. Nestled in twelve million acres of forest known as the North Woods, Callihax wasn't exactly accessible. Desolation was the rule, the kind of place where "middle of nowhere" earned its name. June meant the spring rains had ended and the snowmelt had all but run its course, but still, the journey was never easy.

At the airport in Bangor, I settled on the last all-terrain vehicle in the lot: a black Land Rover, which would fuel the fire of my "city lifestyle," but better that than a breakdown. The terrain in northern Maine could be ruthless: mountains, lakes, rivers, all obscured by a disorienting sylvanian sameness. Even in summer, temperatures could dip below freezing when the sun went down. And forget cell phones—there was no service in the woods. No park rangers or adventuresome tourists, either. On these forest roads, you were on your own.

An hour outside of Bangor, the signs of suburbia began to fade. Exxon and Sunoco stations became single-pump affairs with a garage out back. Chain restaurants become diners. The Holiday and Comfort Inns disappeared, and roadside motels took their place.

Then came the perverse sense of abandonment: rusted signs and toppled garbage cans. Mailboxes with chipped paint, no numbers. Side roads that deteriorated into gravel, then dirt, then shadows. I passed campsites with weeded parking lots and hotels with punched-out windows. And woods. Millions upon millions of woods. There was something terrifyingly claustrophobic about all those woods.

At dusk, I stopped at the Tree Pine Inn, a landmark of sorts that had achieved almost cosmic significance over the years. Six rooms in total, all of which I'd stayed in at one time or another. Each had a double bed, a desk, a massive crucifix on the wall, and a seventies-style bathroom. Despite the décor, it was better than the alternative. I never drove the final stretch at night; in fact, I rarely drove anywhere in these parts after dark.

The timeless Mr. Sanderson, who emerged from the back room with impressive enthusiasm, must have been ninety by now. No sons. No real employees that I could see, though there used to be, when families took their RV's through the wilderness.

"Ah, Aubrey. Welcome back." He glanced at my bare ring finger. "Room for one, I presume?"

"Yes, thank you."

"How about Room 4? A lovely view of the river this time of year."

"I think 1 would be fine." Room 1 was next to the office—the well-lit, always-open office, above which Mr. Sanderson slept.

"Of course," he said. "Need any assistance with your luggage?"

"Oh, no, I can manage." I paid my forty dollars and he handed me the room key, which must have been fashioned in 1948. A tiny "1" had been carved into the brass.

"Enjoy your stay."

"Thank you."

My luggage was a tiny carry-on, appropriately sized for an overnight trip. Light, too. I hoped that by the time my clean underwear ran out, I could go home.

Home. As in Los Angeles. As in my apartment, and my career, and my life. I hadn't told anyone I was even leaving town. That way it felt insignificant, a blip in the routine. My residency graduation was more or less a fancy dinner—nothing like the cap-and-gown affairs of my youth. The truth was, no one would miss me until two weeks from now, when my new employer expected me on the job. Two weeks to bury my father and make peace with my mother and return home without lasting psychological damage.

Once inside, I closed the blinds and lay on the floral-print bedspread. The stuffy air smelled like broken-in shoes and other people's clothes; like time gone by. I wondered who had stayed here last. A family? Me, some fifteen years ago?

I lay awake for at least an hour, sorting through memories like a deck of cards. Some were fresher than others; crisper. Certain images had faded altogether, leaving nothing but a faint thread of remembrance. The smell of my mother's strawberry Chapstick. My dad's easy, contagious laugh. Their special way with each other, the kind of love story that would never have sold movies, or novels, or even a Hallmark card, but it worked.

When the sun finally set, it happened all at once, brash and unforgiving. I turned on all the lights to fend off a chill.

Sleep came eventually, and then the dreams. Black nights. Blood red dawns. The wretched howl of unseen beasts. A forest with no end; a town with no roads. Yes, it was true: I was afraid of this place. Afraid of where I came from.

At dawn, I packed up my things and ventured deeper into the woods—toward Callihax; toward the soul of the Great North Woods.

Toward nowhere.

TWO

Thursday dawned misty and cold. At check-out, Mr. Sanderson warned me about the conditions of the roads: pot-holed and crumbling in places. Visibility would be poor. Beware wrong turns. Exactly the way they'd always been, essentially. "Take your good ole time," he'd said. No suggestion to stay another night, though. No, he would judge me for that.

I turned on the fog lights and drove north on County Route 27. In some places, the road slanted toward a deep ravine that sheltered the river; in others, it wound through valleys and over hills. Moosehead Lake marked the halfway point, at least in my mind. Another three hours on a clear day; five or six today. The fog had that thick, settled quality that made it durable.

I stopped on the north end of the lake to check my bearings. No GPS signal, of course—that had vanished hours ago. The map I'd purchased in Bangor hardly made up for it because every season changed the terrain. If a mudslide or flood or other such natural disaster wiped out the main road, there would be no detour signs. No alternate routes. Definitely no short-cuts.

After another sixty miles, I ditched the map and relied on memory to take me the rest of the way. Landmarks helped. There was Rogerson's Gas, a single-pump station about fifty miles short of my destination that sold candies from the 1950's. I stopped and said hello to the missus, which meant Mr. Rogerson had probably died. No way he'd miss work on a Thursday for any other reason.

Mrs. Rogerson greeted me with a warm smile. "I haven't seen you in quite some time, honey. What's it been, two years?"

"Twelve."

"Oh my goodness. Well, the years go by a lot faster when

you're my age." She counted my dollar bills and made the correct change. Rogerson's Gas had always been a mental math establishment.

"You look the same," I said, which was true. Same snow-white hair and grey-blue eyes. Same red reading glasses that hung around her neck like a prized piece of jewelry.

"As do you, sweetheart. You look just like your mother."

Even though this was one of those things people said to make conversation, in my case, it was precisely true. Physically, at least. When I looked in the mirror, I saw my mother's face—but I didn't see *her*. This would take hours of psychobabble to explain, so I never bothered.

"Thank you," I said.

"How is your mother, by the way?"

"Oh, the same." I peeled off a dollar bill and purchased a bottle of Coke. Glass, not plastic. I wondered how in the world they stocked fresh soda in glass bottles.

"I know this has been a tough year for them both," she said.

I hadn't heard a word about a "tough year"—not from my father, anyway. We talked once a week over the phone, but he glazed over his day-to-day life. *Oh, you know how it is. Busy as always. Keeps me on my toes.* That was the extent of what he shared. Sure, his voice sounded strained at times, but he was responsible for 432 souls in Callihax. Strain was the norm.

"I'm not sure what you mean," I said.

Everyone out in these parts took pride in playing down their emotions—or, in more severe cases, banishing them entirely—but Mrs. Rogerson made no effort to hide her surprise. She closed up the register and said, "You didn't hear?"

"No," I said.

"Well, it's been almost a year—how the time goes. Last July we had a real honest-to-goodness epidemic in Callihax. Four little boys died."

In a town with only 400-some people? The horror of such a catastrophic loss had the effect of a battering ram. "How?" I asked.

"I don't really know. Some kind of flu, although the news always gets filtered by the time it reaches me." Her sigh almost blew me over. "Just a sad thing. A real sad thing."

As the town doctor, my father would have seen those boys. Treated them. Made the diagnosis. He would have done this all himself, at least until Med-Evac flew them out. *And he hadn't thought to mention it to his medically-trained daughter?*

"Anyway, I didn't mean to upset you," she said. "Those folks are resilient. Been a long winter, but you know how it goes. How is your father, by the way?"

"He passed away three days ago," I said.

Her face paled. "Oh heavens above. I'm so sorry—"

"Anyway, I really should get going." I made a show of glancing at my watch, which had broken weeks before. "So nice seeing you. Take care."

"Safe travels," she mumbled.

I should have been gentler. Kinder. My reluctance to talk about my father with Mrs. Rogerson—with anyone, really—had surprised no one more than me. I remembered the hospital chaplain saying to patients, "We all grieve in different ways," and even though it was true, achingly true, I liked to think those hours and months and years of loss would somehow pass me over. I was glad I'd left the hospital before he had the chance to say the same to me.

With my mind so thoroughly preoccupied, I made my first wrong turn about ten miles past Rogerson's. I realized my mistake fairly quickly: the road narrowed, then disappeared altogether in a grove of aspen trees. Thick, warped branches leaned over the hood, obscuring the view of total nothingness that lay ahead. I put the Rover into reverse, rear-ended a tree, and tried again. The tires spun in the mud. I tried the four-wheel-drive, first-gear, first-gear-amped-up-or-whatever-that-button-meant, and every other feature at my fingertips. The tires kept spinning. Overhead, a lone vulture circled the sky. I hated those birds, with their fat necks and soulless eyes.

With both feet on the accelerator, I rocketed out of the ditch.

The front fender rammed into yet another tree, but I didn't care. I spun the steering wheel and shifted into gear and found the road somewhere behind me.

As the Rover settled into its lumbering rhythm, I turned on the radio and listened to static to calm my nerves. The noise helped; always had. I kept my eyes on the road rather than the forest on all sides, which helped to narrow my focus. After a while, the fog thinned and a weak, scattering sunlight filled the void between the trees.

A mile more, and the road diverged. Years ago, there had been a sign indicating the way toward Callihax, but no more. As my father used to say, *these folks don't want to be found.*

And they weren't, unless you knew the way.

Despite my every attempt to unlearn certain things, I still knew the way.

***

The town of Callihax was one of three established settlements in the entire Great North Woods of Maine. One of the three didn't have a name, and the other had lost its main road to a flood, which meant you could only get there by foot or horse. That left Callihax as the real foothold of civilization in the region. There was a post office, a grocery store, a diner, a pub, a dance studio, a chapel (next to the pub), and a single-pump gas station. Dr. Milnes was the dentist and my father the doctor. A red-bricked school with a baseball field and a gravel track occupied the prize plot by the river. On first glance, one might call the town of Callihax homey, or even quaint. But there were no WELCOME TOURISTS signs in the windows.

Unfortunately for me, discretion was a lost cause in a goddamn Land Rover. The tinted windows might protect the guilty, but my God. *Tinted windows.* I would never live this down.

The kids noticed me first: four of them outside Murphy's Soda Fountain, pointing and shouting as I drove past. *Citsby! Citsby!* Short for *city bitch*, "citsby" fit me and my Land Rover to a tee.

Back home, I drove a used Toyota, but no one here knew that.

The grizzled men loitering outside the pub gave me a similar welcome. All four glared at me from under their worn baseball caps, the challenge obvious: *Go back where you came from.*

I was trying to remember their names when a grey blur darted into the street in front of me. *Brakebrakebrake.* I wrenched the wheel hard to the right. The Rover had a lot of mass behind it, a ton of momentum, and it lurched into a pole in a cloud of dust. The stench of rubber—or maybe it was charred flesh, *Jesus*—came through the vents. I put my hands on the dash and waited for the terrible whine of an injured animal.

Nothing happened. Barely daring to breathe, I turned the key in the ignition. The wheezing engine purred, then went quiet. *Had I hit it? Was it dead?*

"Are you okay?" A hard rap on the window made me jump. "Hello?"

Before I could answer, the door swung open and the smell of Callihax—pine and lilac and pure, elemental air—swept over me.

"Aubrey?"

I remembered him then—his voice, his face, his everything— as if no time had passed, as if we were still seventeen, sitting in the circular booth at Murphy's, sipping ice cream sodas and holding hands under the table and saying things like, *I love your laugh because it makes you blush and then I want to kiss you.*

"Luke," I said, and all those memories came and went in the span of a single breath.

Like me, he bumbled his first attempt to speak. "Are you okay?"

"Yeah, I just...I'm so sorry."

"*You're* sorry? Mazie's a terror. I'll pay for the damage to your car—"

"It's not my car."

"It's not?"

"Just a rental."

"Ah."

I looked past him toward the chapel. "Is your dog...is he...?"

"Oh, she's fine." He called her name, and a few seconds later Mazie-the-very-bad-dog emerged from the woods with her tail between her legs.

"Silly girl," he muttered, but he seemed incapable of any additional discipline. She licked his hand as if it were covered in bacon.

I rubbed the contrite dog's ears while Luke watched. He was probably wondering why I'd developed such issues with human eye contact over the years. Trauma? Personality change? *Actually, it's just you.*

"Anyway, it was nice seeing you," I said, which sounded like the lie it was. "I'm only in town for a few days, so..."

"I know," he said, with sudden seriousness. "I'm sorry about your dad."

"Thanks."

I tried for a quick exit, but the car wouldn't start. Luke and his naughty dog watched me flood the engine twice. I got out of the car and popped the hood—or at least tried to. The damage to the frame had locked it in place.

"I could give you a ride up the hill," he said. "My house is right down that way...you probably remember..."

"No, that's all right," I said.

He still lived with his parents? No wedding band on his finger, which meant no wife and probably no children. I had to admit, I'd expected more from someone as charismatic and attractive as Luke Ainsley. Maybe he was divorced. Or sterile. He certainly hadn't shown any signs of sexual issues while *I'd* known him...

"Can you at least let me know how much I owe you? Joe Reed could fix it while you're in town—"

"I'll let you know." I gave up on the hood and walked around to the trunk. "Anyway, thanks."

"You keep saying that when I'm the one that caused all the trouble."

"It's not your fault." I wished he would go. If he saw my suitcase, he would insist on carrying it because the wheels were broken and it was a long way uphill. That, and because he was "raised right," as my mother would say.

"Here, let me help." *So much for not seeing my suitcase.* His shirt rode up a bit as he lifted the suitcase out of the trunk. In a desperate effort to look elsewhere, I settled on his face; his silver-grey eyes, like a pair of marine moons. He had aged, yes, but he still looked seventeen—because weren't we all still seventeen, somewhere, a teenager scrambling for value and truth and love in a body that was supposed to know better? *Twelve years.* I had never rued the passage of time more than I did in that moment.

"Traveling light," he said.

"Yep."

His gaze lingered on my face. It didn't roam; didn't wander. I wished he were more like those sketchy L.A. dudes that scoured my figure at each and every opportunity, sometimes in plain sight. Luke did no such thing. He would not look at me that way unless I invited him to look at me that way. And *that* would most certainly not be happening.

Mazie started to whine, which broke the stare. Luke ruffled the thick fur behind her ears and under her neck, and I remembered the dog he had in middle school, Caesar, who disappeared in the spring floods. Luke and I barely knew each other at the time—he was a year ahead of me in school, which put us worlds apart—but I'd never forget the way he had searched for that dog. He must have hiked hundreds of miles that spring.

"Anyway," I said. "I should really go—"

"It'll be dark in an hour, though. Hard to see at dusk." *So he remembered my fear of the woods at night*—or maybe it showed on my face.

"I can't just leave the car here."

"Sure you can." He registered my hesitation and said, "Trust me. It's not a problem."

The truth was, he had me at *it'll be dark in an hour.* "I guess a ride would be fine."

He smiled—a boyish, open smile that made me feel a little guilty for arguing with him. He hoisted my suitcase out of the trunk and set it on his right shoulder as if he were carrying a log. No surprise there. He had learned from his father, who had learned from the lean, indomitable men that came before him.

Although Luke lived on the south end of town, which should have meant a miserable walk down Main Street, he took me instead through the churchyard and behind the brick buildings lining the western side of the street. No one seemed to notice us, and even if they did, Luke functioned as a kind of shield; a temporary immunity against the masses.

He waited until we had left the downtown area before attempting conversation. "How was your trip?" he asked.

"Long."

"I bet. How's LA?"

"Who told you I live in LA?"

He laughed. "Aubrey, everyone in town knows where you live. Hell, most people know what *street* you live on. Don't be surprised if someone starts asking you about the lattes at Intelligentsia."

"How did you…"

"Your dad tells us everything about your life out there." He tried to catch my gaze, but I looked away. "He was so proud of you."

"Well, maybe he shared too much."

"Nah. He only talked about certain things."

"Like what things?"

"Like your job. The hospital. Your neighborhood. The city. Restaurants you liked to go to. General things."

"As opposed to personal things?"

"I wasn't fishing for information, if that's what you mean."

There was no graceful way to respond to that, so I changed the subject. "How's your family?"

"Good."

I waited, but he didn't elaborate.

"Cold winter?" I asked, taking the hint.

"One of the worst we've ever had. Snowy, too."

"It's pretty warm today."

"This is the nicest day we've had since last year." As we came to the bottom of the hill, he turned down a driveway that led, seemingly, toward nothing. "Maybe you brought a bit of California with you."

The conversation stalled there, as it always did when two people—now essentially strangers—started talking about the weather. We walked on in silence, our journey ending at a quaint colonial that had belonged to the Ainsley family for generations. I braced myself for the invitation to stay a while, but it never came.

"Here we are," he said, and pointed toward his car, a Subaru with Maine plates and a Boston, MA decal. *Boston?* I couldn't picture Luke in such a dirty, crowded, noisy place; to be honest, I couldn't picture him anywhere but here.

"You lived in Boston?" I asked.

"Eh, just for a little while."

"Why?"

"Long story," he said, which told me he didn't want to talk about it. Fair enough.

Mazie clamored into the backseat while I rode shotgun. The interior smelled strangely pleasant: rugged and fresh and outdoorsy—or maybe it was just him. Luke had always smelled delicious as a teenager, which set him apart from the boys in his class that never showered and wore their salty stink as a badge of pride.

"Do you remember how to get there?" I asked, regretting the question instantly. Of course he remembered. In a town this size, a toddler would remember.

"I think I can manage," he said, sparing me the obvious retort.

Two-point-two-four miles from his driveway to mine. Six minutes driving and thirty-eight on foot. Each of these numbers had long since ceased to matter, and yet I remembered them. In the last eight years, I'd studied for three board exams and two licensing exams. I'd learned how to prescribe medications without killing people. I'd convinced random strangers to trust me with their lives. *How in the world had I remembered 2.24, 6, and 38?*

The drive still took six minutes. We didn't speak, though Mazie provided plenty of background noise with her enthusiastic panting and the occasional bark. Luke told her to sit, and she sat. He told her to stop barking, and she stopped. He asked her to shake my hand, and she held out a paw and did so.

"I thought you said she was a terror."

"She is," he said. "A well-trained terror."

"But she ran out into the street."

"Well, she has one weakness."

"Which is…"

"I, ah…you know, it's just a theory. I'd hate to throw her under the bus with a false claim."

"I won't hold it against her."

"How about me?"

I shrugged.

Luke had a habit of studying his knuckles when he didn't want to answer something. *Are you taking Sara Siles to prom? How did your mom die? When did you realize we were over?* He glanced at them now, but the challenge of driving these roads meant he didn't linger long.

"She gets a little crazy around outsiders."

"Crazy enough to get herself killed?"

Mazie barked once, which made me wonder if she understood English.

"She wouldn't have gotten hit no matter how you reacted."

"Did you not see what happened? She ran out in front of me!"

"You didn't hit her."

"Because I swerved."

He abandoned the knuckle-study and put his hands on the wheel. "Look, I'm really, truly sorry. If anything had happened to you—"

"Then I'm sure you would have paid for my hospital bills, too."

Mazie fell quiet, as if stricken by the insult. Luke looked wounded, too, but what did he expect? Thanks to him, my worst fears had been confirmed. *You're an outsider now. Even the dog knows it.*

"I'm up here on the left." I didn't care that he knew the way. He needed to remember that my childhood in that house counted for something.

He parked the car a hundred yards short of the front door and helped me with my suitcase. I practically wrenched it out of his hands before he could take it any further.

"Thanks for the ride," I said.

"Anytime."

There won't be another time, I thought, but stayed silent to keep the peace. Mazie barked as I trudged the final distance up the hill. Luke told her to shush, and she shushed, but the people of Callihax would not be so easily tamed.

In the town down below, the vultures were gathering.

THREE

My childhood home had occupied the summit of Lews Hill for 150 years. My grandfather built it in the years after the Civil War, a self-professed patriot who saw the North Woods as a peaceful escape. The house reflected his mood at the time: dark hallways and cavernous rooms, with tall windows that afforded sunlight on only the brightest days. My mother had added a sunroom when she moved in, which had eased the house's generations-long depression. She sat up there now, watching me as I made my way to the front stoop.

I waited a small eternity for her to open the door. In those tense, drawn-out seconds, I ran a hand through my hair and rubbed a toothpaste stain off my pants and cursed myself for wearing such impractical shoes. She would have expected more.

Finally, the door lurched open. The hinges groaned as they always did, a warning of sorts. Nothing about this house had ever said *welcome.*

"Hello, Aubrey," she said, with as much warmth as she could muster.

"Hi, Mom."

She studied me while I did the same. There was no denying I had inherited her features, which were so strong as to completely subsume whatever I might have inherited from my father. Red-blonde hair on sun-washed, lightly freckled skin, with honey-colored eyes that radiated a shallow warmth. There were no crow's feet around her eyes, which should have been the first clue that smiles came rarely; laughter almost never.

We didn't embrace. Hugs had gone out of fashion in the Lane household sometime in the late-nineties. Instead, she patted my arm and took my suitcase from my hand.

"Mom, I got it—"

She left me on the landing while she carted my suitcase upstairs. I could see that the house hadn't changed much in the last decade: the walls were still sparsely decorated, blandly painted. Photographs were scarce, but those that did make it to the wall or onto a shelf *meant* something. And not just those of my major life events—graduations, in particular—but landscapes, too. My mother's garden in full bloom, dusted with snow. A shadowy path to the river, first blazed by my great-grandfather. The willow tree behind St. Rita's where my father proposed. I had no such photographs in my own apartment; not even a postcard.

"You must be hungry," my mother said.

I hoped my fascination with my own home didn't show on my face. "I'm all right."

She escorted me into the kitchen anyway, where a tidy meal of spaghetti and meatballs awaited us. My favorite, and therefore strangely sentimental. I decided not to comment on it.

"Have a seat," she said.

There were only three chairs around the kitchen table—the fourth had been removed decades ago when my older brother, just two at the time, died unexpectedly. My father's chair was empty, and I wondered how long it would be before my mother removed that one, too.

I took my proper place at the table and helped myself to a clump of spaghetti. "Clump" was perhaps the kindest way to describe her presentation. The pasta itself tasted like butter and carbs and salt—my mother loved salt. She didn't even bother with salt-and-pepper shakers. She poured it right out of the tin.

"Did you stay at the Sanderson place last night?" she asked.

I nodded.

"How is he?"

"Good. The same."

"And the Rogersons down by Moosehead?"

"Mr. Rogerson wasn't there."

"Oh, yes. Well, he died ages ago."

"He was alive when I left."

She coiled a single strand of spaghetti. "Like I said, ages ago."

This response packed the same punch it always had, even after years of silence. As my mother refused to forget, I was the first in a long line of Riennes to leave this place. My betrayal used to be her favorite topic of conversation before we stopped talking altogether.

"Fair enough." She sipped her water. "Still like Los Angeles?"

"Yep."

"You finished your residency?"

"Two days ago."

"Congratulations."

"Thanks." I reached for the glass of milk she had set out for me. Thick and full-bodied, probably milked from a cow that morning. I thought about my gallons of skim in the fridge and shuddered.

"Your father told me you have a job lined up." Her voice caught on the word "father," but she used her ice water to swallow it down.

"Starts in two weeks," I said.

"That's wonderful."

I chewed with a deliberate slowness, avoiding her gaze. If my father had been sitting here, he would have cut the tension with a joke, and it would have worked, because it always did. Maybe I needed to take *his* chair away.

"Why didn't you call me?" I asked.

"Aubrey—"

"Might have been nice, you know, to hear about Dad from you instead of Jim Ranson."

She put her utensils down and folded her hands. Much to my surprise, her eyes betrayed a rare, but very real sadness.

"I'm sorry for that," she said. "I wasn't sure how to tell you."

"'Your father's dead' would have worked."

She sighed, which for her was never dramatic so much as anti-climactic. "To be honest, Jim Ranson was more than happy to play the villain, whereas I knew you'd blame me if I told you to come home."

"Blame you for what?"

She heaped a second pile of spaghetti on my plate. As she did so, the briny taste in my mouth turned dry.

"For the inevitable."

***

The inevitable arrived the next morning with a stiff knock on the front door.

Jim Ranson, in all his white-haired, cowboy hat, jeans-and-boots glory, greeted me like a prodigal daughter. "Ah, the illustrious Aubrey Lane!" he bellowed, and in the same breath, "Again, my condolences."

He peeked over my shoulder, no doubt searching for my mother. I blocked his path, though he didn't seem to notice my deliberate maneuverings. "Where's your lovely mother?"

"Out," I said.

"Ah, well that's a pity."

I closed the door and stepped out into the porch. "What can I help you with, Sheriff?"

"Well, you see..." He scratched his head until fat flakes of dandruff settled on his shoulders. "I'm in a bit of a bind, if you hear what I'm saying."

"I don't, actually."

"I want you to know I respect your grief and all that, but the good folks of this town have needs. Pressing needs." He hooked his fingers around his belt loops and said, with all the gravitas his position afforded him, "Medical needs."

I hadn't expected this conversation to come so soon. I wasn't ready; I would never *be* ready. I hated Jim Ranson and his shiny gold star and his false sympathy. Couldn't he see my crossed arms and cold stare? Couldn't he *feel* the ire rolling off me? How dare he come here and demand my services on the eve of my father's funeral. How dare he even ask.

"Sheriff, excuse me for saying so, but your timing is egregious

—"

"Call me Jim. You're all grown up now, after all."

I would never be calling him Jim. "I can't take my father's place."

He laughed, all red-faced and jolly. "Oh, I know that. We *all* know that. Your father was an icon. A hero! No way in hell could anyone take his place, especially you! Just a little baby doctor, you are."

The insult didn't faze me as much as his brazen confidence did. I sucked it up and said, "So you understand then."

"I just need somebody to ease the fears of these folks for a little while. See some patients, listen to some hearts, hand out some painkillers. Whatever it is you doctors do, I just need you to do that for the next few months or so."

"Do what, exactly?"

"You know, fill in."

"Sheriff, it's not that easy. I'd need a license to practice in Maine, for one thing."

"A license!" He chuckled at this. "All you need out here's your pretty head and a thick skin. Trust me on that one, honey."

Honey. I wanted to slap him. "I won't practice without a license."

"Actually, I already filled out the paperwork." He crooked his arm behind his back and pulled out a stack of papers, rolled up like a thick newspaper. "This here's for an emergency license. Expedited processing 'cause this is an underserved area."

It appeared Jim Ranson had actually done some homework— this was new. Talk about desperate measures. "Here, take a look," he said. "All's you gotta do is sign."

As I paged through the application, the death of my future career took shape in my mind. Not in a blaze of litigation, as every doctor feared, but with a signature. He had even marked the place for me to sign.

"Look, the license is moot," I said. "I'm not taking the job."

"Why not?"

"For one thing, I have a job in LA."

"Jobs in those big cities are a dime a dozen. Not to mention those people got resources comin' our their ears. These folks need you."

I gritted my teeth. "People are people, Sheriff. I don't make distinctions."

"Fair enough. But if you quit your job there, somebody takes your place. You quit here, these folks go without."

"I'm not quitting because I'm not starting."

"Sounds awful selfish if I do say so myself."

"*Selfish?* Sheriff, I've been in school for twelve years. Four of them working nights, weekends, holidays. Eighty-hour weeks on a salary that's barely minimum wage if you compute it hourly. I have three-hundred-thousand dollars in federal loans, which means I *need* this job. I need it to pay off my loans and put something away for retirement and do all the things I should have done ten years ago. I don't have a choice."

"Well, actually..." He reached into his other pocket and produced yet another crumpled stack of papers. "This here's the paperwork for federal loan forgiveness. This being an underserved area and all."

I didn't even look at the papers this time. "Jim, the answer is no."

"Look, I wouldn't be here right now if I didn't need to be, believe me. But this is easy-peasy. I did all the work, all's you gotta do is give me your John Hancock." He leaned in close before delivering the final blow. "What would your dad say, Aubrey? Think about it."

My father would have told Jim Ranson to go to hell. He had always stressed my autonomy, even though it probably killed him to see me leave home for a city 3,000 miles away. My mother was the one who made her thoughts known—if not with words, then with silence. I knew what she would say. *Some things in life aren't all about you.*

"You don't have anyone else?" I asked.

"No," he said. The smile was gone, as were the pretenses of "offering" me the job. We both knew this was a full-on assault.

"But—"

"The folks that live here don't trust just anybody. They need a familiar face; a tie to the community." He spread his arms wide like a king presiding over the land. "And you, my dear, fit the bill."

"I won't do it," I blurted. Jim Ranson could offer me the world on a platter and I would turn it down. There would be no negotiating. No *maybe*, or *I'll think about it*. I had already thought about it; I'd thought about it since the day I started medical school.

"Well, alrighty then." He tossed the papers on the floor at my feet and grunted his good-bye. "Sorry to waste your time, then."

He got into his truck and drove off. My hands had started to shake and my throat had that numb, closed-up feel that always ended in tears. I stumbled back into the house and slammed the door. The walls shook with the force of it.

I wiped my eyes and cleared my throat of the sobs lodged way down deep. Dazed but not yet destroyed, I walked toward the kitchen to face my mother. As a child, I had avoided her during times of discipline, or even just need. As a teenager, I'd slammed doors and called her names and vented my frustration in all kinds of self-destructive ways. Now I was too shell-shocked to do either.

"Here." She nudged a mug of hot chocolate in my direction. This wasn't the only thing she offered me. Jim Ranson's ready-made licensure application and loan-forgiveness forms had somehow been salvaged from the porch steps.

"I'd rather not."

"Please don't tell me you're a coffee drinker now."

"No." I sat heavily in the chair across from her. *My* chair. The empty third one was still there. "I drink lattes to look cool."

"Well, that's disappointing."

I watched her fold her fingers together in that tidy, prayerful way she sometimes did, her mind working in mysterious ways. "Dad knew this would happen," I said. "Didn't he?"

"He intended to find a replacement before he retired."

"I don't believe that."

"Does it matter? He's dead now, and this is the situation we're faced with."

"The situation *we're* faced with? Since when did Jim Ranson ask you to drop *your* life?" I pictured myself hurling the mug through the window that overlooked the garden, even though I knew dramatics wouldn't solve anything. The echoes of Jim Ranson's bidding would follow me across the globe.

"Why should you care what he wants? He's a dirty old man who likes to play Sheriff every once in a while."

"It's not just him, Mom. You know he speaks for the town."

"It's still your choice. Whatever he wants of you, it's your choice."

"I don't want to stay here."

"Then don't."

I went to the window and traced an oily finger down the pane. If I were fourteen, my mother would have set me to work cleaning all the windows in the house. My father would have lifted the punishment after about an hour and said, *Don't tell your mom.*

"And if I go back to LA? What happens then?"

"Life goes on."

"What about us?"

She wiped a few stray crumbs off the table with a cupped hand. "We went the last five years without talking, surely we could go another thirty."

Yes, we surely could. She would never call me every Sunday afternoon like my father did. She would take her daily hike and make her own meals and die in her own bed, alone in a silent, empty world. The angry teenager in me would say she deserved it.

She loves you, my father used to say. *She loves you so much it scares her.*

"I can't stay," I said.

"Then don't. Your father would understand."

And just like that, I was seventeen again, a lost, angry soul with no defense against my mother's psychological mastery. She went upstairs before I could scream or rant or rave, but I wanted to. Good God, I wanted to. It wouldn't change things, of course. After the funeral, I would do what that scared, confused girl had always threatened to do:

I would run away.

FOUR

Word of my father's death reached the farthest reaches of the county. On the day of the funeral, Callihax had its first real traffic jam. People traveled in droves to pay their respects —most in rusted old trucks, some on foot. A few on horses. My mother received them all before making her signature move: as the processional hymn began to play, she turned to me and said, "Would you say a few words about your father? I need some air." I couldn't entirely blame her. The woman had social anxiety that put most hermits to shame.

I hadn't prepared a eulogy, but that was probably for the best; these folks didn't want a stilted performance. And so, before a crowd that extended into St. Rita's courtyard, I talked about my father's humble beginnings and big dreams, the son of a coal miner father and a bread-baking mother in the Ohio River Valley. He had seen workers crushed in the mines, but it wasn't the dead that inspired him. It was the living—the vibrant young men who turned into frail, sickly shadows as the fruits of their labor consumed their lungs.

He moved to the North Woods after residency and made his life here. The people of Callihax became his patients, but they also became his neighbors, his friends, his family. As I spoke, the women dabbed at their tears; the old men hung their heads, hiding the same. They had known my father; they knew how much he cared about them. I hoped my words had done him justice, but I would never know for sure. No one said a word to me after the service.

The luncheon was a spirited, chaotic affair—essentially my mother's worst nightmare. Again she greeted the guests with obligatory politeness, and again she disappeared. Her natural tendency to do so made perfect sense given the Rienne family line and their choice of residence. For not the first time, I admired her gall.

I was planning a similar exit when Mrs. Cobalt—four feet tall, hunched almost to her knees, with a shawl wrapped around her flowy white hair and leather-skinned skull—hobbled up to me. Her cane was nothing more than a stick, warped from however many years of use. My father often told me about his attempts to provide the elderly with walkers and even wheelchairs. Some said no to be polite; the rest whacked him with a cane like hers.

"Hello, Miss Lane," she said to me.

"Mrs. Cobalt." I tried to smile. "Thank you for coming—"

"So you're leavin' on Monday," she said.

I ditched the smile; she wouldn't stand for false courtesies. "Yes," I said. "I am."

"Well, that's a pity."

"Ma'am, I'm sure Jim Ranson will find you a fine replacement —"

"That dope? I don't think so." She shot a nasty glance at Jim that would have been funny if it weren't so sincere. "Listen, honey, I know we're crusty. I know it's been a while since you been up here. And I know you got a life down there in Hollywood, but these folks want you here. They're just too damn proud to say it."

"Mrs. Cobalt, with all due respect, these folks *hate* me."

"Fooey." She swatted the air with her rheumatoid fingers. "That's what they want you to think. Gives 'em the upper hand."

"I'm not negotiating with them. I've already decided—"

"I walked into your father's clinic the week he moved up here. Introduced him to your mother, in case you didn't know."

I didn't know, but my parents had never spoken about their unusual courtship. Such was family life in the North Woods: each generation had its secrets, its own history. Privacy was mostly an illusion, but not within families. A strange dynamic, but one I'd grown accustomed to.

"No," I said.

"Well, I did. Had to. People without roots to a place don't stay in that place for long."

"So you intend to find me a mate? Is that what you're saying?"

She smiled—a crooked, toothless, ancient smile. Warm, though. I didn't know Mrs. Cobalt had it in her. "No, honey. You've already got your roots. That's why *you* should be the doctor of the Great North Woods."

"I appreciate the sentiment—"

"That, and it's been a tough year here. I'm sure you've heard."

The change in topic was so abrupt I nearly missed it. "Not very much," I said.

"Well, let's just say folks got their theories."

"Theories?"

"Your father most of all."

"What do you mean?"

The Jim Ranson crowd was migrating toward us. In another minute, they'd descend on me with their cigar smoke and veiled insults, and Mrs. Cobalt would hobble right out that door. Maybe she'd get a good word in first, but she wouldn't stay.

"Oh, it's a long story. Not worth tellin' if you leave Monday."

"Mrs. Cobalt, please. What did my father tell you?"

"He didn't tell me a damn thing—you should know that. He never talked 'bout his patients. Back when George had the cancer, he wouldn't talk to *me* unless George was right there, tellin' him to go ahead."

"Yes, but you mentioned a theory..."

Jim had located me from across the room. He gave me one of those perfunctory nods, which I ignored. Mrs. Cobalt had noticed him, too.

"I hope he chokes on a cigar," she grunted.

"Mrs. Cobalt—"

"Sheriff said your father died of a heart attack," she said. "That right?"

"I..." Again with the subject change. I took a breath; tried to keep up. "That's what he said over the phone."

"Mm." She patted my arm and leaned in close. The thick scent of Werther's Originals fanned my face as she whispered, "I don't think so, honey."

***

Moments later, Jim Ranson entered our orbit. Mrs. Cobalt commented on his cancer sticks, then his body odor, which she described as "Cuban ash." He wondered aloud how she, in all her worldly wisdom, could possibly know how Cuba smelled. That's when I left.

With the old woman's cryptic words reeling in my mind, I retreated to the sunroom upstairs. This had always been my grandmother's favorite room, even though my mother was the one who put it there. She used to sit on the sill with her reading glasses around her neck, her rosary dangling from her fingertips. "Look at that view!" she'd say, and then she'd pull me onto her lap and whisper in my ear, "Look, sweetheart. See that sky? Those trees? Today is going to be a *great* day." And somehow, it always was.

She was gone now, but I still looked at the sky everyday before work and thought, *Today is going to be a* great *day.* It wasn't, of course. There were dark, hard, terrible days in my residency. Brain deaths and overdoses and terminally-ill children. There were days that started with tragedy; days that ended with a crippling sense of futility and loss. But Gran had taught me the value of seeing each day as a new start, and she had done so here, in this place I'd come to hate, and resist, and fear. I wondered what she would say to me now. *Look, sweetheart. Look how beautiful the world can be.*

And it was. The bay window offered a sprawling view of northern Maine; a rush of sky, trees, and mountains. On a clear day, you could see for a hundred miles. On a spectacular day, you could see Canada. Gran would have relished a day like today.

I opened the window to get some air, only to hear the hushed voices of old family friends. Jim Ranson was among them. A dozen other "public types," as my father used to say. He had resisted their cigars and card games for years.

Jim Ranson was the most vocal: *Oh, she'll come around. No doubt about that.*

She's awful young, though. Aubrey is what, 22?

Nah. Turned twenty-nine last week.

How the hell do you know that?

I do my research.

You sure she even has a medical degree?

Her residency program said so.

I dunno. That girl don't look all that doctorly to me.

I shut the window with a defiant slam. So much for patient confidentiality—the doctor's office was the hub of town gossip. How my father had weathered it for so many years without going mad was perhaps his crowning achievement as a physician.

As I stepped back from the window, the door behind me opened. Not cautiously, but with the full, confident force of someone who did it often. For a wonderful, terrifying moment, I thought it was my father.

Instead, Luke Ainsley walked in the room.

The sunlight made him somehow more real; more *him*. His eyes shone in the afternoon light. "What are you doing up here?" I asked.

"I, uh...I just thought I'd say hello." He made an awkward move for his tie. It already had that casual, loosened look, his top two buttons undone. Luke had never relished the confines of a suit, even though he wore it well. Beautifully, in fact. Better than most of the bankers and lawyers I knew.

"We already said hello," I said.

"True..."

"You were pretty bold coming up here."

"I know," he said. "I'm sorry."

More silence as he waited for me to accept his apology.

"Do you want me to leave?" he asked.

"I don't care what you do." All I really wanted was someone to *talk* to. A friend. A confidante. A neutral presence. Someone who would heartily agree that, *Yes, Jim Ranson's an asshole,* and *Yes, Ellie Fields looks like she cut her hair with garden shears.*

"I was just about to head back downstairs anyway," I said.

He didn't move. I didn't either.

Instead, we watched the crowd two stories beneath us, as the Samson kids trampled my mother's garden, a bunch of grey-haired cronies sipped their brandy, and the old ladies in the Callihax crochet club exchanged their gossip while looking appropriately somber. Father Meade was a bit of a lone ranger over by the fish pond.

"Jim Ranson is a piece of shit," he said.

Had I been thinking out loud? No, Luke just knew me. *Still* knew me. "You think so?"

"I've thought so since he arrested me in sixth grade for kissing Spoons."

Spoons. Red hair. Gap teeth. I couldn't even remember her real name. "You kissed her? You told me you two were never a thing."

"Oh, we were a thing," he said. "A couple of eleven-year-old slobberers."

"No need to be so graphic."

He smiled. "At least I improved."

Oh how he'd improved. "What happened to her?"

"Lives up on Spur Hill. Two kids."

"Who'd she marry?"

"Tom Jenks. They were at the funeral."

"I always liked Tom," I said. "I should have said hello."

"I'm sure you still could." We watched three-year-old Sammy Samson take a spill in the rosebushes. I waited for him to get up. *Please don't be hurt. Please don't need a doctor.*

He got up, but the thorns had left a mishmash of red marks across his face. I saw his mother, Moira Samson—definitely remembered *her* name—dab at the blood with her sleeve. She hadn't changed a lick since high school. Same stark black hair, same glass blue eyes. Wiry and thin and deceptively strong. If it came down to me versus thug or me versus Moira Samson, I'd choose thug.

"How many kids does Moira have?"

"Four," he said. Then: "Three."

"Is it three or four?"

He looked uncomfortable for a moment. "She had four. Her oldest passed away a year ago."

Moira's son was one of the four? She had always seemed impermeable to life's tragedies. Or if not impermeable, then at least resistant to them. I had never seen her cry in the ten years we'd shared a classroom—and before that, a playpen. Our mothers were unlikely friends before Moira's died of breast cancer at thirty-three.

"How?" I asked.

Unlike Mrs. Sanderson, who had rushed to share the ugly details—those she knew, anyway—Luke studied his knuckles until the silence turned awkward. "It's a long story," he said, which seemed to be the standard answer around here—for me, anyway. Privacy and loyalty comprised two sides of the same coin in Callihax, and I had earned neither.

"Is that her youngest?" I asked. The rambunctious little boy spun out of her arms and pitched headlong into the azaleas. This plant was kinder to him.

He nodded. "Sammy. Give that kid a lollipop and he's yours forever."

"All three-year-olds like lollipops."

"Not like Sammy."

"I'll keep that in mind," I said. I hoped I didn't have to.

I asked about a few more people—names, ages, forgotten details—and Luke pointed them out to me. So many names, so much time gone by. Babies were now teenagers. Newlyweds were either happily or miserably married. The old were still old, unless they were dead.

"So," Luke said. "Jim Ranson give you his pitch yet?"

The directness of the question hit me like a physical blow. "What do you mean?"

"He offered you the job, didn't he?"

"How do you know?"

"Because everyone knows."

All I had to do was look at the scene in the yard and know this to be true. The whisperers had turned more vocal. A few were waving their hands and yelling. *We need a real, honest-to-God doctor in this town. We deserve it!* Then someone else would talk about how inappropriate it was to discuss politics at a funeral, and they would quiet down, and it would start again. Everyone had an opinion, but on one thing they agreed: I wasn't their man. Or woman. Or doctor or hero or whoever they imagined me to be. Maybe Mrs. Cobalt was finally losing her touch.

"Sounds like they don't want me anyway," I said.

"Trust me, they want a city snob even less."

"City snob?"

"Sorry," he mumbled. "I didn't mean you..."

"Well, I'm not a city snob. I'm a citsby."

He laughed, which made my facial muscles twitch. One more solid joke and I might actually crack a smile. "The argument could be made," he said.

"I get the feeling your people hate me."

"My people? As in, my cult followers? My minions? I'm not sure what you mean..."

I smiled—weak, barely there, but enough for him to notice. "You know what I mean."

"They don't hate you. They're just...wary."

"Why?"

"Because you left."

"That's it?"

"That's it. If you move here, eventually people accept you. If you leave and come back, they forgive you. If you leave for good..."

"They hate you."

"Nah. They wonder about you."

"Do *you* wonder about me?" It wasn't a fair question. In fact, I'd surprised myself by asking it. I had thought about Luke every day for the last twelve years—not obsessively, nor even intentionally, but those memories didn't fade. I sometimes wondered about the course his life must have taken without me: a wife, kids. A home of his own on Racharde Hill, which he'd always loved because of the way the light scattered on the boulders up there. My mind had assigned him a completely different reality than the one he actually inhabited.

"You know I do," he said, and I did, *I do*, but his answer stirred something in me just the same. Nostalgia, maybe? *Hope?* That was a dangerous thought.

"So," I said. "Now that we've talked ad nauseum about my job, what do you do?"

"Your dad never told you?"

"No," I said, skipping the part about my asking him not to. Getting over Luke would have been impossible with constant updates.

"I'm a biology teacher."

"Here?"

"Well, no, I commute to Portland," he said with a boyish smirk. "About a thirteen hour drive each way."

Given his love of nature, it made sense. His resistance to the outside world, less so. Luke had never intended to leave the North Woods. Whatever it was that had changed his mind must have changed it completely.

The attic stairs creaked with someone's weight—probably my mother, who always seemed to know where I was. Yet another hardwired Rienne trait: stealth. I hadn't inherited that one, either.

"I should really go back downstairs," I said.

"Yeah." He reached for his tie again. "Yeah, go for it."

"Okay."

"Okay."

He moved aside so I could pass. At least he realized it was better if we left separately. Trying to explain the necessity of why we had to do so would be awkward.

"Your Land Rover's ready, by the way," he said.

"It is? Where?"

"I parked it out back."

"How much?"

He waved me off. "Don't worry about it."

"It must've cost a fortune to ship those parts—"

"I said don't worry about it. You fly out Monday, right?"

I didn't ask how he knew. *Everybody knows.*

"Yes."

"Then you should be able to make it back."

I dreaded that drive through the North Woods, but I didn't dare say so. The only thing worse than a solo ride through the wilderness was a ride with Luke. What would we talk about? Failed relationships? Sports? Probably the weather. A ten-hour conversation about the weather.

"Absolutely," I said.

I heard it then: a strange, skewed note in my voice that hadn't been there before. It had crept in sometime during the conversation with Mrs. Cobalt, as sly as the snakes conspiring beneath my window, raising questions that no one but this town, these people, these Woods, could answer. *I don't think so, honey.*

The sound I heard was doubt.

FIVE

When the invaders left, I searched the house for my mother. Afternoon had given way to a dusky twilight, which cast the walls in an eerie autumn glow. Never had this house felt emptier; darker. I lasted about twenty minutes before venturing outside.

After a brief survey of the garden, I finally found her in the barn. My father had turned the loft into a studio of sorts the year after they were married to foster my mother's creativity. Her artwork sold well in cities she'd never visited—well enough to make a name for herself, if she'd so desired. She wanted no such thing, of course. The canvases were signed *S.R.*, and whoever bought them knew nothing else about her identity. At least the kids in town benefited from her talents; she'd taught art classes since her teen years.

She acknowledged my presence with a curt glance in my direction, then it was back to the canvas. A bold, streaked red sky dominated the scene, its palette more firelike than cloudlike.

"They're gone," I said.

"Finally," she said. "What time is it?"

"Almost eight." The sun had finally dipped below the tree line, which turned the oranges of dusk to a stark, sudden violet.

"Did you have dinner?" she asked.

"I had part of a casserole."

"Such a waste," she lamented. "We're only two people. And you'll be gone tomorrow."

Tomorrow. Sunday. A long ride through the woods, back the way I'd come. A flight from Bangor to Boston on Tuesday, then on to Los Angeles. All booked; my plans set. I could acknowledge this fact and move on, and we would likely never speak of it again. Maybe she'd start using the phone. Maybe she'd visit, or travel, or ask me to do the same.

Except she wouldn't, and in ten, twenty, thirty years, I would hate myself for taking the easy way out. I was hating myself now.

"Mom, how exactly did Dad die?"

She paused before her latest creation: a dreamlike cityscape, sketched in otherworldly reds, greens, and blues. The oil paints were rich and textured, as sublime as the scenes she painted. For a woman so rooted in hard reality, her art was anything but.

"Mom?"

She put her paintbrush down and looked at me. "What did Jim Ranson tell you?"

"He said it was a heart attack."

"He said that?"

"He said he was 'pretty sure' it was a heart attack."

The whisper of a chill slid down my spine as she said, "I think you should let this go."

"Let *what* go?"

"He's dead and buried. Let's leave it at that."

"You can't just say something like that and expect me to *let it go*. He's my father."

She walked over to her desk, a block of oak that could probably withstand the apocalypse. From the bottom drawer, she pulled out a starched envelope.

"Here," she said. "Have a look."

At first I thought she'd saved those damn licensing papers, but no, this was something else entirely. The seal was still in place.

It was a will. Dated two weeks ago and written in my father's hand—a rough, blockish print that resembled an epitaph. The ink was thick and smoky black.

I leave my home and all my personal possessions to my wife, Sarah Rienne Lane.

I leave my practice and all my professional possessions to my daughter, Aubrey Rienne Lane.

And lastly, I wish to lie in peace in my beloved North Woods, which have sheltered me from foes near and far.

It was a strange piece of literature, especially for my famously verbose father. I wondered if my mother had helped him write it. My instincts said no, but that final line threw everything into question. *Foes near and far?* The only foe in these parts was Mother Nature.

Then there were the first two lines: my mother's rightful inheritance, which prefaced my unwanted one. My father knew I didn't want to practice here. He had said as much in his first will, a 20-page document prepared by a lawyer and thorough in every aspect. In that version, he had left the clinic building to my mother and made no mention of my professional aspirations whatsoever. *What had changed?* The answer was everything. *Everything* had changed, and I didn't know why.

"Did he show you this before he died?" I asked.

"Yes."

"When?"

"When he wrote it two weeks ago."

The timing seemed strange, if not downright bizarre. "Where is the original will?"

"He destroyed it."

"And you waited until now to mention it?"

"I didn't want you to stay here for the wrong reasons," she said, an excuse that might have passed as genuine if it weren't so evasive. After the way our relationship had gone, I couldn't begin to imagine why she would want me to stay at all. Maybe some deep-down part of her wanted me to stick around and honor the family name. Maybe she wanted to punish me for leaving. Only I wasn't doing this on her terms, or even my own. This was about my father.

"Tell me about what happened last summer," I said.

She dipped her hands in a basin of water and dried them on the folds of her apron. Her answer came with some reluctance. "Four little boys became ill and died," she said. "Last July, it was. I imagine you've already heard that much."

"I heard it was a flu."

"Flu. Virus. Ebola." She pinched her lips into a sad, humorless smile. "If you stay here long enough, you'll hear it all."

"So no one knows how they died?"

"The official diagnosis was Parvovirus."

"'Official' according to whom?"

"The CDC."

"The *CDC* got involved?"

"Briefly. Four deaths in a town as small as this is considered an outbreak."

I could almost picture it: my father in his tiny clinic, watching little boys get sicker by the day. He would have called Med-Evac, of course. Specialists. And then, later, the Department of Public Health. He must have really been desperate—or fanatical—to contact the CDC.

"Parvo isn't often lethal," I said.

"Well, your father knew that. He wasn't happy with the way the CDC handled the case, so he pulled those boys' files and interviewed everyone in town and tried to figure it out on his own. It consumed him for months."

"Why didn't he tell me?" Just thinking about all our conversations over the past year made me question the strength of our relationship. My father had always asked about my patients; in return, I asked about his. He told me about the little old ladies with colds and the lumberjacks with bad knees, but never those boys. *Why?*

"He felt like a failure," she said.

"It sounds like the CDC failed *him*."

"Maybe." She blew out a soft, almost defeatist sigh. "In any case, he had a change of heart two weeks ago. He buried the files and told me never to speak of those boys to anyone. The town had moved on; he would, too."

"So he changed his will, then had a heart attack."

"Heart attacks happen to men in their sixties."

"You don't think the timing is a little suspicious?"

Her voice tightened. "There was nothing suspicious about

it. Both your grandparents on his side had heart attacks—his mother at sixty, his father at forty-two. He knew his odds."

In an actual city, his odds would have been better, but I didn't say that. Remoteness was what my father wanted; like everyone else in Callihax, he was willing to pay the price that came with limited access to specialized care. "What about an autopsy?"

"And ship his body all that way for no good reason? Your father would have reincarnated himself to stop such silliness."

"I'm not sure it's 'silliness' given what happened up here last year."

"You sound like a conspiracy theorist."

"I just want answers—"

"What kinds of answers? A diagnosis? A nasty little bug you can see under a microscope?" For the briefest of moments, she looked on the verge of screaming or crying; I couldn't tell which. "Those boys died tragically, and if your father had accepted that, he might not have worked himself to death. Because that's what happened, Aubrey. He wanted so badly to give those parents 'answers' that his heart gave out."

For the last twelve years, my mother had blamed me for turning my back on this family. For many of those years, she had wielded an array of weapons—guilt, anger, bribery—to entice me home. And now, finally, I stood before her, ready to be manipulated; maybe even willing to stay.

And she wanted me to go.

I could see it in her eyes, in the rare note of desperation that colored her voice. Fear, too. I never imagined my mother could experience such an emotion. I thought fifty-five years living in the bowels of a twelve-million acre forest had beaten it out of her. It occurred to me then that I had never been so wrong about something in my life.

She stood and went to the window, captivated by the darkness that made her feel at home. I made a point of looking away from the night; anywhere but the night.

"I don't know why your father changed his will. Maybe he was desperate. Nostalgic, perhaps. I don't know, Aubrey, but the fact is, he was proud of the life you'd built for yourself in Los Angeles. He wouldn't have wanted you to stay."

I thought of his soft laugh, his easy smile. I remembered the way he always said *Take care* when it came time to say good-bye.

"Yes, he did," I said, and with those words, my voice broke. It should have happened hours ago, with the funeral. The eulogy. The thousands of kind words spoken about a man I loved more than anyone, yet saw just once a year.

I met my mother's gaze and said, "He just never asked."

***

As the sun came up on northern Maine, I rang Jim Ranson's bell.

I hoped the early hour would unnerve him, but no, the sheriff was a decidedly morning person. Despite our strained relationship—which had been strained for some time now, he radiated sunshine and energy and the zing of black coffee. A whiff of bacon and lard escaped the front door as he swung it wide.

"Come to say good-bye, eh?" He waved me inside. "Shoulda slept in."

I followed him into the kitchen, where he poured me a cup of black tar. No sign of his wife, but she was never around when Jim "talked business." This included town hall meetings, elections, and the like. I had always thought they were an odd pair.

"Secret to a zesty life right there," he said, pointing to the slop he called coffee. "Go on. Drink up."

I unfolded my well-worn stack of papers and laid it out on the kitchen table. Signatures in a dozen places. Personal information all confirmed. The stamp on the cover letter said *Expedited*, with an address in Augusta. "I have a proposition," I said.

"Eh?" His bushy eyebrows narrowed. "What's that?"

"I'd like to stay on as the local physician—"

"What the goddamn—"

"—until I can train someone who can take over for me."

He finally seemed to notice the licensing application, his fat lips curling into a smirk as he paged through it.

"What's so funny?" I asked.

"You're a bit late, honey."

"Late? I just talked to you two days ago."

"Turns out we've got a real, high-class, Harvard-educated doc to come help us out."

Whiplash. That's what this felt like. Not so much a bomb blast as a sudden snap of the spine, which made the rest of my body numb. I should have been relieved. Elated. Thrilled. Instead, I felt that rare, telltale rush of fire in my veins, a defiance so raw it could only have come from my mother. Apparently I'd inherited the Rienne tendency to fight tooth-and-nail for something once you set your sights on it. Harvard or not, I wasn't going to fold my cards.

"A Harvard-educated doc wants to practice here?" I asked.

"Harvard. Princeton. Whatever. Somewhere good. Real good."

"Princeton doesn't have a medical school."

"That's what you think."

I didn't know what to say to that, so I let it go. "I thought you said you needed someone with ties to the community."

"We can make an exception for a guy like him."

"You may want to hold that thought." I reached into a different pocket and handed him a copy of my father's will.

"What's this?"

"Read it."

He reached into his jeans pocket for his reading glasses and put them on. Then he laughed. "This a joke?"

"Does it look like a joke? You know my father's handwriting. He's written you enough prescriptions over the years."

He bristled at this. I had no doubt Viagra was among them. "Your father and I worked closely together, Aubrey. We had an understanding that I'd help out if anything ever happened to the practice."

"Well, I *own* the practice. So your point is moot."

He wagged the sheet of paper in my face. "I don't like this."

"It's notarized."

"Uh huh."

"By your wife. You can check with her, if you like."

"There's no need for that." He handed it back to me, the edges damp with his sweat. "In any case, this isn't a problem. My man will just set up shop elsewhere."

"Really? Because it could take months to get the right equipment, medications, ancillary staff..." I ticked them off on my fingers. "Maybe years. In fact, your 'man' may change his mind when he finds out he has to see patients in his living room."

His stubbled cheeks flared red. "Two days ago, you were ready to hike outta here blindfolded if you had to—"

"Well, I've changed my mind."

"*Shit.*" He pounded the table, which made me smile. Poor form, sure, but I couldn't help it. "This ain't fair."

"Look, this isn't a competition. Two doctors is better for this town than one."

"Not if he's got no place to work!"

I sighed. "Then he can work with me. In the clinic." A sizable concession, and not one I was thrilled to make, but Jim Ranson could make life hell for me. And I needed his help in more ways than one; he just didn't know it yet. "We'll be a team."

"Until you bail on us for greener pastures."

"If this man is as good as you say, you won't care if I bail." I caught his gaze over the brim of his mug. "How did you find him, by the way?"

"Find him?" He barked out a laugh. "He came to *me*, sweetheart. Turns out a lotta docs are sick of the old insurance-paperwork-whatnot and want to practice old-school medicine."

"I see." Something about this reasoning didn't sit quite right with me—it should have taken weeks for the real world to hear about a vacancy up here, for one thing—but I decided to let it go. When this fancy-pants doctor showed up, I'd ask him myself.

"Anyway, I've got to get my day going before my wife ruins it." He finished his coffee and showed me the door.

"Just one more thing, Sheriff."

"What's that?"

"I'd like a copy of your investigative report."

"Investigative report? What the hell do you mean by that?"

"My dad died unexpectedly. Surely you did *some* police work."

"This ain't LA, honey," he said. "A heart attack's a heart attack."

I studied him for a moment, gauging the reproach in his voice, the flicker of unease in his eyes. He shuffled past me toward the stairs. "Look, my man starts next week, so if you'd be kind enough to let him in, I'd appreciate it."

He didn't bother walking me out. I stood in the kitchen, alone, pondering his parting words: *A heart attack's a heart attack.*

I had decided it wasn't.

SIX

The battle lines drawn, I steeled my resolve and made my inaugural visit to the clinic. There weren't many people out and about this early, which was good. I didn't want to be seen fumbling with the lock to the front door.

The building that housed the clinic was actually an old brick house, erected sometime around the turn of the 20th century by a leathermaker. The years had been good to it, thanks in large part to its perch on high, shaded ground. The lofty oaks protected the roof from heavy snowfall, and the slope of the hill kept the rain waters at bay. In May, the most spectacular dogwood tree in Maine bloomed out front beside my father's American flag.

I parked the Rover out back where it couldn't be seen from the street. The spare key was in the azalea bushes around here somewhere. My father had always taken great care to hide his keys somewhere other than "under the mat."

As I circled the building, it was my father's hand-painted sign —*JOHN LANE, M.D. – GENERAL PRACTITIONER*—that sparked an uneasy nostalgia. I remembered the day we put it up, a ceremonial father-and-daughter event that belonged not just to us, but to the whole town. A few hundred people came to see us hang that sign. I must have been four, maybe five-years-old. Afterwards, we had ice cream and lemon sticks to celebrate. I remembered because little Luke Ainsley had licked his ice cream right off the cone, and I'd given him mine.

I found the key right where my father said it would be, buried three inches deep under the fourth azalea bush, the one with the "mohawk." By then my hands were muddy and my fingernails caked with dirt.

My father had always been fanatical about patient privacy. He kept all the charts on the second floor behind a locked door, which he opened twice a day—once in the morning to retrieve the charts he needed, and again in the afternoon to put them away. When I asked him once why he went to such extreme measures in a town with little-to-no crime, he said, "Would you want everybody knowing how Jack died?" The answer was no —a horrified, rattled no. The story around town was that my little brother had been kicked by a horse. The truth was that my mother had tripped on the stairs and landed on top of him.

The front door opened into the reception area, a fifteen-by-fifteen foot space that prioritized that elusive blend of comfort and functionality. Clean, durable chairs lined the walls, and a small assembly of children's blocks occupied the corner. My father had been a huge proponent of infection control and the like. Hand-sanitizer dispensers were everywhere.

The registration desk was pretty much a table, a chair, and a computer that would have made a nice addition to an antique shop. Knowing my father, it hadn't been turned on in months. He had an assistant, but no assistant worth her salt would use a machine like that. Maybe she had a laptop. Or maybe they still did everything by hand. I shuddered at the thought.

I meandered through the waiting room and down the hall. There were three exam rooms, labeled 1, 2, 3, and 4. Room 1 was the "birthing suite," so named for the stirrups rigged to the exam table. Few women actually gave birth here. A midwife lived in town, and she delivered most of the babies at home unless a complication arose. In that case, my father would go and lend his expertise. This room was mostly for pre-natal visits.

Room 2 and 3 were standard exam rooms. On a busy day, both were used—but this happened rarely. It was easier to alternate every other day for cleaning purposes.

Room 4 was the procedure room. As a kid, I'd called it the torture room. Actually, every kid in town (and some adults) called it the torture room, which had driven my dad crazy. He had tried to make it as non-threatening as possible: soothing yellow walls, pastel landscape paintings, cabinets that hid the horrors inside. It hadn't worked.

As I explored each of the rooms, I wondered which had been the site of my father's demise. Not 4, I hoped. Maybe his assistant would tell me tomorrow.

I recalled Jim's words on the phone: *He was in with a patient.* No one had mentioned that person by name—not even at the funeral. If I had watched my own doctor die in front of me, I would have expressed my condolences to the family. I might have even reassured them that he had died peacefully.

Then again, if he *hadn't* died peacefully...

Jim Ranson had denied me once, but he had his weaknesses. I had a right to know what happened. If he didn't know, I would go straight to the source.

Whoever that patient was, he couldn't hide forever.

***

On Tuesday, the medical board granted me an emergency license to practice medicine in the state of Maine. On Wednesday, I called my employer in LA and explained that my father had died unexpectedly, and as a result, I would not be able to start on our mutually-agreed upon date. *Would you like to renegotiate the contract?* Yes. *When?*

I didn't know. These phone calls and licenses and federal loan-forgiveness forms were not a permanent solution. I had an apartment, and rent, and obligations in Los Angeles. No boyfriend worth mentioning, but I had friends—concerned, mystified friends. I e-mailed them and delivered the same spiel: My father passed away, and I would be taking a sabbatical of sorts. Timeline uncertain, but probably a few months. I didn't tell them about the job in my father's old clinic, nor the Maine license, nor even Callihax. No one knew the name of my hometown, just that it was "in the woods somewhere."

After the logistics were in order, I told Jim Ranson that the clinic would re-open on Wednesday. By 9 AM, there was a line out the door.

I had arrived early to prep the rooms and tidy up the reception area, but it wasn't nearly enough time to prepare for the onslaught of sick people that showed up. There were old men and babies and a painter clutching his hand and a pregnant woman holding her belly. A wiry teenager had something nasty poking out of his left leg. A mother with six kids in tow had quite the whooping cough, as did her six kids.

Run.

That was my first thought. *Run away.*

My second was *breathe.* Then: *put on your white coat. Check your teeth in the mirror. Smile. Shake hands. Use the hand-sanitizer. Be confident and open with patients. Open the front door. Smile. SMILE.*

"Good morning—"

The herd uttered a collective greeting as they barreled past me into the waiting room. A pretty blonde with no obvious injuries or illnesses winked at me. "Hi," she said. "I'm Corinne."

"Hi, Corinne. Uh, if you'll just join the others—"

"I'm the secretary."

"Oh. You mean the administrative assistant?"

She gave me a blank look. "Huh?"

"Never mind. Great. I'm glad to have you. Did you bring your laptop?"

"My what?"

I ushered her toward the desk, but she veered off toward the back room. "Where are you going?"

"To make coffee. You want some?"

"Corinne, there are fifteen people out here—"

"Yeah, well, I can't think without caffeine. They can wait."

I took a deep breath, which would surely be the first of many today. *Concede battles when necessary; focus on the war.* I could room the patients myself.

I stood at the head of the waiting room and waved my arms like an auctioneer. "Do any of you have an appointment?"

Everyone started shouting at once. "Okay, stop." I yelled above the din, "*Stop.*"

A few more grumbles and the crowd quieted down.

"Raise your hand if you have appointment. Please be honest because I can check the schedule." *When I find it.*

Two hands went up: the pregnant woman and Moira Samson. While everyone else fought over those sturdy plastic chairs, Moira stood by the door with her accident-prone little boy perched on her hip.

"Thank you," I said. "Now, I'm just going to take a quick look at each of you."

"Here?" someone barked.

"Right here."

I knew better than to try and educate these folks on the finer points of *triage*. That concept had never flown here and probably never would.

A brief assessment told me that the lady and her whooping kids could wait. So could the elderly couple who had caught each other's cold. The painter needed stitches. The kid with the broken end of a golf club protruding from his thigh probably needed a surgeon, but he was stuck with me for now. I'd take an x-ray and see.

"Okay, you two first," I said, gesturing to the two traumatic injuries. A dissonant groan filled the room. "Those with appointments will be next."

I escorted the kid to Room 4, the painter to 3. The painter applied pressure to his bloodied hand while the kid got his x-ray. The golf club had missed the bone, and from the looks of it, his artery, too. He was lucky. *I* was lucky, because calling Med-Evac on my first day would not inspire confidence in the masses.

"What's your name?" I asked him.

"Jeremy," he said.

"Okay, Jeremy. I'm going to pull this out and stitch it up."

"This is gonna hurt, isn't it?"

"Yes." He looked about seventeen, which meant he could handle it.

"Do it fast."

I did my best. He grunted, but didn't scream. A few stitches took care of the rest. I gave him a tetanus shot and ibuprofen and pushed him out the door.

"Can I get something stronger for the pain?" he asked. The tough-guy routine was gone, replaced by a sheepish, pandering look I knew well.

"Hell no," I said.

He shrugged. At least I'd sent *that* message loud and clear. *Please God don't send me too many teenagers looking for oxycodone.* Not today, anyway. Tomorrow, maybe. Next week would be better. Never would be ideal.

Except for a curt "No" when I asked if he was in pain, the painter didn't say a word while I sutured his wound. He didn't want lidocaine either, but I gave it anyway. There was something barbaric about sticking needles in people's bodies without anesthetizing them first.

"Thank you, ma'am," he said, and that was that.

Two down, more to go. I saw that someone else had slinked into the waiting room: a white-haired gentleman with a dry cough. He had his reading glasses on and a newspaper under his arm. He looked okay.

I waved at Moira to come on back. She hoisted Sammy a little higher on her hip and followed me into Room 2. *Where was the nurse? Was there a nurse?* I'd have to ask Corinne as soon as she finished her critical beverage.

Once we were settled in Room 2, I held out my hand for Moira to shake. "Uh, hi, Moira. I'm not sure if you remember me—"

"You've changed, hon, but not that much." She looked me over like a prospective purchase at a flea market. "So you're a doctor now?"

"That's right."

"How long you been an *actual* doctor?"

"Well, I did four years of a Med-Peds residency—"

"I know what a resident is. I mean a *doctor*."

I tugged at the stethoscope around my neck, as if that might grant me some credibility. "A day," I said. "One day."

Moira barked out a laugh. "Ha. Great." She wiped Sammy's nose with the sleeve of her shirt. "And my boy here's your third patient. *That* makes me feel good."

I smoothed the pleats of my white coat, a feeble attempt to cultivate Moira's respect. Judging by the look on her face, it didn't work. She probably thought of my outfit as a costume.

"May I examine him?" I asked.

"I ain't decided yet." She let this sink in until it had the desired effect.

"All right."

"Well, shit. I thought the new doc would be here today."

"He doesn't start until next week."

"You know how hard it is for me to get off work? It don't happen with the snap of my fingers like it does for some people." She demonstrated this with a violent snap of her fingers two inches from my face. I managed not to flinch.

"As I said, I'm happy to take a look at him."

"He ain't a car."

"I understand that."

"I hope so, 'cause he's the nicest kid I got. You hurt him and I'll kill you."

Doing my best to ignore what sounded like an actual threat, I took the empty stool; the "doctor's stool." Moira eyed me with her usual calculating distaste, as if to say, *You don't belong there.*

"So what's going on with Sammy?"

"He fell into your mama's rose bush, and now he's got an ear infection." Her tone was flat, laced with a challenge.

"When did it start?"

"When he fell into the bush," she said, toneless.

"How did it start?"

"What is this, twenty questions?"

I looked at Sammy. His eyes where rheumy and wet, his gaze unfocused. He must have spent the last few days crying himself into a stupor.

I listened to his lungs first. Clear as a bell. Good. His heart was beating furiously, but kids' hearts ran quite a bit faster than adults, so this wasn't necessarily cause for alarm. I examined his skin: no rashes or bites, just a few healing scratches on his face. His mouth and throat and nose looked clear. The ears would be a battle.

"So," she said, "you like the big city?"

"It's fine."

"I bet you hate being back here."

"It's home," I said. "It's good to be back."

"Uh huh." More of that cold stare as she watched me rinse my hands a second time. I was stalling and she knew it.

With nothing left to do but look in the poor kid's ears, I braced myself for Sammy's flailing arms. It was all for naught because I couldn't get the light to work on the scope. Through it all, Moira just watched and rolled her eyes.

By the end, even Sammy had reached his limit. Newly energized by the failed ear exam, he fought me with kicks and slaps. The last one caught me square on the side of the head.

"Oh for godssakes." Moira pulled the boy toward her. "You're just making it worse."

I rubbed my temple, feeling the sneaker-print that would appear there later. "Maybe we could focus on the history—"

"Seriously, Aubrey. Don't waste my time."

"If you could just tell me what's been going on—"

"His ear's draining stuff and he keeps pulling on it." She wiped Sammy's nose with her sleeve again. "Ain't it obvious he's uncomfortable?"

"Yes, but—"

"Just give us some antibiotics."

"I'm not sure that's what he needs—"

"That's what he needs. Come *on*. I gotta get to work."

I left the room, my white coat skimming my calves with each stride. The damned thing was far too big, the pockets crammed with pocket books and useless instruments. My father, on the other hand, had carried only two things: a stethoscope and a pen. He didn't need anything else.

The in-house pharmacy was on the second floor, adjacent to the file room. On my way there, I had no choice but to pass by my father's old office. The sign on the door said, *You're Lost.* As a kid, I used to think his cheeky wall hangings were funny. Now, not so much.

I used the key to let myself into the file room, which led into the pharmacy through a second door. This door was also locked, a feature my father had added after someone worked the lock on the first door and broke in. The next week, he treated five teens with overdoses.

Moira's voice bellowed through the halls. "Helloooo! We're still down here! You better hurry, Aubrey. I didn't come all the way over here to pick my fucking nose!"

Christ. So much for a patient patient.

I measured the appropriate amount of liquid amoxicillin and made my way downstairs. Moira was waiting for me outside the exam room. "Took long enough."

"I don't know where everything is yet—"

"Uh huh." Moira poured out the first dose and helped Sammy gulp it down. "You got any cough syrup? I'll wait."

Dejected, I went back upstairs to hunt down the cough syrup. *Anything to get Moira out the door.* Of course, it took me a small eternity to realize that the over-the-counter medications were stored on the opposite side of the room. In my rush to get back downstairs, I lost my tuning fork and most of my pens.

Rounding the corner, I waved the green bottle like a trophy. "Here it is—"

But Moira was gone. I glanced toward the waiting room. The usual chatter of waiting patients who knew one another had gone quiet.

No.

No.

I nearly tripped on the rug trying to get there. The man with the cough lay face-down on the floor, his newspaper crumpled beneath him.

"He's not breathing!" someone screamed.

I felt for a pulse: radial, femoral, carotid. There was none. The man's lips had gone a pale, delicate blue in the span of a minute. I pictured the blood pooling in his veins; the inertia of an organ that was meant to beat. Death made me slow, and scared, and useless.

"Jesus," Moira spat, and shoved me aside. She got on her hands and knees and started doing chest compressions. They weren't good—pretty awful, to be honest—but at least she was *doing* something. Along with everyone else, I stood and watched her for a full minute.

When my brain finally kicked into gear again, I noticed Corinne spectating from one of the waiting room chairs. "Where's the AED?" I asked her. No, shouted at her.

"The what?"

"The defibrillator!"

"Oh." She thought for a moment. "I think it's in 4..."

I tore through the hallway and proceeded to open every cabinet, door, and box in Room 4. The AED was under the sink, covered in cobwebs. It looked like a video game console, with its leads and wires and palm-sized screen.

I found Moira still in the throes of CPR. Her mascara leaked down her cheeks in purple rivulets, which gave her a ghastly, almost witchlike quality. I had never seen her devote herself so completely to something in her life.

"What the hell is that?" she asked.

"A defibrillator." I got down on my knees and attached the pads to the man's chest. His collar was neatly-pressed; his shirt starched. I ripped it open and sent buttons flying. The sound made me want to weep.

"Somebody call 9-1-1!" The lady with whooping cough bawled.

"This *is* 9-1-1, dumbass," Moira said, and resumed compressions.

The AED took a moment to power on, and another few to register the rhythm. I told Moira to stop compressions. *Shock shock shock.* The urgency of that word pulsed through my mind.

She sat on her heels, transfixed by the plastic box. It started to beep.

We waited. *One...two...three...*

There was no mistaking the thin red line that spooled across the screen. No blips in the rhythm strip; no signs of life or hope or anything. Asystole. I had always hated that word. Hated the finality of it.

"Aren't you gonna use it?" Moira barked.

"It's not a shockable rhythm..."

"Fuck that." She reached over and tried to hit the red button, labeled *SHOCK*. "Clear!" she yelled, just like they do in the movies.

The current from rolled through him, an awful convulsing that broke one of his teeth. The rhythm didn't budge. The line stayed flat.

Again Moira reached for the button—

"Stop," I said.

"We have to try—"

"Just *stop*," I said, choking on the words. "Please."

She muttered something under her breath, then got to her feet. Everyone in the room was watching us. Watching *me*.

"I should have triaged him," I whispered. "I should have talked to him when he came in—"

"Too late for that," Moira said. The look in her eyes was damning.

While the others looked on, Moira scooped up her son and walked out, my father's sign jingling as the door slammed. In slow procession, they followed her out the door.

When it was just me and Corinne, I got on my hands and knees and tried, for a full hour, to save this stranger's life. The compressions were technically adequate; the algorithm for a pulseless rhythm followed to perfection.

An hour later, I pronounced my first death in Callihax.

***

Jim Ranson and his deputy—who also happened to be his son —came to collect the body. The sheriff informed me that the man's name was Jedediah Walsh, age seventy-four. He had a wife, six kids, ten grandkids, and eighteen great-grandchildren, all of whom showed up within the hour to talk to me.

After the awful routine of describing their patriarch's final moments and the efforts that had been made to save him, Jim Ranson cornered me in the hallway.

"I'd ask you what happened," he said, "but ten people already told me everything. Sounds like you just—"

"Stood around and did nothing."

My brutal honesty seemed to please him. "Seems so."

"They're right. I panicked."

"Moira Samson, though. What a hero."

I thought of her parting words: *Too late for that.* So merciless, yet so true. There was no place for hindsight in medicine. Mistakes could mean death, especially in Callihax, where the closest "back-up" was hours away.

"I guess we'll never know what got him, then," Jim said. "Family declined an autopsy."

"I guess we won't." As much as I wanted to throw his line back at him—*a heart attack's a heart attack, asshole*—I resisted. In any case, maybe it wasn't a heart attack. Maybe it was a pulmonary embolism. Or an aortic dissection. Or a fatal arrhythmia. I would never know and forever wonder. Such was the nature of this job.

"So I take it clinic's cancelled for the rest of the day?" he asked.

Although I wanted nothing more than to walk out that door and cry in a corner somewhere, Jim Ranson expected that. The whole *town* expected that. Today's events had proven my ineptitude. It would be a steep uphill climb from here on out, with no guarantee of a summit.

With that thought, I put my white coat back on and propped the door open.

"Nope," I said. "I'm here till five."

***

The elderly couple with colds didn't come back. Neither did the whoopers. Everyone with afternoon appointments cancelled except Ophelia Sinclair, the pregnant woman who insisted on holding her belly like an extra appendage.

Corinne checked Ophelia in, then escorted her to Room 1. I listened to their conversation behind the door:

You sure she's a doctor?

Oh, yes. I saw her diploma.

Diploma's just a piece of paper. I could type it up myself.

It's got that fancy cursive and Latin and stuff.

Still sounds fishy.

Doc wouldn't raise a fake doctor.

A long pause as Ophelia pondered this. I knocked on the door and barged right in. Corinne mouthed "Good luck" to me and left.

"So," I said, and tried to smile. "Pregnancy going well so far?"

"No," she muttered. "Being pregnant's hell. *Hell.* I want to die sometimes."

Wait till childbirth. "Hm."

"I feel like it's sucking all my energy right outta me. And even though your dad tells—sorry, *told*—me it uses all my nutrients, I keep getting fatter, so I dunno."

"Not all your nutrients—"

"I just want it to come out."

I flipped through her tattered paper chart. *Twenty-two visits since her first ultrasound?* God Almighty. I tried not to let my horror show on my face.

"Do you know the sex?" I asked.

"Are you nuts? I don't have sex anymore."

"No, I mean the baby. The sex of the baby."

"Oh," she said. "Boy."

Then why are you referring to your child as it? "That's exciting," I said.

"Whatever. I just want it born."

"Just four more weeks."

"Four?" She held up a calendar containing eight-months' worth of black marks. "According to this, I've got 26 days."

"Okay, 26 days. My mistake."

"You sure you know what you're doing?"

"Yes," I lied.

"You ever birth a baby before?"

"Not my own baby, but I've delivered some, yes."

"How many?"

I honestly had no idea. Thirty? Forty? Best to allay her fears a bit—no harm in inflating numbers.

"About fifty."

"Fifty?" She looked skeptical. "Doc said thirty."

Dad sold me out? Great. I put the chart aside.

"In any case, the midwife usually delivers the babies here."

"Not my baby." She patted her belly like the head of a dog. "I've had four miscarriages, so Doc wanted to do it himself."

I gave up on the smile. "Well, I can assure you I'm qualified to deliver your baby," I said, which sounded like the false reassurances of a car salesman.

"Well, I doubt that. It's a good thing they're sending that guy from Boston up here." She prattled on, oblivious to the vague insult. They just kept coming.

I interrupted her with the standard maneuver—yanking the stirrups out of the table. The metallic groan distracted her enough to reroute the topic of conversation.

"I thought I didn't need a pelvic today," she said.

"You don't. You don't need anything today, in fact."

"Yeah, but Doc said—"

"Doc's dead."

Something in her expression softened, only to tighten right up again. She rejected my offer to help her as she hobbled off the table.

"I got my next appointment on Friday," she said. "It's always on Friday. I had to reschedule last Friday 'cause your dad passed."

"I know. I'll see you then."

"Don't cancel this one."

No promises if my mom dies, I thought, but kept my mouth shut. "I won't."

"Good." She shuffled toward the door. "And don't tell anybody I said anything about that Boston doctor."

"Oh, I won't."

As it turned out, I didn't have time.

Dr. Sheldon Kline was knocking on my door by lunchtime.

***

He found me in my "office," a closet-sized hovel behind the reception area. Among its perks were a tiny window overlooking the dumpster, a water heater that released steam at insanity-inducing intervals, and the relentless stench of old coffee and cashews. It was the only part of the entire building that felt like *mine*. And, of course, the bar was set extremely low. Here, I could do my paperwork and feel less like an imposter.

That said, it was not the kind of place in which I had hoped to encounter my first, honest-to-God professional rival. I wasn't even sure how Sheldon Kline had gotten in. Ophelia must have left the door open to spite me.

He introduced himself with a firm handshake and a thunderous baritone. "Sheldon Kline," he said. "Are you the illustrious Aubrey Lane?"

"I'm Aubrey Lane," I said.

"Ah. Excellent. Your father spoke very highly of you."

"You knew him?"

He hesitated for a shade of a second. "I did, in fact. Not well, but I knew him."

"How?"

"We met at a conference years ago."

"Which one?"

He raised an eyebrow. "Am I being interrogated?"

"Sorry." I gestured to the plastic chair in the corner, which looked as though it had aged out of the waiting room. "You can sit down if you like."

"Thank you." He sat down in a genteel way that fit his age, his name, and his undoubtedly stellar credentials. Sheldon Kline, M.D. He sounded like a genius. I wondered what in the world had drawn him here. The North Woods weren't exactly for the faint of heart.

"I'm very sorry about your father, Dr. Lane," he said. "Very sorry indeed."

"Aubrey." I forced a smile. "Please."

He responded with a prim purse of the lips that told me he never intended to call me by my first name. "You don't seem very surprised to see me here," he said. "I'm getting the feeling someone told you I was coming."

"Jim Ranson told me."

"Ah."

"He said it would be next week."

"Well, here I am! I wanted to get a lay of the land."

"I see."

"Please don't get the wrong impression." His good cheer never faltered, even though my mood had clearly tanked. "I'm not trying to trespass on your turf. When Jim called to tell me that you had decided to stay, I was delighted, but surprised. "

"Well, I felt similarly when he told me about *you*."

"I can explain the whole chain of events if you like."

"Please do."

He propped his ankle on his knee and proceeded to gesticulate like a librarian at story hour. "As I mentioned earlier, I knew your father. He asked me months ago to consider the job if something were to happen to him."

Months ago. The timing fit with the old will, but not the new one. Maybe Sheldon Kline hadn't gotten the message.

"How did you hear about his death? Jim Ranson called you?"

"No," he said. "Your mother called me."

The shock must have played on my face because he smiled and said, "Ah. She didn't tell you."

"No, she didn't tell me." She hadn't called her own daughter to relay the news of my father's death, but she'd called *him?* I now knew what Mrs. Rogerson felt like, always on the filtered end of critical information.

"Well, perhaps she thought you weren't ready to undertake the care of an entire town."

"I finished my residency."

"Last week?" His dainty English was making my blood boil.

"Does it matter?"

"I believe it very much does. Look around you, Dr. Lane. You're in way over your head."

"Everyone has to start somewhere."

"A fine point," he said. "Although a failed resuscitation isn't the *best* place to start."

As he indulged in the propulsive force of this comment, I assessed my adversary for a moment. In terms of experience, this man had it in spades. His hands were wrinkled and mottled with sunspots. His hair had gone a snowy white. Maybe he wanted to retire up here. Maybe he genuinely feared for the welfare of these patients. Maybe he was right to worry. It didn't surprise me in the least that he had heard all the grisly details of poor Mr. Walsh's demise.

"How many patients do you see in a week?" he asked.

"Depends on the season."

"Last week, then."

I glowered at him. "I wasn't here last week."

"Ah. Of course. Based on the books, though. Say four or five a day?"

"About that."

"Perhaps twice that in the winter?"

"I don't know, Dr. Kline," I said. "I haven't gotten that far."

He plucked my diploma off the wall. *Dammit.* I'd debated putting it there in the first place for just this reason. His lips twitched as he read it.

"I should be careful," he said. "I do believe the ink is still wet on that thing."

I swiped it from his hands and fumbled with the hook for an inordinate amount of time. "So, are you just here make fun of me in my own office? Because if so, I can rescind my offer to take you in."

He spread his hands wide. The smug smile held strong. "I apologize."

"How about this. You see your patients and I see mine, and we'll see how things go."

He smoothed his tie and stood up. A nautical-themed tie, sweater vest, and ill-fitting khakis. Fit for an older man, too. I'd known a lot of doctors like this in medical school, none of them particularly likeable. No wonder he'd waltzed right in like he owned the place.

"Oh sure," he said, chuckling. "We can give that a go."

***

By Thursday afternoon, it was obvious who was "seeing" patients. My public failure with Jedediah Walsh had done its damage, and every single patient requested Sheldon Kline, i.e. "the man doctor," "the Harvard doctor," and my favorite: "anyone but *her*." To comfort me, my father would have taken me by the hand and bought me ice cream and told me to head on back to LA, take an easier job, forget all about these people. My mother would think me a coward. And so I stayed, if not to spite her, then to see this through.

Even without Jedediah Walsh's sudden death under my watch, it wouldn't have taken long for the mutiny to happen. Sheldon Kline's crazed wild hair and impeccable blue ties radiated confidence. He never fumbled with his stethoscope; didn't even wear a white coat. He talked to patients without rushing them. He gave advice without sounding paternalistic. He was good. Very good.

Better than you.

The nagging voice became a chant by the time we filed the last chart. I hadn't seen a single patient independently, and I knew that from now on, I probably wouldn't. Sheldon Kline had stolen the hearts (and bodies) of Callihax. I could leave tomorrow and no one would care, nor even notice. They *wanted* him as their doctor. Screw "ties to the community." No one seemed to give a hoot that he drove a Prius or had a British accent or asked where the recycling bins were. They liked him. Accepted him. Mutiny, indeed.

Shortly after the last patient left for the day, he poked his head in my office. I knew it would only be a matter of time before he confiscated the second floor, but for now, he seemed content with the entire reception area. Corinne gave him a wide berth.

"Well, then," he said, "I think everything went splendidly today, don't you?"

"Yep."

"We're quite the team."

"We are."

He dusted off his trusty beret and plopped it on his head. "I suppose I'll be heading home, then. By the by, how do after-hour calls work around here?"

"Well, people call after hours..."

He gave one of his rollicking belly laughs. "Quite funny. Now, do you come in the office for emergencies? Or do you do house calls?"

"It depends on the call." This was a bit of a lie, since I hadn't yet encountered a true medical emergency. Of the two people who called the house last night, one was Ophelia ("My butt hurts") and the other was Fanny Dirkstein, who agreed to wait another twelve hours to have her ingrown toenail addressed.

"Just to be safe, I think you should notify me of any calls that come in." He glanced at the phone on my desk. "Don't you have a pager system?"

"No. My dad hated pagers."

"Don't we all," he said, as if this were some grand inside joke. "Cell phones?"

"No service up here."

"So how do people reach you in cases of emergency?"

"They come running."

Again, the belly laugh. "I'm being quite serious," he said.

"So am I."

He twirled his fingers as he stood there, looking pristine in his sweater vest and tie. In a span of two days, my white coat had gone from white to grungy. Coffee on the sleeves. Vomit on the breast pocket. Something brown and goopy on the back. I would have to do an emergency load of wash tonight.

"Well, we'll have to address this once we've settled in a bit."

Once you've *settled in a bit.* "Sure," I said.

"Until then, please let me know of any calls that come in."

"I will." By next week, everyone in town would have his home number. He just didn't know it yet.

"Excellent."

He pulled his scarf—pashmina?—around his neck and walked out. There was no rush in his stride; no barely-restrained urge to escape. He'd had a good day. An *easy* day. He'd told stories and shook hands and sent people away feeling calmed and reassured. After it became clear that none of the patients scheduled for that day wanted to be seen by me, I had taken to shadowing him like a clingy med student. Essentially, I stood in the corner and took notes. A few patients said hello, but not a single one had called me *doctor.* Most ignored my presence entirely.

I leaned over the desk and pulled my diploma off the wall. It sat in an expensive wooden frame, courtesy of my proud father. The letters were sloped and antique-looking. *Doctor of Medicine.* And there, below that, was my name: Aubrey Rienne Lane. Four years of endless study and long nights and inhumane hours. Residency was even worse. But it wasn't enough, was it? I thought it would be. My father had assured me it would be.

I shoved the diploma in the drawer alongside expired condoms and broken pens. Sheldon Kline hadn't paid much attention to "charting," but I liked to keep things in order. If I couldn't take a history or perform an exam, at least I could write a damn note.

Subjective: *Mr. Rinehardt presents today with a sore left*

shoulder. He believes he may have injured it while playing "Bomber" with his three-year-old son. Patient also spends 8-10 hours per day felling trees and carrying heavy loads. He has had this pain for almost a year, but it acutely worsened after the "Bomber" incident. Pain is sharp, localized to the joint, and 8/10 with certain activities, including overhead motions. Denies instability or weakness.

I looked at Sheldon's note:

David Rinehardt. Dx: biceps tendonitis. Rx: cortisone injection. RTC prn for sx's.

Judging by the chart—Rinehardt's was fairly thick given that it dated back 32 years—my father's dictations fell somewhere in between Sheldon's militaristic style and my literary one. He had used medical lingo, but not to the extent Sheldon Kline did. Maybe he liked to inject a little personality into his charts. Or maybe that was just me.

I was finishing up Dave Rinehardt's note when the phone rang. Probably a test, courtesy of my supervisor-disguised-as-colleague. It wasn't difficult to imagine the exchange: Sheldon would say a jolly hello and ask me about any dubious activities, oblivious to the hit on my ego. It was also past seven and I hadn't eaten since the stale bowl of granola at lunch.

I rather liked the idea of blowing him off, but my father had never missed a call since residency, and he would have expected the same of me. Patients were instructed to call here first, and to call him at home *only* if it were a true emergency. Far as I knew, most people actually heeded this advice.

"Hello?" I skipped the typical greeting. It didn't much feel like "Dr. Lane's Office" anymore.

"Oh, hey. Is this Dr. Lane?"

Luke. He really had a lovely voice; always had. Husky in ways that reminded me of late nights and teenage misadventures, but lush, too, like a fine wine.

"This is she."

"Uh, this is Luke Ainsley."

"I know."

"Oh."

"You know you shouldn't be calling this number after-hours, right? It's just for emergencies."

"I know," he said. Much to my satisfaction (and surprise), he sounded chastened. "It's a bit of an emergency."

"It is?"

"Could I come by the office?"

I wanted to scream. There goes dinner.

"Can this wait till tomorrow?"

"I don't think so."

"Can you be here in ten minutes?"

"Yeah. Yeah, no problem."

"Fantastic," I growled, and hung up.

Seconds passed. A minute. I stared at the phone, hearing Sheldon Kline's chortling in my ear as he requested—no, *dictated* —that we do things his way. The truth was, Sheldon Kline had already taken over my father's practice. Sure, I could sit in that hovel and do paperwork until the end of time, but he was the doctor. My father's sign would come down eventually, only to be replaced by one that read *SHELDON KLINE M.D. AND HIS BOARD-CERTIFIED ASSISTANT.*

*If he found out about this...*Then what? He couldn't fire me because I owned the building and, technically, the practice. Sure, Jim Ranson was probably already working on the plans for a state-of-the-art medical facility to please his "man," but for now, Sheldon Kline was stuck under my roof. If the patients wanted him, fine. I had to concede it was probably better for them anyway. But Luke hadn't called Sheldon; he'd called me.

I left the phone where it was.

SEVEN

Luke lived almost two miles away, so when he showed up eleven minutes later looking winded, it aggravated my miserable mood. Anyone who could cover that distance in eleven minutes needed a medal, not a doctor.

I let him in without so much as a hello and escorted him to Room 4. My hope was that the various gadgets and tools might make him uncomfortable, at the least. Scared shitless, at best. I had left a Foley catheter dangling over the sink.

"So," I said, with about as much enthusiasm as I could muster. "What's the problem?"

"Well…" There were no chairs, and the examining table was a clear no-go. He stayed where he was by the door.

"Well?"

"I wanted to talk to you about your dad."

"Now? *Here?*"

"Look, I'm sorry." He sounded genuinely contrite. "I know you're probably tired—"

"Really tired."

"Right. I know. But I needed to talk to you, and this was my first real opportunity."

"The funeral wasn't appropriate, I suppose?"

He searched my face for understanding, which I denied him by looking away. There were boundaries here. He needed to know that.

"Aubrey…" he started.

"What?"

"I was the patient."

Silence. A tense, spiraling silence. "What did you say?"

"With your dad. When he died. I was the patient in the room

with him."

"*You?*" It was the only word I could manage.

"I should have told you sooner. I tried. In the sunroom." He looked at his muddy, grass-stained shoes. "I'm sorry."

"Please stop apologizing. It's lost its luster."

"Yeah. Sorry. I mean…" He sighed. "I'm in a tough position here."

"That would be an understatement."

"Can we go to your office?"

"No."

He rubbed his chin with his thumb, an old habit that reminded me of the early days of our courtship. His nervous thumb, he called it. *Why was he nervous now?*

I studied him for a long moment: the otherworldliness of his eyes, the hard slope of his jaw. In the physical sense, he was still the Luke Ainsley I remembered. But there was a remoteness about him now, the kinds of walls that came with time, and experience, and hurt. I supposed he might say that about me, too.

"Which room were you in?" I asked.

"The OB room. He called me at 1:30 and told me he needed to talk."

"In the middle of clinic?"

"I figured it was a domestic dispute or something strange like that. I sure as hell don't know anything about pregnant women."

"And you went?"

"Right away. I got there and went straight in."

I folded my arms to fend off a chill. "And?"

He looked pained as he met my gaze. "I was too late."

"Too late for *what*, Luke?"

"I don't know."

"You must have an idea."

"I don't. I wish I did." He dipped his hands in his pockets to calm his nervous thumbs. "I did compressions, but no one could find the defibrillator."

First order of business: *put the damn defibrillator in plain sight.*

I would rectify that tonight. "How long did you try to save him?"

"Till my arms gave out."

I could picture it in all its agonizing detail: my father on those slick white floors, his limbs sprawled out in every direction. Mouth open, eyes rolled back. Death was never dignified, no matter how hard people tried to sell it that way.

"This isn't what you wanted to hear," he said.

It wasn't, but what could I say? That I wished he'd done compressions a little longer? Found the defibrillator? Called me the moment it happened? We all had regrets; we all could have done things differently. I couldn't crucify Luke for his mistakes when mine had been worse.

"You did all you could," I said.

We sat in silence for an uneasy beat. I resisted the urge to ask questions because it wouldn't change anything. My father had died in his own clinic, as far from his only daughter as he'd ever been.

To Luke's credit, he didn't argue with me. "Aubrey, it looked like a heart attack."

"What?"

"Your dad…" He rubbed his neck as he looked down. "I heard rumors that maybe…I dunno. That it looked suspicious."

Despite the whirl of unease in my gut, I stayed standing. "Go on."

"Well, it didn't. Look suspicious, I mean. He clutched his chest and went down. That was kind of it."

"Did he say anything to you?"

"No."

"Nothing about why he asked you to come in?"

"No," he said. "I'm sorry."

I believed him, but there were gaps in his story. Luke and my father weren't exactly close, which I imagined had something to do with our teenage romance. I supposed it was possible they had *become* close over the years, but his story didn't support that.

"I did run into him in town a few weeks ago," Luke said. "He told me he was looking into converting everything into an electronic medical record."

"And you think that's related somehow?"

"I'm not sure. I'm no techie, though—hell, I'm lucky if I can find the power button."

"Well, I highly doubt he was interested in your technical services. He's a dinosaur. Hates technology." I cleared my throat. "Hated."

"Why would he lie, though?"

"I don't know." I tried to remember my father ever being deceptive. Nothing came to mind. "He never talked to you about anything else before he died? He never called you? Left a message? Mentioned something then said to forget it?"

"No..." He stopped, his gaze drifting toward the window as a distant memory migrated somewhere more accessible.

"What is it?"

"Two months ago. At the pub."

"The pub? He didn't drink."

"I know. But he was drinking that night—gin and tonic. I remember because he asked what kind of gin I liked."

"Are you sure you were talking to my dad?"

"I wasn't *that* toasted." He paused, his voice finding a more serious tone. "It was late, though. Almost closing."

I was tempted to ask what Luke was doing at the pub so late, but that would convey interest, and officially, I wasn't interested.

"What did he say?"

"Well, not much at first. He didn't like to talk about..."

"Last summer," I finished for him.

He nodded. "I think he just wanted someone to talk to. Your dad treated all four of those boys—everyone knew he took it especially hard. The CDC's bullshit Parvo diagnosis just made it worse."

So he knew about the Parvo theory? Parvovirus wasn't all that common anymore, and the rare parent who was familiar with the virus knew it by another name, Fifth's disease. I was surprised he'd come right out with the medicalese.

"How fast did it come on?" I asked.

"Fast. Each of the boys was sick for a few days, and that was it. Two died on Med-Evac en route to the hospital. The other two never made it out of town."

"Was anyone else sick? Or just those four?"

"There were others," he said. "Your father kept count, but he didn't share that information with me—with anyone, really. You know how he was; very protective of people's privacy."

I understood this. It didn't matter if you lived in South Central LA or in the North Woods of Maine; the death of a child made you vulnerable. Fragile. My father would have been even more protective of grieving parents.

"Anyway," he said. "That was almost a year ago now. People don't talk about it much for obvious reasons, but they're also a touch superstitious."

"So you're saying not to bring it up with anyone."

"I wouldn't."

One day in clinic had made up my mind in that regard. I was about to tell him this when the phone rang down the hall.

"It's probably Sheldon," I said. "Checking up on me."

He started toward the waiting room. "I'll get it—"

"No!"

"No?"

I didn't feel like explaining "Sheldon's rules" to Luke, of all people. Part of me worried that Sheldon already knew Luke was here. Cameras, maybe. A casual drive by the office. Every minute with him felt like a test.

"I'll be right back," I said. "Stay here."

I hurried down the hall toward the ringing phone. Without the benefit of daylight, the waiting room had that dark, closed-in feel. Add that to the list of tasks: *add warmer, softer lighting.*

I answered on the tenth ring. "Hello?"

Static.

"Hello? This is Dr. Lane."

No response.

"Hello? Is anyone there?"

Somewhere down the hall, a door creaked open. I listened for footsteps, but the silence held. I knew it had to be Luke, but why was he just standing there?

"Hello?" I said into the phone again.

As I went to hang up, the static abruptly cleared and a voice, hushed and unrecognizable, spoke: "Get out."

I waited for more, those lonely two syllables ringing in my ears. Then, from somewhere behind me: "Aubrey?"

I whirled around, my heart in my throat.

The line went dead.

EIGHT

I hung up the phone and told Luke it was time to go. Our conversation in the car stalled early, probably because my mind was elsewhere. *Get out.* Maybe it was just a prank call, of which there would be many. Bored teenagers could be nasty.

Except it didn't sound like a prank. It sounded almost malicious.

"Are you sure you're okay?" he asked.

"I'm fine."

"Who was that on the phone?"

"No one. A wrong number."

"You seemed pretty upset for a wrong number."

"I'm upset because you insisted on seeing me for a fake 'emergency' and I missed dinner," I said, trying hard not to snap at him.

"I've got some leftovers—"

"No thanks."

I turned into his driveway, which continued for a while before ending at the river's edge. Luke's ancestors had lived a little dangerously, in my opinion. His house always looked like it was about to topple over and drown.

As he got out of the car, he asked, "Was it something I said?"

"No."

He hesitated before closing the door. "You sure?"

"I've just got a lot on my mind. Don't take it personally." I tried to smile.

He would, though. And he should. Twelve years wasn't enough to erase the nuance and hurt and psychosis of a first love. A hundred years wouldn't be enough.

"Luke..." I trailed off.

"Yeah?" His eagerness weakened my resolve.

"If you don't mind, I really need to focus on things in the clinic. I have so much going on, you know…" I watched his expression change; saw his face register understanding.

"Sure," he said. "No problem."

"I hope that didn't sound callous—"

"It didn't." His smile—stiff, a little sad—made me wince. I watched him walk down the drive with his hands in his pockets, his shoulders braced against a stiff breeze. He had a smooth, easy gait. I missed that about him. The way he walked. The way we walked together.

By the time I shifted into gear, he had disappeared into the shadows.

***

The next week proceeded in what could best be described as The Sheldon Show—Sheldon Kline saw, evaluated, diagnosed, and treated patients, while I took notes. It was like the first year of medical school all over again. Sometimes he read my notes and scrutinized them. Sometimes he commented on the lack of equipment, and medications, and general resources. Whenever the opportunity presented itself, he told me we needed to "change things around here."

In this regard, I actually agreed. My father had been a two-finger typist with a physical aversion to technology, and it showed. The paper charts were quite literally falling apart. They were organized alphabetically, but only in the most general sense. All the "A's" went in the same pile. *Pile* meaning a heap on the floor. The charts had overtaken the office like a plague. Shelves were overrun. Desks jammed with billing forms and other slips of paper that were probably important. It was only a matter of time before Medicare hunted us down.

But it would take years to convert everything to an electronic medical record. Even if I managed to recruit a staff of twenty, the real obstacle was the inevitable backlash against my efforts. *Fancy-pants Aubrey Lane thinks she can just change medicine.* I'd be chased out of town with pitchforks.

In the meantime, I did what I could to optimize the messy medical records. I started with the patients who were being seen that week: fourteen in all. I gutted all the irrelevant crap from their charts—old notes, x-rays, receipts—and filed it in the archives, ie. the attic. The result was a slim paper chart with key information, emergency contacts, allergies, current medications, and relevant medical history. Notes from the past three years were organized in chronological order in the back of the chart. Sheldon didn't notice this improvement because he didn't actually handle the charts—he just asked me what he needed to know.

Every morning, I pulled the charts for those patients who appeared on the schedule. On Monday, there were four: Sammy Samson (1 week follow-up), Ophelia Sinclair (pre-natal, 37 weeks; also "psychological distress related to pregnancy"), Lois Ainsley (New Patient), and Carter Reed (trigger finger).

Lois Ainsley?

Luke had a sister, but her name wasn't Lois. His parents were Philip and Nancy, and in any case, they were definitely not new to the practice. *So who the hell was Lois?*

She was scheduled for noon—the lunch hour. A popular slot for people who worked during the day; stay-at-home moms usually preferred the mornings and kids came after school. Luke, for instance, would come at noon. Was he related to her? *Married* to her? The absence of a wedding band on his finger didn't necessarily prove anything (although Mr. Sanderson and just about everyone else in town might disagree).

I didn't have time to think about much more than that because the Samsons had arrived early. For not the first time, I wondered about that family, with its stoic matriarch, a non-existent father, and four-now-three children. Which of those dead boys had been her son? Tristan? Kyle? Had she wept for him? Of course she had; just because I couldn't imagine her doing so didn't mean she grieved any differently than anyone else.

Three generations of the Samson family awaited me in Room 1. It took me a moment to recognize Dirk Samson, Moira's father and the grizzliest dude in Callihax. He reminded me of a birch tree—sinewy and lean, his plaster-white face speckled with sunspots. His beard was blond, but the hair on his head had gone a savage, bone-white. He had the body of a teenager and the face of an old man, which gave him the look of an alien woodsman.

Sheldon bungled in without so much as a glance in Sammy or Moira's direction. He shook hands with Dirk, then promptly washed them, because Dirk's hands were a filthy black.

"Fine boy you have here," Sheldon said, his attention still fixed on Dirk.

"He's my grandson," Dirk snarled.

"Ah." Sheldon's face bloomed red. He tried to recover by reaching for the boy, but Sammy recoiled in Moira's lap.

"Man up, Sam," Moira said, but her voice lacked its usual bite. I wondered if Dirk's presence had anything to do with that. "Come on now."

Sammy started to wail. I remained at my perch by the door, while Sheldon tried to get the kid under control. Despite Moira's attempts to bribe him with lollipops, chaos ensued. Sammy screamed and cried and kicked Sheldon away. Dirk, meanwhile, looked on in silence.

"Aub-eee!" Sammy yelled.

Sheldon froze. Even Moira looked a little stunned.

Sammy crawled to his feet. "I want Aub-eee," he sniffled.

"Honey, this here's the real doctor." Moira pointed to Sheldon. "Aubrey hurt you last week, remember?"

"Aub-eee!"

"For Chrissakes." Moira scooped him up and plopped him in my arms. "There. Happy?"

Sammy beamed.

My heart skipped a beat—or three, or ten. "Hi, Sammy," I said.

"I'm better!"

"Yes you are," I said, and the smile that found my face touched my soul. I held him while Sheldon explained to Dirk that the kid was fine, no need to bring him back to clinic unless his symptoms returned.

Dirk responded to this with a series of blinks. No nod; certainly no words. His gaze cut across the room to me.

"You seen him last week?" he asked me.

"Yes," I said, swallowing hard.

"He look better to you?"

"Yes." *And I gave him antibiotics he didn't need,* but no need to mention that.

"Good."

He gestured to Moira, who gathered up Sammy's Matchbox cars and followed her father out the door. The fire hadn't yet gone out of Sheldon's cheeks.

"Ah, the terrible twos," he said, chuckling. "Moodier than a goddamn woman."

He peeled his stethoscope off the floor and strode out.

Next up:

Lois Ainsley.

NINE

A miracle of sorts happened five minutes before noon: Sheldon got the runs.

He was examining Mrs. Parson's tonsils when he grabbed his belt buckle and bolted for the door. "Pardon me for a moment, would you?" he asked. He didn't wait for her answer.

"Oh, dear," she said.

Oh yes, I thought.

With Sheldon otherwise occupied, Mrs. Parsons was more than happy to tell me all about the roses she'd already ordered for the Christmas season. Poinsettias were no longer in vogue, she explained. The real reason she'd nixed the poinsettias was that she had discovered they were poisonous—which didn't faze most people, but Mrs. Parsons feared the living world. Judging by the massive size of her chart, she was one of my father's regulars. *Incurable hypochondria*, he used to say. *Listen; don't indulge.*

Sheldon poked his head in as the clock struck noon. "Would you join me in the hallway for a moment, Dr. Lane?" He smiled for Mrs. Parson's benefit.

The windowless hallway lighting did him no favors, emphasizing the wan, sickly sheen of the gastrointestinally distressed. "Are you all right?" I asked.

"I've got a bit of a bug." He admitted this with as much cheer as he could muster. "Must've been the omelet I had for breakfast."

I tried to feign sympathy, but this was victory. Four whole hours with my own patients. Yes, it would go terribly. Yes, I would want to quit by the end of the afternoon. But I desperately needed a breather from Sheldon Kline.

"Would you like me to take over for a bit?" I asked.

"No, no." He wiped the sweat off his brow with an old-fashioned hankie. "I think we should cancel clinic this afternoon. Tell them all to come back tomorrow."

"But I can just see them now—"

He muttered something about "nonsense" as he hustled into the bathroom for the third time. A waterfall of gastrointestinal distress ensued behind the closed door. Still, he kept talking.

"Double-book them if you must. We'll start early."

"But tomorrow is St. Rita's feast day." I had given up on trying to sound civil.

"Pardon?"

"The church has a parade. They won't like it if we open for business—"

"You think Ophelia Sinclair will care? That gal would come in on Christmas if she could." He released a long, tortured moan, then went on: "Carter Reed has had that trigger finger for years. He can wait a day or two."

"What about Lois Ainsley?"

"New Patients are never urgent." The sound of running water joined the sounds of the ceiling fan and a host of other noises going on in there. "She can reschedule."

"But 'New Patient' also means 'not sick.' I'll just take a history and do the exam."

"Dr. Lane, you know I have the utmost faith in your abilities —"

"I won't prescribe anything," I said. The hopefulness of the afternoon had started slipping away from me, as had my pride.

"What if Ms. Ainsley *asks* you to prescribe something?"

"Then I'll tell her to come back tomorrow."

"What if she has an acute issue?"

"Then I'll tell her to come back as soon as you're able to see her."

The toilet flushed and the door swung open. The smell was atrocious. Eggs, indeed. Maybe some sardines thrown in for good measure.

He blew his nose, which completed the pathetic picture. I

eased him toward the reception area, and from there, the front door.

"I can handle this, Doctor."

"I just think it would be more practical—"

"Go home. I'll call you with any emergencies." My hand had found a nice foothold in the crook of his elbow. I was ready to push him over the threshold if I had to. "How about I have Corinne give you a ride home?"

"I really think—"

"Corinne!"

Corinne rounded the corner at her usual lazy pace, her golden bracelets and anklets and hoop earrings clanging with each step. For twenty-eight (certain personal factoids, like age, were readily circulated by the masses), she dressed extremely young —or maybe I was just old. "What?" she drawled.

"Can you drive Sheldon home, please?"

She blew out a breath between her teeth. "Seriously? Now?"

"He lives five minutes away."

"Then can't he walk?"

"Corinne, he's sick."

She looked at his mutilated hankie and beaded brow. "Oh."

"Thanks," I said.

As they stepped out into the sunshine, Corinne threw me a glance. "By the way, your twelve-o'clock's here."

***

Lois Ainsley was one of those rare humans that belonged in a Renaissance painting. Among her striking features were a perfectly oval face, soft blond ringlets, and a slender gap between her two front teeth. According to Corinne's intake notes, she was fifty-two inches tall and weighed forty-eight pounds. Her date of birth made her seven-years-old.

Luke sat in the chair beside her. *Her father?*

They both had that uncomfortable, stiff-legged look to them, but Luke was worse. His eyes were bloodshot, his usually clean-shaven jaw covered in scruff. He looked in desperate need of a good night's sleep.

"Hi," he said to me. The warmth with which he had greeted me days before was gone.

"Hey." I looked at Lois. "Hi there. My name is Aubrey."

"Dr. Lane," Luke clarified. He patted the girl's hand, but she continued to study me with arresting blue eyes.

Luke tried again. "Lois, can you say hello to Dr. Lane?"

No response. The stare—incredibly—intensified.

I took the stool Sheldon had occupied for the past week. No point in reading Lois' file while we sat in the room together; it was completely blank. For the purposes of our office records, Lois Ainsley was a seven-year-old ghost.

Luke finally gave up on trying to coax her into an introduction. He peeled off the girl's pink coat and folded it haphazardly in his lap. For whatever reason, Lois Ainsley seemed transfixed by me. Maybe it was the white coat, or my stethoscope, or the assembly of tools in my pockets. Maybe it was the mysterious yellow stain on my collar. Maybe she could smell fear.

"Here." I handed her my penlight. "Have a look."

She accepted it with great caution. After a careful inspection of its tiny bulb, she gestured for the tuning fork. Then my prescription pad. My stethoscope. It wasn't long before I had everything in my pockets laid out for her on the examining table.

Together, we identified the items—or rather, she pointed, and I confirmed: Book. Pen. Stethoscope. Ophthalmoscope. Syringe. Change purse. Note cards. Prescription pad. Broken watch. Ten-dollar bill. My insurance card.

She didn't miss the last item, which was poking out of my change purse. She held it up.

"That's a St. Christopher medal," I said. "It belonged to my dad."

I watched Lois inspect everything before chancing what felt like a very awkward conversation with her ride. There was no real way to ease into this, so I just went for it.

"Is Lois your daughter?"

Luke rubbed his knuckles until the skin turned red. "My niece."

"Oh."

"You remember Ellen, don't you?"

Ellen Ainsley, Luke's older sister, would be thirty-three now. I hadn't seen her since my eighth-grade graduation.

"Of course."

"Lois is her daughter."

"I see." I didn't dare ask what had happened to Ellen—at least, not with her seven-year-old in the room. Another lesson learned the hard way in residency.

"Anyway, Lois is going to be staying with me for a while."

"That's…a big deal."

"Yeah." He smiled, equal parts weary and genuine. "It's an adjustment for both of us, but we'll get there."

"How about…how about your dad? Is he helping out?"

"No," he said.

His curt answer said everything. Before Mrs. Ainsley died, Ellen's troubles had sent both her parents into a period of permanent retreat, which I thought had more to do with shock than humiliation—but there were those that disagreed.

"What happened?"

"Dad went down to New York, tried to help Ellen out…" He brushed Lois' hair out of her face as he spoke. "Anyway, he gave up eventually, moved to Florida…"

"I'm sorry," I said.

"It happens."

I silently thanked him for not bringing up my own family. Those wounds were still raw, the reality of my father's death having yet to settle in.

I looked at Lois. What a strange, precious little girl. Ellen had been the same way: aesthetically pleasing, but with a personality that seemed to float on the whims of other people. Mercurial was perhaps the best way to describe her. Mercurial, and tragic.

"So…I just have a few questions I have to ask to establish Lois as a patient here."

Luke's face brightened. "Sure."

"Was she full-term?"

"Full what?"

"Born at term, I mean."

"Oh." He rubbed his neck. "Shit, I don't know. Is that important? I might be able to find out—"

"No, no, it's fine." I hurried onto the next question: "Any chronic health problems? Disorders? Major childhood illnesses that you know of?"

"Uh, no. Not that I know of."

"Is she generally healthy?"

"Very healthy."

Lois had discovered a diagram of the male anatomy in my Pocket Medicine book. Luke distracted her with a box of band-aids.

"Does she speak?"

"Speak?"

"She hasn't said a word since she's been here."

"She's a little shy."

"So she does speak at home?"

His silence gave me my answer.

"Not at all?" I asked gently.

"I figured it's just the trauma from all the change in her life." We watched as Lois decorated the walls with band-aids. "She lived with my dad for a while before..." He trailed off. "Anyway, just a lot going on."

In an attempt to sound nonchalant, I said, "I see."

"It's a long story."

"Would it be all right if I checked her hearing?"

"Sure, sure. Now?"

"We can do it now if you like."

Sheldon would have vetoed the hearing exam—"*Are you sure that's really necessary?*"—but Luke trusted my judgment. He sat in respectful silence while I put the headphones on Lois's ears. She responded in perfect sync to the sounds.

"Hearing's fine," I said.

"Good. I thought it would be. She's a light sleeper."

"Nightmares?"

He nodded. "Sometimes."

I didn't pursue it. Unlike most kids her age, Lois was very cooperative with my exam. I wondered if she'd ever had a vaccine in her life. I'd ask Luke about this later, when he was feeling a little less like a total failure.

"Well, she's a lovely girl." I offered a sticker to Lois who, after some deliberation, chose the truck over the unicorn.

"Good choice," I told her.

She looked at me with eyes that were intense and intelligent —not the glazed, empty look I'd seen in some children who had been abused or neglected all their lives. Someone had cared deeply for this girl for most of her life.

"Is that it, then?" he asked.

"That's it."

"Great. Thanks for, uh, seeing us."

"Sure."

Lois's presence had eased the tension between us, but the undercurrent of strain remained. Strain and hurt and a whiff of betrayal. I just wasn't sure who had betrayed whom.

Before I could figure that out, Corinne appeared at the door.

"Oh, hey!" She whipped her hair and flashed her smile at Luke. "Your little girl is so *cute*." Her next thought was so obvious it may as well have been spoken aloud: *Just like you.*

"My niece actually," he said.

"Oh! Well, still." She held out her arms for Lois, but the little girl retreated towards the wall. She slinked out the door like a miniature spy.

Luke started after her, but Lois was distracted by the pictures in the hallway and had stopped to look at them. Corinne remained where she was, ogling Luke.

"Corinne, can you put Ophelia in a room please?"

"Her appointment's not till one—"

"Yes, but she's here. Can you please just put her in?"

"Sheldon said not to do that—"

"Corinne!" I bit my lip. "Please."

"Whatevs," she said, and smirked at Luke. "You *have* to let me babysit."

"Yeah, that, uh...that'd be great." His attempt to sound convincing fell flat, but Corinne was charmed nonetheless. "I'll call you."

"Awesome. Here's my number." She'd already written it on the back of Lois' discharge sheet.

"Thanks," he said.

"First sit's free." She winked and finally left.

I was still reeling from her gratuitous flirting when Luke grasped my wrist and pulled me back into the room. The sudden, whirlwind gesture took me a little by surprise. To be honest, it felt almost scandalous. His hand on the bare skin of my forearm; his voice hushed in a darkened room. I hoped to God he couldn't hear my heart racing.

"Aubrey, I have to tell you something."

"What's that?" I asked. Annoyed. Irritated. A little turned on.

"I don't have a clue what I'm doing here." He seemed to realize how inappropriately close we were and backed up a step. "About Lois, I mean."

I eased his hand off me and turned on the light.

"Sorry," he muttered.

"It's fine."

"I'm losing it, as you can see."

"You're doing fine. Kids are resilient."

"What about adults?"

I conceded a smile. "Maybe less so."

"I knew I was screwed." His eyes danced with the joke, though a part of me wondered if he really believed what he was saying.

"You can always call the office with questions," I offered.

"Parenting questions?"

"Any questions."

He shook my hand. "Thanks, Dr. Lane," he said.

Dr. Lane.

When he said it, it didn't sound like my father's name.
It sounded like mine.

TEN

Carter Reed cancelled and Ophelia Sinclair refused to see me, so I spent the rest of the afternoon alone. Sheldon called around four to discuss Lois Ainsley, which ended up being a very short conversation. Except for the peculiar mutism, she was a healthy seven-year-old girl.

After a full run-down of my one and only patient encounter, Sheldon proposed a list of tasks for the afternoon: *pull the charts for Wednesday, get Corinne to wipe down the tables and equipment, change the daily calendars,* and so on. Corinne didn't do "wipe-downs," so I did that myself. Calendars had all been changed. That left the charts.

There were five on the docket for tomorrow: two *B's,* an *I,* and an *S*. It took three minutes to locate the first three. Temptation set in on number four.

To start, I wanted to know how Moira's son had died. Asking questions around town—or worse, of her—would just breed animosity. Reading a file was easy. Clean. No one would ever know. Except the HIPAA gods who, let's face it, didn't play much of a role in this town.

I moved down to the *S's* and sifted through the Samson files. There were a number of them: Dirk, Eloise, Moira, Mary, Margaret, Mary Ann, Marie, Margo...*for the love of God, show a little creativity.* Quite a number of boys, too: Aidan, Blake, Zed, Michael, Timothy, John, Jake, Jacob...

I pulled out every last Samson chart—there were fifty-four in all—and tried to sort them by first name. I looked for Ryan, Kyle, Tristan, or Bo. No matches. I tried alternate spellings. Middle names. Confirmation names.

Nothing. I resorted to organizing the charts by birthdate,

which gave me three boys between the ages of five and fifteen. Still no Ryan, Kyle, Tristan, or Bo. Maybe Bo was a nickname? In which case any of these charts could be his.

It took two minutes to dispel that theory. All three boys had been seen in clinic in the past month—each of them for sports physicals.

Maybe Luke had gotten the ages wrong. I expanded the birthdate range and came up with two more charts. Again, both boys had been seen in the last year. One was thirteen, and per the chart, he'd fallen out of a tree. The other was fifteen and had been treated for chlamydia.

Five dead-ends.

Where was it?

My mother had mentioned something about my father "burying the charts." Did she mean literally burying? As in, with a shovel and gloves? This file room was the most secure place in town, even more so than the Post Office, which didn't lock its doors. Maybe my father had finally gotten around to archiving the charts of his deceased patients, in which case the Samson boy would have been removed from the pool. I tested the theory by pulling Gran's chart. She had died during my sophomore year of high school.

Her chart was still on the shelf, neatly filed next to Jean Rienne, her sister. Both were deceased. Both had a big red slash drawn through the first page. Apparently, this was my father's highly technical approach for differentiating the dead from the living.

I didn't bother to look for the other boys. All the charts were shelved according to Last Name, First Initial, which meant I'd have to go through 2,000 files to find a Tristan, or a Ryan, or a Bo—*if* those charts were even here. Sometimes my father left paperwork in random places: at home, under the reception desk, in his office…

The office.

Unlike the file room, his office door didn't lock. I walked right in, unprepared for the tragic onslaught of the familiar. The room even smelled like him, like carbon and ink and chamomile tea. I gasped at the memory.

The condition of the room, even more so than the smell, came as a shock. The rug was aligned perfectly with the wall. Chairs sat at proper angles. The desk had been moved from the window closer to the door, which gave the space a cold, impersonal feel. My father had always appreciated a nice view. Even though he and Gran weren't related, they were alike in that way. They could sit for hours in front of a window, admiring the simplest things: colors. Trees. Sky. My grandmother used such scenes for inspiration; my father, for that elusive sense of calm.

Maybe someone had come up here and moved all the furniture around, but that didn't make sense. An intruder would have left things alone, seemingly untouched. Anyone who knew my father well could see that the furnishings had been deliberately manipulated.

No, it wasn't some sly ghost in the night. My father had done this. He had moved his desk from the window to the wall; he had stored his personal effects and opted for empty space instead of his characteristic chaos. I wondered what had been going through his mind when he'd dragged that desk across the room, turning his back on a view he had always savored.

The search for stray charts was brief. All his dusty medical textbooks had been cleared from the shelves, probably relegated to a box somewhere in the basement; his desk drawers were also empty. I even pulled up the oriental rug, revealing a glaze of dust. There was nothing there. No charts. No hundred-dollar bills stashed under the rug. Nothing at all.

I was on the way out the door, feeling dejected and not a little confused, when a figurine on the windowsill caught my eye. As I drew closer, I saw that the statue—which, oddly, faced the street—was in fact two people molded together: a burly, massive-shouldered man, and a small child on his shoulders. The rushing waters at the man's feet cast aside any doubt: it was definitely St. Christopher, the patron saint of travelers—and something else that eluded me.

Christopher's lush red cloak had gone a spotty orange, his facial features rubbed nearly flat after years of rough handling. The little Jesus on his shoulders was in even worse shape. I wondered who had given my father such an oddly sentimental gift. A patient? Father Meade? Not my mother—she didn't believe in religious relics.

As I placed it back on the sill, I watched a large SUV drive past, heading south. It slowed as it passed the corner store, then stopped directly across the street. I spun away from the window, cursing myself for staring so long. All the lights in this room were on. Whoever was in that car had definitely seen me.

Why did it matter? It didn't; everyone in a two-hundred mile radius knew I worked here. Hell, I owned the building. I turned off the light and left the room.

I had more to do, but the spidery chill at the base of my neck told me it could wait until tomorrow. I packed up my things and threw on a coat and made my way out back. I tucked my keys between my knuckles and hurried across the lot.

Ten paces...twenty...I started to jog...

Footsteps.

Behind me. Close. Moving faster.

I was nearly to the Rover when my keys slipped from my fingers. *Shit.* I couldn't see a damn thing on the concrete. No moonlight; no stray glow from neighboring businesses. My father had never bothered to install exterior lights.

There. I pried them off the pavement and ran toward the Rover's hulking mass. The footsteps behind me matched my pace. I knew sounding a car alarm at this hour would rouse the whole damn town, but whatever. I hit the button.

The sound was tremendous, like a bullhorn. Big European lights started flashing. The whole vehicle seemed to vibrate with the noise.

Footsteps. Louder. *Close.*

I jerked my left elbow toward the sound. The crook of my arm landed with a sickening crunch—flesh against flesh, bone against bone. My technique was good. Something warm and wet sprayed my sleeve.

"Aubrey! What the…"

The blinking lights of the Land Rover caught Luke at a truly cinematic moment as he bent forward and cupped both hands over his nose. Blood seeped through his fingers.

"I'm so sorry…I thought you were somebody else…"

He held up a hand as he pinched his eyes shut.

"Here. Stand up." I tilted his head back while he kept both hands on his face. Yes, definitely broken. Even in the flickering headlights, I could see the damage.

"Jesus," he groaned. "L.A. turned you into a badass." The blood gave his voice a puckered, nasal quality.

"Sorry," I mumbled. "Let's go inside and I'll set it."

"Set it?"

"You'll be fine."

He let me escort him back inside—not so much a display of trust, perhaps, as a concession. The blood leaking between his fingers left a trail on the pavement.

In the shadows across the street, the SUV was gone.

***

I put him in Room 4. This time Luke had no qualms about sitting on the exam table. He climbed right up there and tilted his head back until the blood oozed down his throat and made him cough. I handed him some gauze and told him to apply pressure for a few minutes.

"I must've scared the hell out of you," he said.

"Just a little."

"I get the fear of dark parking lots, but this isn't exactly—"

"LA?"

"I wasn't gonna say that."

"Keep your head back." I tipped his chin with my fingers.

"Is it still bleeding?"

"It's slowing down." I removed the saturated gauze and shined a penlight up his nose. A bad break, but a clean one.

"Good thing I trimmed those nose hairs yesterday," he said.

"*That's* what you're worried about?"

"Why? Should I be worried?"

My first thought was *probably*, but I ignored the question and said, "I have to set your nose."

"That sounds painful."

"I can give you something for pain beforehand."

I expected Luke to answer with a quick, tough-guy *no*— all men under the age of thirty-five did—but he surprised me. "What would you recommend?"

"I'd take something for pain."

"Then let's do that."

A whiff of fentanyl later, he had relaxed, his shoulders and arms and tongue noticeably looser. "Miracle worker," he slurred.

"I haven't done anything yet."

"Then let's get on with it."

The whole ordeal took three seconds, but it felt far longer. A soft crunch, and it was done. Tears welled in his eyes, but he didn't make a sound.

"Can you breathe?"

He inhaled deeply through his nose. "Yeah. Thanks."

"I broke your nose, and you're thanking me?"

"Well, you fixed it. So it's a zero-sum game."

"Hardly. You're going to look like hell for at least a week."

He shrugged. "Gives me some street cred."

"I won't tell anyone I did it."

He laughed, then winced. "I appreciate that."

I stood back to assess the damage: bloody shirt, blood-spattered jeans. An impressively swollen nose that would be all sorts of colors tomorrow. I felt awful.

"Why were you lurking in the parking lot?" I asked.

He gave me a sheepish look, made even more pitiful by the mangled nose. "I came back for Groovy."

"Groovy?"

"Lois' stuffed frog. She can't sleep without it."

"Oh." Now I *really* felt awful.

"I saw the lights on as I came up the hill, but they were off when I got here. I figured you'd just left."

"You drove here?"

"Ran. Why?"

"No reason." The SUV couldn't have belonged to him anyway, seeing as it was gone now. Or maybe I'd imagined the whole thing—the North Woods had that effect on people, especially after dark. Gran used to call it *woodsanity*.

Luke climbed off the table. I had to steady him as he bent down to tie his shoe.

"I'll drive you home," I said.

"I can walk."

"I'm sure you could, but I'd hate for Lois to find you passed out in the driveway tomorrow morning."

"Hey, if I make it to the driveway, that's a victory."

"Let's go." I helped him with his coat even though he didn't really need it. On our way out the backdoor, I grabbed Groovy from the lost-and-found bin.

"Are you gonna give me the same leave-me-alone lecture when we get there?"

"That wasn't a lecture."

"A speech, then?"

"I just think it's better if we do our own thing. Don't you?"

"Sure. I mean, that's what I told Anna and lemme tell you—"

"Who's Anna?"

"A girl...I tried to marry her, to be honest."

I felt my cheeks flush. "Your fiance."

He laughed, albeit gingerly. "Nah, I wouldn't call her that. Sounds so pretentious and French. I don't speak French. I speak English. Then again 'fiance' sounds better than 'betrothed,' which sounds like a vampire bride. Don't you think? Or is that just me."

He started toward the front door. "I'm this way," I said, steering him toward the back. "So you're not engaged now?"

"No. You?"

"No."

"I gotta say I'm surprised." He opened the door with his bloody hand and held it for me. Always a gentleman, even after my assault on his face. Once outside, I made sure to lock the door behind us.

"Why?"

"You fishing for compliments?"

"No, I just want to know why."

"Let's see. You're dumb as bricks, for one thing. Hideous, too. You smell bad. Not at all funny. You dress like a homeless person —"

"Okay, I get it."

He smirked as he opened the car door for me.

"What about you?" I asked. "Surely your winning sarcasm would have won somebody over."

"Not in the way I might've hoped."

I made a point of averting his gaze as he eased into the passenger seat. Whatever that comment meant, I didn't want to know the details.

"So is it just Lois and you in that big house, then?" I asked.

"Used to be just me, but my aunt moved back in. You remember her, right?"

"Sure."

"She's helping out."

"That's good."

We trawled through town at a slow speed, while Luke babied his nose and I watched for the SUV. The streets reflected the dim, scattered lights of the empty storefronts, mirroring the starry sky overhead. Callihax never felt as desolate as these lonely hours after dusk.

After about a mile, we turned onto County Route 42, where the Ainsleys lived. The blue mailbox signaled the place to turn, and I made it automatically, a function of tried-and-true muscle memory. Every light in the house was on, even in the attic.

"Lois prefers the lights," Luke explained.

"Can't blame her," I said, thinking to myself, *She's not the only one.* As soon as the tires crunched gravel, Lois bolted out the front door.

"She's excited to see you," I said.

"Nope. It's this guy." He held up Groovy. "Thanks for grabbing him, by the way."

Lois glimpsed the stuffed frog, but her freckled cheeks paled when she saw Luke's face.

"He's okay," I said to her. "Just a broken nose."

"Just a broken nose," he muttered. "Hurts like a goddamn—"

"Luke! Oh my word." Luke's aunt—the only woman on his father's side, and known to us "kids" as Ms. Ainsley—approached the passenger-side window. "What happened to you?"

"It's a long story," he said. "I'm tired and I'm going to bed."

Ms. Ainsley looked past him at me.

"He's okay," I said. "It'll just take some time to heal."

"He looks like he got hit by a bus."

"It'll get better," I said, more to convince myself than her.

"I certainly hope so." Her mood swung the other way and she flashed me one of her matronly smiles. "Take care now, dear."

I watched Luke trudge toward the house with Lois at one side and his stodgy aunt at the other. He would definitely hate me tomorrow—not just for the broken nose, but for the fentanyl, and my "lecture," and his loosened tongue.

Still, he hadn't said much, especially about himself. I never thought Luke Ainsley would leave the North Woods, but he had, and then he'd returned, and I didn't know why. I wondered about Lois, too. Her wordlessness deepened the mystery of who she was; where she came from. Luke had opened up to me only once about his mother, and even then, whiskey-drunk and bone-tired, he'd stumbled over every word. He was eighteen then. Something told me the years had fortified, rather than weakened, his emotional barriers.

In time, I might figure out how to get those answers—if not from him, then from someone else. As for the SUV, I'd chalk that up to a creepy coincidence. My father used to tell me never to interfere with strange folks who passed through town. *Best to just let them go*, he'd say. I only ever knew they were around when my father locked the doors and windows for a night or two. I locked the doors that night.

***

Wednesday broke with a temper, blustery and cold. The trees outside my window keeled in the wind as if trying to escape some unseen force of nature, wayward branches scratching the panes. I pulled an old pair of thermals out of the closet and padded downstairs.

The day held so much promise in the early hours—at least it used to, when my father woke at dawn to "carp the day," as he liked to say. First thing he did was make a pot of hair-raising coffee, which woke you up whether you drank it or not. Then he sang—Christmas carols were his favorite, even in July. Coming downstairs to a quiet kitchen didn't sit right, even though it had been years since I'd spent any significant amount of time here.

Jax, my father's old coonhound, seemed to rue his absence in much the same way. His large, sad eyes blinked up at me as I opened the backdoor. He loped toward it, none too anxious to do his business on cold wet grass. I padded after him in my slippers, thermals, and robe—one of the perks of living a few thousand feet away from the closest neighbor. Jax didn't wander far, and I was about to call him back inside when his ears perked up, and he bolted. He was gone within seconds.

"Jax!" *Dammit.* The mist snaked through the trees and a thick frost crunched underfoot. I stopped after about a hundred yards, knowing that to go any farther would risk disaster. In any case, he knew his way back better than I did.

My trudge uphill turned brisk as I recalled the events of the previous night. More than likely the SUV had already left town, but even so, its presence gnawed at me. If I saw it again, I'd swallow my pride and ask Jim Ranson to keep an eye on it.

The sun had not yet crested the trees, and my grandfather's manic depressive house still indulged its early-morning gloom. There were no comforting lights in the windows, no spirals of smoke from the fireplace. I had left the back door open.

"Mom?" I dead-bolted the door behind me. "Mom!"

The knives winked at me from their perch on the countertop. *We may as well cut our food with our fingers if we're going to have dull knives*, my mother said once. She sharpened them once a month using her own tools.

I pried a paring knife out of its stand and held it flush against my thigh. I crept up the stairs, hips angled sideways. There was no one here. *Jax just ran off. You're acting crazy—*

"Aubrey?" My mother materialized at the top of the stairs with such stealth I screamed.

"Have you lost your mind?" she cried.

"No, I just—"

"Give me that."

She grasped the knife in the safety-first position and brushed past me. I followed her into the kitchen because it seemed like that's what she wanted me to do. "Sit down," she commanded.

"I'm sorry—"

"You're white as a sheet. What did you see?"

"Nothing."

"Where's Jax?"

Damn, she was sharp.

"He ran off."

"That dog's a thousand years old. He doesn't just 'run off.'" In a startling deviation from the norm, her auburn hair was a tousled mess, her flannel pajamas rumpled from a truncated sleep. Everything about her had that sleepy, early-morning look. Except, of course, for the electric terror in her eyes.

"Tell me what happened," she said.

"I overreacted."

"Prior to that."

I thought about the SUV—black, bulky, non-descript. It could have been a Ford or an Escalade or a Honda. It could have been anything. And yet here I was, wielding knives at dawn after chasing a decrepit coonhound in a bathrobe.

"I saw an SUV outside the clinic last night."

"An SUV?"

"Yes. A black one."

She gave me a look that made me feel ten-years-old again. "Do you realize how many people drive SUV's?"

"Several?"

"More than several," she said. "You, for one—"

"Mine's just a rental—"

"Surely you must realize the American obsession with their big cars."

"Even up here?"

"Especially up here. Snow makes people skittish."

I considered this. "Okay, fine. But this one stopped in the middle of the street. The driver was looking at me."

She laughed.

"What's so funny?"

"Sweetheart, can you think of anyone in town who *doesn't* want to get a good look at you? You're the newcomer. The talk of the week. The month, maybe. People are curious."

"Something just seemed off," I said sullenly.

Her voice softened a touch. "Let's say it was an outsider. You thought the driver of this mysterious SUV distracted that old coonhound and stole into our home to terrorize me?"

"Something like that."

"I see."

"It sounds stupid when you say it like that."

"Is there a better way to say it?"

I poured myself a cup of hot cocoa. Maybe the sweet taste would dampen my mortification. "Dad always locked the doors when strangers came through town. I guess I got a little spooked."

"I noticed you locked them last night."

"Habit, I guess."

"You haven't been here long enough to form a habit."

"Nostalgia, then."

"There you go."

She helped herself to a cup of cocoa and drank it in a

pensive silence. Her fingers were long and slender—"musical," as my father used to say. My mother had abandoned the piano and violin some years ago, which had devastated him almost as much as my leaving home.

"I didn't mean to start your day like that," I said. "I'm sorry."

"It's fine. I've had worse."

"What about Jax?"

"He'll come home."

"You sure?"

"With all the goodies you slip him under the table?" Her eyes betrayed a strange mix of humor and sadness. "I'm positive."

But this time, she was wrong.

ELEVEN

Sheldon was delighted when I called to tell him I'd be missing clinic. "Search as long as you need," he said, loosely translated as, "Search indefinitely!" I'd have to get there at dawn tomorrow to clean up his mess, but that was tomorrow. Today I intended to find my father's dog.

My hiking boots from high school still fit—at least well enough to wear for a day. I laced them up and canvassed every inch of woods within a half-mile radius of my house, an effort that required three hours of steep climbs and bushwacking. I called Jax's name until my throat was raw. No answer. Not even a lonely set of paw prints in the mud.

After lunch, I tried the downtown area, the school grounds, a meshwork of dirt roads, and finally, the river. Former neighbors and old classmates ignored me, their heads down and hands shoved in their pockets. No one asked me who Jax was, even though I suspected some of them knew. Only one person offered to help, and that was sixteen-year-old Zach Shears, who appeared to be operating on some kind of dare. His friends snickered as I passed them by.

With dusk on the horizon, I called it quits. Jax was an old dog —possibly senile, and therefore lost, and weak, and somewhat low on the food chain. Such was life in the North Woods. Survival of the fittest. Maybe a mountain lion had gotten him, or a bear. I didn't allow myself to consider the third possibility. *Human.*

After a dinner of canned soup and potato chips, I collapsed in bed with my flannels and boots on. Some hours later, the phone trilled in my ear. 2:13 AM.

"Jax?" I pinched the bridge of my nose to summon some

clarity. "Sorry, I meant...never mind. Who is this?"

"Is this Dr. Lane?" A high voice; childlike. I didn't recognize it.

"No, this is Aubrey."

"Oh."

The long pause nearly lulled me back to sleep.

"You're the doctor though, right?"

"Sorry again. Yes, this is Dr. Lane." I turned on the bedside light. "What's wrong? Who is this?"

"This is Kyla."

"Kyla..."

"Samson."

*Kyla...Kyla...*I couldn't keep all the Samson kids straight, but she sounded young enough to be Moira's daughter. I couldn't picture her face, though. Freckles? A white scar teasing her bottom lip? Or maybe that was Francine...

"How can I help you, Kyla?"

"Well, I didn't know who else to call..." Static peppered the line. "I just kinda had your number..."

"Kyla, it's two in the morning. Just tell me what the problem is."

"I think my mom's in trouble."

"What kind of trouble?"

"Like, she's on the floor."

"The *floor?*"

"Yeah, like, asleep. Kinda."

"Kinda?"

"Her eyes are rolled back in her head and she's shaking all over."

Seizure. That word and all its associations—grand mal, post-ictal, Ativan, Keppra, EEG, Neuro consult, prolactin—bloomed in my mind. Most of those words didn't mean anything out here; I sure as hell couldn't call a neurologist to sort this out. I could call Sheldon, though.

"Are you home alone, Kyla?"

"Yeah. Well, except for Sammy and Francine, but they don't count."

"Okay. I need you to roll your mom onto her side."

"Right now?"

"Right now."

The sound of Kyla's shuffling footsteps permeated the static. I tried to picture the scene: Moira on the floor, limbs seizing and eyes rolled back, while her nine-year-old tried to roll her over. *Where the hell was their father?* Moira was such an imposing figure that I hadn't even considered his absence until now. She had three kids at home. That wasn't an insignificant number.

"Okay." Kyla was sniffling now. "Okay, I did it."

"Is she still seize—shaking?"

"Yeah." She let loose a sob. "It's bad, isn't it?"

"I'll be over in a couple minutes. What's your address?"

"Cooley Road. The green mailbox."

I knew it well. Moira had grown up in that house, a sturdy old farmhouse down by the creek. I'd never been inside, but everyone knew *about* that house. As kids, my friends and I used to ride our bikes past the gate and speculate about all the ghosts that lived there. Why else would Moira never invite anyone over? She had a ton of friends. Liked parties. And the house was a good size, not a trailer like some kids had. The "Samson Mansion"— an exaggeration, but it had a nice ring to it—was one of the great mysteries of Callihax.

"I'll be there in eight minutes," I said.

"Can you hurry?"

"I'm already on my way."

"Okay." Kyla sniffled and hung up.

I was almost out the door when my mother appeared in the doorway. She hadn't even gone to bed yet. "What's going on?"

"Someone's having a seizure."

"Hm. Do you have everything you need?"

"Yeah. I mean, I think so."

"Did you call Sheldon?"

Silence. Not a direct answer, but close enough. I waited for her to berate me.

"Just be careful on the roads," she said.

***

It took me twelve minutes to get to the Samson Mansion—four more than estimated because I got lost. Not catastrophically lost, but enough to fray my nerves. I almost rolled the Rover in my haste to get there.

The Samson Mansion hadn't changed a lick in fifteen years: same green shutters and wild, sprawling ivy, set against woodsy white paneling that Dirk had cut himself. Tonight, the windows were cracked open, and heavy white drapes caught the draft. I parked next to the front door and walked right in. My teenage self would have been proud; my 29-year-old self was strangely nervous.

Kyla intercepted me in the foyer and led the way toward the living room. She didn't take my hand nor say a word; the Samsons, even the children, were a stoic bunch.

Seizures were never pretty. The whites of Moira's eyes lolled in her head, lending her an almost demonic air. An undignified trail of spittle glazed her chin. The room smelled faintly of urine, which sometimes happened when the brain went haywire.

"It stopped," Kyla whispered. As it turned out, Kyla was the one with the scar on her lip, which suited her in a way. Although it wasn't on display right then, she had a toughness about her that reminded me of Moira. She stroked her mother's black hair as she sat by her side.

"Moira?" I squeezed Moira's shoulder and peered into her eyes. I'd left my penlight at home, but her pupils looked okay. Equal. Probably reactive. All in all, a really shitty neurological exam. My father would have been disappointed.

I looked in her mouth next. She'd bitten her tongue, but nothing that would require stitches. She seemed to be breathing okay—no gurgles or wheezes. I tried to sit her up.

"Moira? It's Aubrey."

She had that glazed, post-ictal look that might take hours to clear. Kyla stopped crying while I performed the rest of my brief

—and admittedly lousy—exam.

"Is she okay?" Kyla asked.

"She's fine. I need to take her to the clinic."

"Right now?"

"Right now. Is there an adult at home, Kyla?"

"Yeah." She pointed at Moira.

"Other than your mom."

"No."

"All right. Where are your brothers and sister?"

"Over there." She jutted a finger toward a dark hallway, where two kids stood in the shadows. I had to stifle a scream. They looked like little ghosts.

"Hi, Aub-eee." Sammy shuffled into the light. Francine was right behind him.

"Hi, Sammy," I said. "You two up for a ride?"

"A ride!" Francine squealed.

They both had on their cotton pajamas, which would never do on a night like this, but I didn't have time to find their shoes or coats or whatever else Moira used to keep them warm. Apparently the Samsons weren't big believers in layers.

"Follow me, okay?"

Francine started jumping up and down. "Okay!"

Kyla told her to be quiet because "Mama's sick." Francine didn't seem particularly concerned, now that the prospect of a nighttime drive was on the table. Mission accomplished, in that respect.

Moira couldn't really walk, so I had to carry her to the car. Fortunately she weighed about 95 pounds. The Samsons were a wiry breed, all gristle and bone. Four pregnancies hadn't changed her frame whatsoever.

It took ten minutes to get to the clinic. By then, Moira had roused enough to walk. She had also roused enough to start spewing questions.

"What the hell am I doing here?" she demanded, her words slightly slurred, like a ranting drunk. "You *kidnapped* me."

I eased her into the chair in Room 4. The bright lights hurt her eyes, so we sat in near darkness while the kids entertained themselves on the floor.

"I smell like a urinal," she said, averting my gaze for maybe the first time ever. Her voice was strangely quiet. "Fuck me."

"You had a seizure, Moira."

"Yeah, I know."

"You *know?*"

"I stopped taking my meds a week ago, so yeah, I know."

"Meds? For what?"

"Epilepsy. Ever heard of it?" She tried to sneer, but her voice had lost its bite.

"Why did you stop taking your meds?"

"None of your damn business."

"Okay, well I need to give you a dose of something now—"

"I'm fine. We're leaving."

"Moira, please—"

"I'm outta here. Kyla, get your brothers and sister. We're gonna wait in the waiting room till Grandpop picks us up."

Moira's withering stare stirred Kyla to action. She started to obey, but the trauma of the night's events slowed her response time.

"Are you aware that Kyla found you?" I asked. "She called me."

"Well, she shouldn't have—"

"She was scared, Moira. *Look* at her."

Moira looked. Kyla's lower lip started to tremble, and she ran into Moira's arms in a flailing rush. Any and all impressions of Moira as a tough-love parent softened in that moment. With surprising tenderness, Moira whispered into her daughter's ear, "I'm sorry, baby," and used her thumb to wipe her tears. "You're my strong girl, Ky. You know that, don't you?"

Kyla nodded.

"What does Mama tell you?"

"That I'm strong as they come."

"That's right."

Kyla abandoned all sense of big-girlness and nestled herself in Moira's lap. I was an only child, or at least raised as one after my brother died, and I'd never had to compete against siblings for my mother's attention. With three children, it seemed inevitable that one of the Samson kids would need more attention, more care, more love. Such was not the case with this family; I realized that now.

"I hate those meds," Moira said. "I've always hated them."

It took me a moment to process the unexpected breach of silence. "How long have you been on them?" I asked.

She shrugged. "I dunno. Fifteen years, I guess? I had my first seizure in high school." She grimaced at the memory. "Homecoming. What a shitshow."

"It was for me, too."

"'Cause you had a seizure?"

"Because it was high school."

She allowed the hint of a smile. "Got better though, didn't it? College and all that? Time of your life, they say."

"It had its moments."

"I don't see the appeal. I got my kids. Life's pretty good."

The light caught her in such a way that for the first time, I noticed the tears on her face. She wiped them away with bony knuckles.

"I gotta get these kids home." She climbed off the exam table to rouse her kids. Francine had fallen asleep on top of Sammy. "Let's go, baby."

"I'm *tired*."

"I know. That's why we're goin'."

"I want a cookie," Sammy said.

"Don't even start with me, Sam."

"A lollipop?"

"Jesus Christ." Moira pulled the boy into his arms with the same tenderness she had comforted Kyla. Whatever had ailed him last week had ebbed, and he looked himself again. Even the rosebush scratches had healed.

"Please, Mommy."

"I can't even..." Moira dug into her pockets and pulled out a pink lollipop. I couldn't guess where she'd gotten it from; she must have had it at the ready.

"Savor it, bud," she said. The four of them trudged toward the waiting area.

"Wait," I called out.

"I gotta get home."

"You need a ride?"

"Pop'll come get us."

"You sure?"

She gave a non-committal shrug which told me she'd probably wait all night before calling her father. Dirk didn't strike me as an up-and-at-'em kind of guy.

"I'll drive you," I said.

"You already done enough." The bite was back.

"I have to drive home anyway. Plus I can't just leave you here—Sheldon'd kill me."

Sheldon. I never called him. He'd find out, too. I had to document everything that happened here, and Sheldon had a real penchant for surveillance. I sometimes wondered if he'd retired from MI-6.

"Uh huh."

I expected more of an argument, but she didn't offer one. Maybe she was tired. Maybe the seizure had sapped her energy, although even if it had, she didn't dare show weakness.

I ran up ahead and started the car. That was one nice perk about living out here—parking restrictions didn't exist. No red zones. No fanatical meter maids.

"Nice ride," Moira said, as she settled into the Rover.

"It's a rental."

"Whatever. City folks always go for these boats."

"I'm not city folk."

She instructed her kids to belt themselves in, then she did the same. Maybe my father's lectures had really hit their mark. "If you say so," she said.

The clock on the dash showed 3:13 AM, the dead of night. A streetlamp offered the sole shred of light, a flickering orange streak in darkness. There was no moon, just shadows.

As I made the turn off Main Street, Moira said, "Stop."

"What's wrong? Did you leave something?"

"Over there." She pointed at a narrow, closed-off road that led to Moon Pond. The rusted barricade that had fallen over it said, DANGER. DO NOT ENTER.

"There's a car, Mama," Francine said.

A car?

"Past the barricade," Moira said. "See it?"

I saw it: a black SUV. *The* black SUV. The tail-lights were on.

"Keep driving," Moira said.

I resisted the urge to floor the accelerator and instead continued down the road at low speed. Moira's gaze flicked to the rearview mirror, as did mine. I kept expecting to see high beams —or worse, someone running after us on foot.

Moira must have sensed my unease because she stopped glancing at the mirror. Kyla was singing a pop song to herself in the backseat, while Francine and Sammy had fallen asleep again. Moira plucked the half-eaten lollipop out of Sammy's hand.

"What do you think that was?" I asked.

Moira proceeded to finish off the lollipop. "I dunno."

"You looked worried for a minute there."

"I don't worry. Now *you*, on the other hand…"

"I wasn't worried."

She laughed. "Uh huh. I think you left some prints on the wheel there."

I peeled one sweaty hand off the wheel. "I was just a little spooked."

"Well, it's spooky all right. I don't trust the place."

"Moon Pond?"

"Yeah."

"Why not?"

"Maternal instincts, I guess," she said, glancing over her shoulder at her threesome, asleep in the backseat. She rubbed her temples and stifled a yawn.

"I've got a hell of a headache," she said.

"You should sleep in tomorrow. Take a day off."

"Can't. I gotta be in at seven."

"Moira, that wasn't a suggestion. Sleep deprivation lowers the seizure threshold—"

"Look, I'll take my meds. Happy?"

"Not really. Have you ever seen a neurologist?"

"Yeah. Your dad."

"He's not a neurologist."

"He sure was. He was also an OB, a pediatrician, and a shrink. Damn good one, too. I hoped you learned a thing or two from him."

"I didn't have much of a chance."

"That's a shame," she said, and seemed to mean it.

I almost missed the turn onto Cooley Road, but Moira pointed me in the proper direction. In my rush to get over to her house, I hadn't fully appreciated the significance of trespassing onto the Samson property. Dirk had fences everywhere, hidden in the brush. A pack of Rottweilers roamed the yard out back, but they shushed at the sound of Moira's voice.

"Here's good," she said. I brought the car to a stop about fifty feet from the front door.

"You sure you're okay?"

"Fine."

"Take your meds."

"I'll think about it."

She roused the kids and hurried them up the gravel drive. I watched them go, Kyla leading the charge. Sammy fell asleep on his feet, so Moira hoisted him up and carried him the rest of the way. Her other children gravitated to her like cubs surrounding a lioness. In all our years of school together, I'd never once pictured Moira as a mother. As a pregnant teen, sure. But a mother? She was too caustic. Quick to judge and withering in her methods. A child would never survive under such a regime.

I was wrong, of course.

I started to wonder if I was wrong about everything.

TWELVE

The rest of the week passed uneventfully. Sheldon and I bonded over things like the brands of our stethoscope and the preferred dimensions of gauze. Beyond that, we didn't say much to each other. He never asked me for my medical opinion, and I never volunteered it. I stood in the corner and took notes and replayed Jed Walsh's demise in my mind, like a pop song on loop. For me, it was the sound of failure.

The good people of Callihax seemed to feel similarly. No one who walked through that door intended to see me and me alone. They all requested Sheldon. *Dr. Kline is so smart. Dr. Kline is so knowledgeable. Dr. Kline has such good hands.* The only compliment I received all week was, *Aubrey dresses good.* This came from Lily Deneau, age fourteen. I corrected her grammar and she thanked me with a death stare.

On Saturday, I went back to the office to search the file room during the day. Eight hours and 1,923 charts later, I still came up empty. Those four boys, whoever they were, had vanished from my father's medical record.

As much as it pained me to admit, Jim Ranson was my best hope. My father may have passed the files along to him—or at least made copies for him to hold onto in case criminal charges were ever filed. Might as well mention the mysterious SUV, too. Moon Pond was closed for the season, and I couldn't fathom why anyone would be out there in the dead of night. I'd file a formal trespassing complaint if that's what it took to get him to investigate it.

The real challenge was how to approach him. As soon as I started asking about those boys, he would want to know why. And I didn't have an answer for that. Morbid curiosity? Genuine concern for the community? He wouldn't buy that.

I had to find some common ground. Something that would interest him no matter who brought it to his attention. There were two things that would qualify. One was my mother, and I had no interest in using her as a bargaining chip.

The other was me.

***

My mother invited me to go to Mass with her, and for the first time in fifteen years, I said yes. She didn't bother to inquire about my motives. She would know soon enough. We took our usual seat near the middle on the left side. Church seating was as ingrained as the sign of the cross; it didn't change unless you really wanted to make a statement (or commit sacrilege).

She looked regal in her Sunday best: a soft blue dress with matching flats and a sheer yellow scarf. The colors lended her an almost whimsical beauty. It was these church outfits that had shaped my sense of style growing up.

Admittedly, I may have gone a little overboard on *my* Sunday best. A cotton-knit white dress with summer sandals and a flame-red cardigan. Although my mother and I could have been sisters, even twins, red worked for me in ways it didn't for her. My theory was that it had something to do with that fine line between saucy and sultry. For me, red achieved the latter. Maybe not the best choice for a religious service, but I had other priorities here.

"Where did you get that scarf?" I asked her. "It's nice."

"Bluefly."

"Is that a store in town?"

"The website."

"You use websites?"

"Electricity, too, if you can believe that."

I almost smiled. Point taken.

"Did you plan on talking to Jim today, or Luke?" she asked.

I tried to keep as straight a face as humanly possible in the company of my mother. She would notice the slightest flinch; the trace of a blush. "Why do you ask?"

"Because you look like a siren."

"Uh, thanks?"

"You're welcome."

The opening hymn started with the blast of organ music, which jolted everyone in the whole pew. The organist, Mr. Hamm, wore hearing aids when I was growing up; he was probably stone deaf by now.

I surveyed the crowd. The Samsons weren't Catholic, but the Ainsleys were. I had seen Luke and Lois in their usual seats—second-to-last row, right side. The people who sat that far back usually left Mass a few minutes early. My father used to call them the cheaters, and my mother would wholeheartedly agree, even though he'd meant it as a joke.

Luke had a good reason to cheat, though. Curious onlookers tried to steal a glance at his striking blond niece as they filed in line for Communion. Few succeeded. Lois was under the pew, either hiding or entertaining herself. Luke waved when he saw me. His face looked awful, to say the least—purple, swollen, distorted. He didn't smile because it was probably excruciating to do so. I waved back, which elicited a snort from my mother. She *hated* gestures in church. When people clapped (even at weddings), she ranted about it for days.

After the recessional hymn, we gathered outside under the eaves. The deep freeze had broken, giving way to a mild, overcast morning. I didn't see anyone unfamiliar in the crowd. The vehicles parked on the street were sturdy and weather-beaten, caked in a winter's worth of salt.

The elderly Mrs. Dougherty brought out her usual lemon cakes and tea, always a hit in the church-going crowd. My first memory of solid food was a lemon cake. It was delicious then; it was divine now. I savored every bite, although my stomach lurched at the sight of Jim Ranson making his approach. This was my opportunity, as distasteful as it now seemed.

His gaze swept my bare legs and right on upward, lingering

for a beat on my cleavage. I let him look. "Hi, Sheriff," I said.

"Hello, Dr. Lane. Looking lovely on this fine Sunday."

"Thank you."

He admired my chest for a moment more. "How goes it at the clinic?"

"Oh, fine. Dr. Kline and I get along very well."

"He's said as much. Tells me you're quite the little note-taker."

The smile on my face stiffened. "Fortunately for me, I have excellent handwriting."

"Well, that's important. You always hear about doctors writing prescriptions in illegible scrawl and some poor schmuck dying because he got percocet instead of penicillin—"

"Sheriff—"

"Please, call me Jim."

I did as he asked through gritted teeth. "Jim, speaking of handwriting, I'm hoping to convert all the charts at the clinic into an electronic medical record."

He looked like I'd just killed his cousin. "Now listen here, just because we don't do things the way you do things—"

"The government provides very generous incentives for us to convert to an electronic system. It's safer. Better for patients. Papers don't get lost. Prescription errors don't happen as often." I waited for his eyes or face or something else to soften. Nothing happened. "I'm talking about financial incentives. Money. Thousands of dollars."

"Thousands, you say?"

"Yes, quite a bit of money. Dr. Kline is on-board."

Dr. Kline wasn't exactly *on-board*, but men like Jim Ranson loved that word. It raised the image of powerful people sitting around a conference table while they talked about fat checks and bottom lines.

"Maybe we should talk it over with him."

"I think that's a fantastic idea." *Stroke the ego.*

"Hm. Yes, perhaps it is."

"But first, I need to do a strict inventory of every paper record. The government requires this before I can even apply for an EMR that qualifies for these incentives."

This was all completely made-up. I didn't know what the government required. I didn't even know what arm of government made the rules. And as for incentives, I knew they existed, but that was about it. In residency, we did what we could to understand the finer points of the healthcare system, but a few presentations scattered over the course of our training wasn't nearly enough. I hoped my spotty knowledge would be enough for Jim Ranson to buy it.

"Don't you have them in that secret room upstairs?" He chuckled at this, but his wording threw me off. Put a lock on a door and people suddenly think it's a "secret room."

"I have most of them, but some charts are missing."

"How do you know they're missing?"

Spending the last few days with my mother had prepared me for this question. "My dad numbered every chart in the order patients were registered. His last new patient was Brenton Kiles, who was born two weeks ago. His chart number was 1943. I only counted 1,923 in the chart room."

"You counted every single chart? By hand?"

"I did."

He laughed at this. "Quite the busy bee over there, aren't you?"

"I'm just trying to serve this community as best I can."

"By filing a bunch of papers? If you say so, honey." He scratched his beard. "Now about those twenty missing charts. You think I have them?"

"I think you may have some of them."

"Which ones in particular?"

"My guess is anyone who died of unnatural or suspicious causes."

"Ah." He wagged a fat finger in my face. "Smart girl."

I didn't feel smart. I felt like gum on Jim Ranson's shoe. "May I take a look at them?"

"You surely may, but I'll need the first and last names of the ones you need."

"First and last? Why?"

"Because otherwise you're just fishing."

I ignored the smirk on his face and said, "Sheriff, I just explained to you that I don't know who the missing twenty are. All I have is a disconnect between the total number of charts and the number in the file room."

"Then you need to do a bit of due diligence."

"I can't apply for the incentive program unless I have all the charts."

"Uh huh." His gaze flicked to my chest for one last good look. "Whatever you say, honey. Whatever you say."

He tipped his obnoxious cowboy hat and waltzed over to his cigar-smoking cronies. Jim Ranson was a lot of things, but stupid wasn't one of them. I buttoned up my cardigan and walked, ram-rod straight, toward the car. My mother was already waiting inside.

"Aubrey!" Luke ran to catch up with me.

I slowed, but didn't stop. He could not make this better, but he could certainly make it worse. St. Rita's on a Sunday was gossip central.

"Aubrey?"

I turned around. "What?"

His face fell. "Hey. Sorry, I know you're probably in a hurry—"

He stopped talking when my mother got out of the car. She *never* got out of the car once inside. She never did anything once she'd closed a door or said no or made a stand.

"Hi, Luke," she said. "You look terrible."

"Thanks."

"I'd hate to see the other guy."

He managed an awkward smile. "She's right here, actually."

My mother's eyes went wide—also a first. "My darling daughter," she deadpanned.

"It's okay. I gave her a bit of a scare in a dark parking lot. Totally my fault."

"Somehow I doubt that."

Luke glanced from my mother to me. "You both look very nice, by the way," he said. Unlike Jim Ranson, he said so without fixating on our busts, hips, or bare legs. I blushed like a teenager at the school dance.

"Thank you," my mother said.

"Thanks," I muttered.

"You know, I can drive myself home," my mother said. She fished the keys out of my purse and walked around to the driver's side. "I've always wanted to know what it feels like to drive a car that costs more than our house."

"Mom—"

"Bye, now."

We watched her drive off. "It's a rental," I said to Luke.

"I know."

"I drive a used Toyota."

"Look, if you drove a Hummer, I wouldn't care. Your mom's just messing with you."

I hadn't even noticed Lois until she was standing right between us, tugging on Luke's sleeve. She pointed to the birdbath. Children were always fascinated by St. Rita's birdbath, with its mossy curves and faceless statue. I had thrown my fair share of pennies into the well as a girl, each of which my mother had scooped out with her bare hands when I wasn't looking. She admitted this to me years later.

The three of us walked over to the birdbath. Lois didn't seem interested in socializing with the other kids, so we stood off to the side by ourselves. Luke handed her a penny. "Make a wish," he said.

He found a dime in his other pocket. "You, too," he said to me.

"My wishes are worth ten cents?"

"Used to be twenty-five, if I recall correctly."

I hadn't thought about those idle Sundays by the bird bath in a long time. He was right, of course—a quarter for my wishes. I only ever made one: to be with Luke forever. How very seventeen of me, but at the time, I'd made that wish with all my heart. I tossed the dime into the water and thought, *I wish my life were less complicated.*

As Lois deliberated her wish, I noticed that Luke looked his usual Sunday best today. Dark pants; a nice dress shirt that he must have ironed an hour ago. The top buttons were undone, but then, they always were. No tie. His hair had that soft, shower-sheen to it, and it damn near glistened in the spring sun. I decided not to resume the conversation with a compliment on his appearance.

"I guess I'm walking home," I said.

"Would you like to join us for brunch?"

"Oh, um..." I ran a hand through my hair for no real reason. He looked entranced for a moment, as if I'd just caught on fire.

"It's a simple affair." He swallowed. "A simple thing, I mean. Just me and Lois and my aunt."

"Are you sure I'm not intruding?"

"I wouldn't have invited you if you were."

This wasn't necessarily true, but I let it go. Maybe a part of me wanted to be invited, or at least included. "Well, thank you. I'd like that."

"Great. We're parked right over here." He pointed to a spiffy little BMW. Must have been twenty years old, but still. *A BMW!* Moira would have had a field day.

"I know what you're thinking," he said with a smirk.

"I didn't say anything."

"You're wondering how I came into such wealth."

I had always loved Luke's sarcasm—dry as a bone, but never mean. He opened the door for me like a proper chauffeur. In a former life, he would have coaxed me into the seat with a gentle hand on the small of my back. Not today.

"Where is Ms. Ainsley?" I asked.

"Oh, she'll meet us at home." He leaned toward me and whispered, "She's being courted by the postman."

I glimpsed the two of them in the church crowd. Talk about an awkward courtship. They had somehow gotten involved in a (mostly silent) conversation with a group of nuns.

"They won't be long." Luke turned around and spoke to Lois. "Seatbelt on?"

She nodded, which Luke acknowledged with a thumbs-up.

Lois tucked Groovy under the seatbelt and took to staring out the window.

Everyone in town seemed to know Luke, and all of them waved as we drove by. Corinne blew him a kiss. He smiled back.

"I think she likes you."

"I thought the busted face might dampen her enthusiasm," he teased. "But no."

"There can't be many single ladies in town." Was I really going down this road? Yes, I was really going down this road. Some nostalgic, tortured part of me wanted to know.

"Oh, there are plenty of single ladies. Most are over ninety..."

"I mean young, attractive single ladies."

"Do you think Corinne's attractive?" he asked me.

This wasn't a strange question. When I first started cruising the bar scene in LA, I spent more time appraising my competition than identifying potential suitors. My female friends did, too. Sometimes we even competed with each other.

For this and other reasons, I quit the bar scene after a while. The hospital scene wasn't much better, but at least it put us all on an even playing field. Romances were more discrete. Flirting never happened—well, rarely happened. People were more discrete about that, too.

"I think she has that waifish blonde thing going for her."

"Waifish blonde? Huh." He pondered that for a bit. "I'm not sure that's a compliment..."

"When did she move here?"

"A few years back."

"From where?"

"California. Hey, look, you have something in common."

I groaned. "Why in the world would someone like Corinne move to *this* place?"

"Sick family member," he said. "You remember Mr. and Mrs. Llewyn?"

It took a moment to summon the image of dwarfish Mr. Llewyn and his rotund wife. They were both old when I left, which meant they must be ancient now.

"I remember them," I said.

"Mr. Llewyn died about five years ago, and Mrs. Llewyn started going downhill. Diabetes. A year later, a stroke. She needed full-time care."

"I thought they didn't have any children."

"They don't. Corinne is their niece."

"Oh." Maybe Corinne wasn't as self-centered as I'd painted her to be. Quite a ways to come for an elderly aunt.

"I think she thought it'd only be a year," he said. "Maybe less. But Mrs. Llewyn is a tough old bird. Corinne is kind of stuck here."

"Did she tell you that?"

"In as many words."

I pictured the two of them having a conversation over vodka-tonics as the grandfather clock in Gargoyle's ticked toward one. The late-night chat with my father made more sense now. Why else would Luke stay out that late? He was thirty and attractive and had the same needs and desires as any other man. Gargoyles wasn't exactly hook-up central, but it wasn't a bad option if you wanted to do the deed drunk.

If not for Lois in the backseat, I might have pursued this distasteful line of questioning. Instead, I waited for Luke to change the subject.

"I saw you talking to Jim," he said.

A peculiar thing to notice, but maybe he was curious. "We had a lovely chat."

"I bet. You looked uncomfortable."

I wasn't sure how much to tell him. *Everything? Nothing?* I needed those names, but to ask him would confirm that I was doing some digging. Luke had never been the type to pry, but something made me hesitate.

"He's making life difficult for me."

"How so?"

"I'm trying to convert everything to EMR, and I need all the charts to do it properly."

"How many is that?"

"Nineteen-hundred forty-three."

He whistled at the number. "Good luck there."

"I need the charts for the deceased, too."

"Huh." His hands moved up on the steering wheel. "Why's that?"

"A reimbursement issue."

Luke had never been gullible, but the lie came more easily now. I sounded confident. Authoritative, even. He seemed to buy it.

"Well, if you need it, you need it. What did Jim say?"

"He needed names."

"Of the dead? That's a strange thing to request, especially if he has the charts in his office."

"As I said, he's making things difficult for me."

His hands shifted on the wheel again. He made the turn onto County Route 42, a straight shot down to the river, and from there, Caucomgomac Lake. We used to swim there in the summer when Moon Pond was overrun with little kids.

"I may be able to help you," he said.

"Really?"

"I can think of a lot of dead people—a lot more than twenty, in fact. That's all you're missing?"

"No." I glanced at the rearview mirror to see Lois sitting quietly in the backseat. The rush of trees and color seemed to captivate her. "I have those. The ones I'm missing are those that died of unnatural or suspicious causes."

He made a sharp turn onto the long gravel drive that led to his house. Maybe a little too sharp. He'd almost missed it.

"Aubrey, that's..." He rubbed his chin with his thumb. "Are you sure you want to dig that up? I mean, are the Feds really gonna care if you're missing twenty charts?"

"No," I said, hearing the whisper of suspicion in his voice. "No, you're right. I'll just tell Jim to forget it."

"You could try the courthouse if you really wanted to. They have death certificates, things like that."

"No, it's fine. You're right. I can find a way around it."

"You sure?"

"Yeah."

His hands slid back down to the six o'clock position as he made the final turn. Lois bounded out of the backseat as soon as we stopped.

"I hope I didn't scare her with the dead people talk," Luke said. He started to pinch the bridge of his nose, then realized what that would do. "She's so quiet, I forget she's there sometimes."

"It'll get easier." I didn't know this for sure—didn't know it at all, really, but it seemed like the right thing to say.

"I hope so."

Brunch was a rather subdued affair, thanks in large part to Lois' silence and Ms. Ainsley's discomfort with my presence at her table. She didn't ask me any substantive questions about my life. We talked instead about the weather, and the church service, and the events planned for that week, now that summer was in full swing.

"Moon Pond opens for the season next week," she was saying. "The children are so excited. It really starts to feel like summer when they take that barricade away."

"I wish they'd leave it," Luke said, and Ms. Ainsley frowned.

"Why?" I asked.

"He's paranoid." Ms. Ainsley encouraged Lois to eat more. The little girl grasped her spoon and proceeded to study her reflection in the silver.

"What's wrong with Moon Pond?"

"Nothing," Ms. Ainsley said. "He thinks he's a hot-shot academic."

"I'm a high school biology teacher, Maggie." Luke had never called his aunt anything other than her first name. My suspicion was that she hated the sound of Aunt and Auntie and its iterations. The way she wore her make-up and hair told me she hated aging, too.

"Well, not by choice," Ms. Ainsley said, turning to me. "He *wanted* to be a virologist." Her eyes rolled as she pronounced *virologist*. She made it sound like a dirty word.

"Wow," I said. "You went to grad school?"

"For three years. I quit because I didn't want to spend my life in a lab."

"He says he prefers those little devils in the classroom," Mrs. Ainsley said. "Always talking back. No manners whatsoever."

"They aren't so bad, Maggie. You were a teenager yourself once."

"Mmhm." She spooned some oatmeal into her mouth. "Not like those hoochies."

Hoochies? Even Luke cracked a smile at her word choice.

"Why viruses?" I asked him.

The question seemed to rejuvenate him. It occurred to me that it must have been months—years?—since someone asked him about a subject he'd considered devoting his life to. "Viruses are one of the great mysteries of life," he said. "They infect all living things—humans, cows, insects, even bacteria —but they die without a host. Are they a form of life, then? Or just an elegant molecule that behaves differently than other molecules? If you look at a virus' structure—"

"I think we've heard enough," Ms. Ainsley said, pursing her lips as she wiped egg off her chin. "You're boring us to tears."

I almost said, "Actually, I'm not bored at all," but Ms. Ainsley cut me down with a look. I hoped Luke could see the sympathy in my eyes.

"Yeah," he said. "Anyway. I'm gonna take a walk. Anybody want to join me?"

"It's your turn to do the dishes," Ms. Ainsley said.

"I'll help." I started clearing the plates before she could protest. With sudden enthusiasm, Lois jumped out of her chair and carried her own plate over to the sink.

"Don't rush," Ms. Ainsley said. "Or you'll have to do them all over again."

Luke took the plates from me and Lois and dried them with startling precision, knowing his aunt would inspect each and every one. No wonder these past few weeks had been hard on him. Lois was one thing, but Ms. Ainsley quite another.

After Lois had dried the last glass, she grabbed Groovy and waited by the door. I couldn't blame her for wanting to come with us.

Luke inhaled the crisp, clean air as we stepped outside. The clouds had cleared, and a spectacular sunshine fell on the bare grass and vanquished the shadows between the trees. Gran would have relished a day like this.

"Lois?" Luke called out to her. She was picking flowers on the hillside. "Stay close, all right?"

She nodded. We started walking down toward the river, a frothing swath of melted snow that always accompanied the late-spring rains. Luke had been drawn to it for as long as I could remember. The path along the river's edge was his, the vines and brush cleared years ago by his own hand. We had walked this very path many times that summer. Memory lane, indeed.

The path took us to the school, past the baseball fields and the track, until we were standing on the brink of the high school grounds. Beyond the fence, there was only woods, woods, and more woods. Principal Howard used to threaten us with "banishment" before it became a dystopian trend.

Luke stood beside me with his fingers linked through the fence. We watched Lois tie the little yellow and pink flowers into a necklace. I realized he hadn't spoken since we left the house.

I was about to comment on Lois' craft skills when he asked, "Do you still sing?"

The question took me by surprise. I hadn't sung in years, not professionally anyway. I sang in the shower when no one was listening—the National Anthem, Christmas carols, the occasional lullabye. Tonight it would probably be hymns.

"Not really," I admitted.

"I heard singing can help with language deficits." He watched Lois lose one of her flowers and try again. "Maybe it could help her."

"Who told you that? My dad?"

"Google."

I looked at his face—his kind, warm, youthful face. He had

softened towards me in the last few days. I wonder what had done it: Lois? His broken nose? The tincture of time?

"You were out of my league," he said.

"What?"

"That summer. I was, what—five-two?"

"You weren't that short."

"I was shorter than you."

"Only if you weren't wearing socks."

"Sadly, that wasn't very often."

I smiled at the memory. Luke's favorite white cotton socks went to mid-calf, which gave him the quality of a deranged tennis player in shorts and sneakers. He took them off during that summer's lone heat wave, which did wonders for our physical relationship. I wondered when he took them off for good. The next summer? College?

"Where'd you go to college?" I asked.

"Bowdoin." He deliberately mispronounced it so that it rhymed with *cow loin.*

"Wow. Fancy."

"I think it was a mistake."

"You going there?"

"Them taking me."

I rolled my eyes. "Uh huh."

"I had a good time there," he said, then paused, and I couldn't help but wonder if he'd met a girl or fallen in love. *Was he thinking about her now?*

"How about you? Was college everything you'd hoped it would be?"

"It was fine," I said.

Luke peeled his hands off the fence, sensing—correctly—that I didn't want to talk about college. My wild days and nights in California seemed self-indulgent in retrospect. For four years, I had done a fine job crafting a bubble that had nothing to do with reality.

"Why did you come back here?" I asked.

"My lab's funding ran out."

"Yeah, but you could have been a biology teacher anywhere. Why here?"

He paused before answering. "For family reasons," he said.

"Maggie? You came all the way back here for *her*?"

"No," he said, hanging his head. "I just...Would you hate me if I said I don't want to talk about it right now?"

He sounded more forlorn than angry, and I couldn't bring myself to push him. We meandered back toward the track, the gravel glinting in rare, unobstructed sunshine.

"I heard your dog ran off," he said.

"My dad's dog," I said. "Jax."

"I'm sorry to hear it. Did you put up signs?"

"No..." I thought about the SUV and the chain of events that followed. The phone call. Jax. The tail-lights over by Moon Pond. I pulled my sleeves down over my knuckles.

"I think he's gone," I said. "Maybe it was a bear or a mountain lion."

"He may come back on his own."

"Maybe."

We walked the mile back to his house with Lois close by, never out of sight. Although we made occasional conversation, the onslaught of new information had thrown me for a loop. Luke was a biology teacher—a virologist, in fact. He had gone to college, and after that, *grad school*. Then he returned, for reasons he didn't want to talk about. And, like everyone else in town, his instinct to protect the dead went deep—extremely deep. I understood this, but it also made me wonder.

When his house came into view, Luke slowed his pace. I couldn't blame him. Living with that woman was clearly no picnic.

"Thanks for the walk," I said.

"Thanks for making brunch slightly less painful." He gave a wan smile.

"If you ever want to talk about viruses..."

"Call the clinic with an emergency?"

"It doesn't have to be an emergency. You could make up a cold or a rash—"

"I'd rather not make up a rash." His teasing smile made me feel sixteen again, all butterflies and nervous energy. Not like the *Okay, let's get on with this* courtship that happened in dark bars and noisy clubs. Innocent. Sweet.

"Or you could just call me," I said.

"I thought you said—"

"Forget what I said. I was being immature."

"Well, wait a minute. I'm not sure I want to be friends with the woman who broke my face."

"Fair enough," I said, hearing the smile in my voice. *Friends.* Could I really be friends with Luke Ainsley? For one thing, friends didn't lie to each other. *Did secrets count as lies?*

We caught Lois engaging in a solo sword fight with sticks. "Lois? Time to say good-bye to Dr. Lane."

"Aubrey."

"Dr. Lane," he corrected me, with a real, honest-to-God sternness.

Lois dropped the stick and ran over. She didn't say a word as she stood on her tiptoes and draped her flower necklace around my neck. Then she ran inside the house.

Luke went suddenly quiet as he admired the flowers around my neck. His gaze drifted ever so slowly to my bare shoulders and collarbone; to my mouth and finally my eyes. He started to say something, but the words caught in his throat.

So I said it for him: "Any interest in walking a little longer?"

***

Somehow, our walk through the woods ended at Moon Pond. In the daylight, the rusted barricade looked tired rather than menacing. The trees swayed in a gentle, inviting breeze.

"Tire tracks leading to the pond," Luke said. "That's odd." He flicked the DANGER, DO NOT ENTER sign with his fingers. A tinny sound rang out in the silence.

We walked on. I couldn't decide how much to tell him about

the other night, so I said nothing. The tire tracks told him as much as I knew anyway.

"Any idea what kind of vehicle those tracks belong to?" I asked.

"Something big." He crouched down and studied the tread. "An SUV would be my guess."

"How many people in town have SUVs?"

"A fair number. Trucks are out of style, and cars are just impractical."

"You drive a Beamer."

"Because I'm a nostalgic moron. Plus I've got the Subaru as a back-up."

"I thought it was because you walk everywhere."

"That, too."

"Does Lois like your BMW?"

"I'm not sure what she likes, to be honest." He took my hand and helped me over a wide swath of mud. I let him go as soon as we reached solid ground.

"You seemed uneasy about this place at brunch," I said. "Why?"

He shrugged. "Maggie thinks I'm a nutcase."

"Who cares what she thinks."

"Well, other folks do, too. No one wants to close Moon Pond."

"You want to close it? For how long?"

"Indefinitely."

Moon Pond was one of Callihax's few beloved landmarks. Families had been swimming in its shallow waters for hundreds of years. I could see why there would be a backlash against shutting it down.

"Explain," I said.

"It's nerdy virology talk."

"I'm probably your best audience in that respect."

"True." The road narrowed as Moon Pond eased into view. The clear water shimmered under a vast blue sky, a network of vines and branches skimming the surface. On days like this, Moon Pond could seduce you.

"Last year, the pond opened a week late. There was something off about the water quality. At least, *I* thought there was."

"I didn't think the water was ever checked."

"It wasn't. The color was a little cloudy."

"That's strange." Although Moon Pond had that roiled, muddy look after a long summer afternoon, it was practically drinkable in the early mornings: cool and clear, as translucent as glass. In five feet of water, I used to count the pebbles between my toes.

"To be honest, no one really cared. They were ready to open up on the Fourth as scheduled. I insisted on testing the pH, measuring ammonia levels, things like that."

"And Jim said no?"

"Jim was actually okay with it. I ran all the tests, and they came back negative."

"Why was it closed for a week, then?"

"That's how long it took for the tests to come back. Believe me, people were pissed. I got hate mail. My house was TP'd. There was even a death threat."

"Yikes."

"Pretty sure Maggie sent the death threat," he said.

I couldn't help but smile. "I could see that."

"In any case, I was last summer's pariah. This year I've decided to keep my mouth shut."

He edged toward the surface of the pond, where the tire tracks ended and the water began. I dipped my fingers in. The temperature was startlingly cool—doable for kids but uncomfortable for most adults. The water itself, though, was pristine.

"The water looks okay today," I said.

"It does. Much better than last year."

I stood up and inhaled the forest air. "So what do you think caused the change?"

"It could have been anything. More algae than usual. A pollutant of some sort. Who knows. I'm a wannabe virologist, not a marine biologist."

"Well, you were wise to do the testing. You never know."

He was gazing across the pond when the crunch of gravel distorted the silence. I whirled around. Luke stood up.

A black SUV was coming down the road.

THIRTEEN

"Hide," I said.

"What—" Then he saw it.

We took off at a sprint through the trees. I made it about five steps before the mud claimed one of my sandals. *Leave it.* I kept running.

We came to a grove of old, thick-trunked trees and crouched behind them. The SUV rumbled up the road, seemingly immune to divots and potholes. Its pace was slow. Deliberate.

"Let's go," he said.

"Go where?"

"Let's get out of here. Come on."

I didn't want to go. I wanted to see who was in that car.

"You know the rules up here," he said, his voice so low it chilled the blood.

There were many rules in the North Woods, but the greatest was, *Stay away from what doesn't belong.* It explained why people didn't trust me. It explained why my Land Rover had drawn such intense attention. And it explained why Luke would drag me out of here if I refused to go voluntarily. People who ventured to these parts unannounced didn't want to be found.

And so, we ran. I kicked off the other sandal and conceded the decimation of my white cotton dress. My feet were bloody and bruised by the time we reached the river.

"Jesus," he said, glimpsing my bare feet. "Why didn't you tell me you lost your shoes?"

"What, so you could carry me?" I turned away from him and sank my feet in the water. He was hardly out of breath, not to mention clean and presentable. My hair was soaked with sweat, and I'd run straight into a bramble of thorns that left my cardigan in tatters. Clearly I was out of practice when it came to running through the woods.

"We shouldn't have run away," I said.

"I didn't recognize the car."

"You flee from all tourists, then?"

"That wasn't a tourist."

"We should call the police in that case."

He considered this for a moment. "Maybe we should."

"Maybe?"

"Jim doesn't get involved in those kinds of things, you know that."

Those kinds of things. I knew what he meant: if it didn't involve a local, Jim Ranson left it alone. Border-crossers, runaways, fugitives...he didn't go near them. If you saw one, you looked the other way. My parents had always advised me to do this for my own safety.

"Why would a fugitive park near Moon Pond?" I asked.

"What makes you think that was a fugitive?"

"I don't know." I rubbed the soles of my feet to ease the pain there. "Just a guess."

"That's not the first time you saw that SUV, is it?"

I shook my head. "No."

"When did you see it earlier?"

"I saw it twice. Once outside the clinic the night you came, and again a few nights ago. I saw it parked just a few feet from the water's edge."

"What were you doing driving around at night?"

"Long story," I said.

He didn't pursue it. "Let me take a look at your feet."

"They're fine." I stood up, but *damn*, they hurt. I must have stubbed all ten toes.

"Here. Lean on me." He offered me his arm, which gave me about thirty seconds' worth of relief. Every step brought a fresh wave of agony.

"I can just carry you—"

"No." I limped toward the river. "Maybe if we swim back?"

"In *that?* The water temp's about 55."

"Okay, then you walk. I'll see ya later."

Luke gave a defeatist sigh and followed me down the bank. I waded in slowly at first, savoring the icy cold that replaced the burning pain. My toes turned pink, then red, then white. My next thought was, *I should not have worn a white dress.*

My house was about a mile downstream, which meant a nice, lazy float on the river. And it was, for about fifty feet. Then the boulders and rapids and various other obstacles entered the equation. Luke hoisted me onto his shoulders and climbed onshore again.

"I don't need to be carried—"

"Calm yourself," he said.

He used to say that to me for all kinds of situations, always in the same teasingly stern voice: an argument about nothing that had gone on too long. *Calm yourself.* A heated encounter in the shed behind the baseball field. *Calm yourself.* Only once did he ever say it seriously; only once did he cry as those words left his lips. *I love you but I'm not coming with you.* I willed the memory away.

Despite the broken nose and my hundred-and-some pounds on his shoulders, Luke hiked through those woods like a regular old mountain man. I almost forgave him for the audible mouth breathing.

"Are we close?" I asked. "I don't have a sense of where we are."

"Almost there."

The final stretch was a steep ascent up Lews Hill. I had to wrap my arms around his chest to keep from falling off, which meant my breasts against his shoulder blades; my bare legs wrapped around his waist. He tensed every time I repositioned myself.

I was starting to think we were lost when the familiar sight of the sun-shy Victorian came into view. Strangely, the sunroom looked vacant, the windows closed. Two o'clock on a Sunday was prime time for my mother to sit with a novel and wile away those lazy afternoon hours. Maybe she was eating a late lunch.

"Here's good," I said.

Luke eased me off his shoulders. I landed on soft grass, but the pain in my battered feet had retreated to the back of my mind. I started jogging toward the porch.

"Aubrey?" Luke hurried to catch up with me. "What's wrong?"

"Nothing." I ran a little faster, no longer caring what my mother might say when I showed up at her door looking like a wet tornado.

I tried the back door, pushing against it with one hand and turning the knob in the other. It didn't give, even with the full force of my weight. The brass rattled in my palm.

"Why is the back door locked?" he asked.

"I don't know."

This door had never been locked during the daytime in all the years I'd lived here. A mistake? Had I left it locked for over a week now?

Not possible. My mother used this door every morning to go on her daily hike. I walked around the porch and peered through the kitchen windows. Everything appeared to be in its proper place, idle and undisturbed.

We jogged around to the front. Was it possible she was having an affair? No, absolutely not possible. Suddenly afraid of wild animals? No. My mother knew how to take care of herself. Tired of having me around? This seemed the most likely explanation.

I tried the front door. Also locked.

Luke checked under the mat. "It wouldn't be there," I said.

"Seemed like the obvious place to check…"

I went back down the porch steps and crawled under them in search of the key. My father had a real penchant for dark, moist places. I felt something crawling up my ankle as I raked my fingers through the mud.

There. I crawled back out, key in hand—

Luke was gone.

FOURTEEN

"Luke?" I called his name four, five, six times, each echo lonelier than the last.

"Luke!"

Then I saw the window—the glass punched out, or in, as there didn't appear to be any shards on the porch floor. A sizable deficit, too. Large enough for someone with Luke's six-foot-two frame to crawl through.

For not the first time since entering the North Woods, I rued the loss of my cell phone. To get help, I'd have to drive to Jim Ranson's house on the opposite side of town and knock on his door and explain to him why his services were needed. He would hem, and haw, and smile that smug little smile of his as he admired the sheerness of my white dress. *Not happening.*

In any case, there wasn't time for that. Ten minutes to get across town, ten minutes to drag Jim Ranson's lazy, cowboy ass out of that house, ten minutes back...*No.* It had taken Jedediah Walsh three minutes to die. If I'd acted instead of waited, those three minutes might have been the difference between a man reading the newspaper and a man dying on the floor. And maybe it was irrational, or selfish, or even stupid, but I would not take those three minutes for granted ever again.

I dismissed the broken window as a viable option for entry. It seemed too easy, a lure that evoked a white, windowless van with its rear doors splayed open. The kitchen, at least, had plenty of light, the layout less conducive to predators lurking in the shadows. I would sneak in through the back and plan my approach from there.

Despite a glaze of rust and a few warped edges, the key still worked. I pushed open the back door as quietly as the hinges would allow. The kitchen smelled like green tea and chives, like my mother's routine. With a slippery chill, I saw that one of the knives was missing.

Other than the missing knife, the kitchen lacked any signs of recent use: no dustings of cocoa on the kitchen table. No dishes in the sink, no pots on the stove. Although I'd never much believed the late lunch theory, I found myself wishing it were true.

I padded through the kitchen and past the dining room. For such a warm day, the windows should have been open, the drapes cast aside to let the air in. Instead, the house had that dark, closed-in feel, like a cave.

My survey of the downstairs ended in the foyer, a large, sprawling space with four dark rooms surrounding it. There was no place to hide in that lonely stretch between hallway and stairs. Here, the floorboards didn't creak so much as scream.

I stopped a few yards short of the stairs. The house was completely still, a brick-and-mortar corpse. With no windows to ventilate the air, the interior took on a suffocating deadness. The house's singular language—creaks, groans, hinges—spoiled the silence. Monstrous shadows played on the walls, and it was this aberrant shift of light and darkness that told me I was not alone.

I ran for the stairs, but my toe caught on the oriental rug that spanned the foyer's prime real estate. I had never tripped on it before. Never once. As my knees hit the floor, I saw that the corner of the rug had been turned up.

Then an arm, tight around my neck. I screamed as my assailant yanked my head back, but he snuffed out the sound with his free hand.

His grip tightened, and all went black.

***

I came to in the bathtub.

Blood. So much blood. I moved my left foot and watched it smear the porcelain surface.

As the buzzing in my head faded, I remembered the barefoot hike through the woods. And Luke. And the broken glass. And someone grabbing me…

"Help!" I scrambled out of the tub. "Help me!"

Luke's hands were on me before I could fully process his being there. My mother put her smelling salts back in the tin. I gulped down air as if it had sprung from a well.

"Take a breath," my mother said. "Go on. Breathe." She lay a calming hand on my forehead, which she hadn't done since I was six. "You're okay."

"I can't…I can't breathe…"

"You're okay," she said again.

"Someone grabbed me."

Her eyes flickered. Luke paled.

"*Who* grabbed you?" he asked.

"I don't know…" My voice came in a series of gasps. "He grabbed me from behind…in the foyer…downstairs…" I tried once more to sit up. "We need to get out of here."

My mother used her other hand to ease me back down. "Aubrey, please."

I noticed then that the window was open. The lockdown had been lifted. *When? By whom?* I tried to ask but the words wouldn't come.

"What time is it?" I asked.

"Almost four."

"Four? But I just—"

"You passed out," my mother said. "Luke said you bled quite a lot from your feet."

"I didn't go into hypovolemic shock from my feet!" I shook them off me and scrambled out of the tub. Admittedly, the blood left an eerie residue on the slick white tub. And judging by the amount that had gone down the drain, I probably needed stitches.

"Why did you put me in the bathtub?"

"Because you're filthy." She wrinkled her nose as she handed me a towel. "I'm surprised you even walked in my house looking like that."

"Walked in? I couldn't *get* in—"

"I locked the doors because of all those bear sightings around town lately," she said, but my mother didn't lie well. Bent truths came easily, but lies sounded rehearsed. I would ask her about it later.

I turned to Luke. "Then what happened to you? I was looking for the key and you just disappeared."

He stole a quick glance at his knuckles. "I broke the window because I thought I heard something," he said.

"So you went inside without telling me?"

"I thought your mom might be in trouble."

My mother clucked her tongue. "A regular old Hardy boy we have here."

"And then what?" I asked him.

"I couldn't find her, so I ran back downstairs to look for you and found you on the floor."

"On what floor?"

"The oriental rug. You looked like you'd tripped."

"You have a nice little bump on your head," my mother added.

I felt for a bump. Sure enough, the left side of my forehead had a new feature.

Luke said, "I already called Sheldon." His eyes added, *I'm sorry*.

"You may need a CAT scan for that head," my mother said.

"I don't need a CAT scan. I'm fine."

Med-Evac saved lives, but it also cost the town thousands of dollars. Only once had my father called them when he shouldn't have, but that mistake had followed him for years. From then on, he had to deal with dispatchers asking, *You ever hear of the boy who cried wolf?*

"I just need a minute to think," I said. "Can you wait outside?"

My mother handed me a bar of soap and a washcloth. "You might consider washing up a bit before the doctor gets here..."

"I'm not all that worried about my appearance, thanks."

She took the hint and walked out. Luke stayed where he was.

"I meant you, too," I said.

"Look, if you think someone grabbed you, I believe you—"

"Thanks for the vote of confidence."

"I shouldn't have gone inside without saying something."

"I had the key in my *hands*, Luke. Why would you just go and break a window?"

"I heard something."

"What, exactly?"

"A thump."

I spared him the rolling eyes. "A thump."

"Yes. Inside somewhere. I thought maybe your mom had fallen."

"And did she?"

"No. I mean, I couldn't find her. She didn't answer when I called her name."

"So you came back downstairs."

He nodded.

"And you found me."

"Yes."

"On the floor."

"I can show you where I found you if that'll help."

"Help with what? It's obvious you don't believe me."

Now that I knew the bump was there, my fingers kept going to it like an itch that needed to be scratched. I would have remembered a head injury. At least I liked to think so.

"Do you have a headache?" he asked.

"No," I lied.

He leaned forward, his elbows perched on his knees. Whatever was weighing on his mind affected his body, too. Even his eyes looked darker; cloudier.

"Aubrey, do you believe I could ever hurt you?"

"Of course I do," I whispered.

It took him a moment to choke out, "You do?"

"You broke my heart when I was seventeen."

"I didn't mean—"

"You mean do I think you could choke me to death?"

"Aubrey," he breathed.

I brushed past him toward the door. Four years working in an inner-city hospital had taught me that human beings are capable of anything. We were capable of great, heroic acts, just as we were capable of murder, and rape, and other terrible evils.

But Luke? I knew him once. I knew his hopes and fears and dreams; I knew his body, his laugh, the way he liked to hold my hand. I watched him hike a thousand miles looking for that dog he loved. I listened to him cry when Ellen left for good.

No, I don't believe it.

Alone in my room, I stripped off my ruined white dress and toweled off my hair. My feet left bloody footprints on the floor, which would dry, and harden, and become a part of this ghoulish, spectral house. I suddenly just wanted to get out of there.

I rummaged through the bureau for a fresh pair of pants and a heavy-duty wool sweater. No socks; the blood would ruin them. I dressed in a hurry, threw a brush through my hair, and glanced in the mirror—

And saw the blur of permanent marker, scrawled on the nape of my neck:

Get out.

FIFTEEN

Luke walked home at his insistence. My mother let him go, and this time, I didn't protest. We both needed some time and space to think.

My mother drove me to the clinic, which had that inert, Sunday afternoon feel. Sheldon had to let us in, which annoyed my mother more than it did me.

For all his glowing attributes, Sheldon was not an Emergency Medicine specialist. He bustled around the clinic in a hopeless rush, hunting down supplies. Sterile technique was not a priority. While he stitched up my feet, I endured his torture with a straight face and a wan smile.

"I don't think you need a CT," he said. "Your symptoms are consistent with post-concussive syndrome.

"Are you sure?" my mother asked.

"I'm quite sure."

Quite sure. He seemed satisfied with his decision, as always. I wondered when his confidence had taken such formidable shape. Ten years after his residency? *In* residency? Maybe birth, for all I knew.

"Now, how did this happen?" he asked.

"I was walking through the woods barefoot."

"Ah. With your boyfriend?"

Sure hadn't taken long for Sheldon to join the gossip-mongerers. "No. With a friend."

"Semantics." He flashed one of his cheery grins. "How about the head?"

"I'm not sure."

"You're not sure?"

"She fell," my mother said. "She tripped on the rug."

"A bit of a rough day for you, eh?" He chuckled at what must have been a hilarious mental image. "Perhaps you should take the day off tomorrow."

"I'll be here."

"Suit yourself." If he was wearing suspenders, he would have given them a casual snap to make his point. I had no doubt he owned a few pairs.

Ignoring my mother's protests to "pamper my feet," I followed him out into the hall, but he stopped short of the door. This could only mean one thing: a lecture.

"You know, I noticed a child's toy in Room 4 the other day."

"Oh. Really?" I tried to distract him with a smile. "Where?"

"On the floor, next to the window."

"Maybe it was Lois'."

"She doesn't seem the GI Joe type."

No, she certainly didn't, although kids could surprise you.

"Is there something you'd like to tell me?" he pressed. The English accent always did me in. It sounded so official, like he was about to interrogate me in the Scotland Yard.

"I saw Moira Samson in the clinic on Wednesday night."

"Ah." He stroked his trim white beard. "For what, may I ask?"

"A seizure."

"A grand-mal seizure? And you didn't think to notify me?"

"I thought about it, but…I forgot."

"You forgot." His smile could have cut stone.

"Yes, Dr. Kline, I forgot. It was 3 AM and I was tired and stressed and she didn't want a fuss. She wouldn't let me do anything for her anyway."

He fished his handkerchief out of his pocket and used it to dab at the sweat on his forehead. "I see."

"I'm sorry."

"It's quite all right," he said.

"I won't let it happen again."

"I should hope not."

I was thinking how humiliating it would be if my mother overheard this conversation when she emerged from the bathroom.

"Oh, hello, Mrs. Lane," Sheldon bellowed. They shook hands; hers were wet and sudsy, his were caked in latex powder.

"I apologize," she said. "You're out of paper towels."

"Is that so? Well, I'll have someone take care of it." That *someone* being me. He gave me a look that said as much. I shoved my hands in my pockets and marched out of the room.

Behind me, I heard Sheldon say, "I think she's just shook up. All that blood, you know."

"I'm not sure that's a fair assessment," my mother said.

I didn't hear the rest because by then, then I was out the door. We piled into the Rover, with my mother at the wheel. It had become clear over the last hour or so that she didn't trust me to drive.

"Did he give you anything?" she asked.

"Oh yes. Got myself a healthy supply of Haldol and tranquilizers."

"Aubrey—"

"You think I'm nuts. You all do."

We drove on in silence. I was so riled up that I almost failed to notice when we passed our mailbox.

"Where are we going?"

"The mill," she said, and then I knew: she didn't think I was crazy at all.

***

The mill had been in my family for eighty years, a steadfast presence on a riverbed roiled by gusty winds and vicious currents. Its days of functionality had long since passed, and some years ago, my grandfather had installed windows, skylights, and a wood stove that made the space inhabitable all year round. Although my father had never liked the place—"*Stay long enough and the walls start talking to you*"—my mother came here often, compelled by solitude.

The mill had no address, and per most maps, didn't exist at

all. There were no roads to its doorstep, no signs pointing the way. We had to park a mile away and hike in, a trek through poison oak, ivy, sumac, and other hazards of the underbrush. By the time we found the old stone structure in its shelter of aspen trees, the afternoon sunlight had gone dusky.

We checked each of the rooms, more out of habit than necessity. Sometimes squirrels, chipmunks, field mice, and other creatures found their way inside to escape the cold. I'd found a skunk under the bed once, which rendered the mill uninhabitable for about two months. This time, though, the place was deserted—except, perhaps, for those whispering walls.

My mother made cocoa, the only foodstuff in the kitchen. We sat at the table, saying nothing as we waited for the water to boil. In another ten minutes, the sun would set, and another cavernous night would envelop the North Woods.

"What changed?" I asked her.

She stirred her cocoa and said, "I found Jax."

Dread flowed through me like a sickness. I pictured Jax's mangled brown and white body, attacked or eaten or even shot. Such things happened to creatures all across the North Woods, but even so, I couldn't bear the thought of my father's arthritic coonhound meeting such an undignified end.

My mother must have finally seen the sad horror on my face because she said, "Not dead. Digging."

"Digging?" The response was so unexpected the word nearly lost its meaning. "Digging where?"

"Down by Moon Pond." She stopped stirring and handed me the spoon. "Jax must have been digging for days, that poor dog. The size of the hole…"

"Mom? What is it?"

"Muskrats."

"Muskrats?" I couldn't decide if I was horrified or amused. "You're sure?"

"I'm sure. I called Jim, of course, but by the time he went over there, the grave—or, hole, I suppose, had been filled in."

"How much time passed?"

"Two days."

"It took him *two days* to investigate? When was this?"

"The morning after you took that call from Moira's girl."

I didn't bother to ask how she knew about Moira because frankly, it didn't matter. A picture of more important, more salient details was starting to come together: the mysterious SUV, spotted twice in two days. Moon Pond. A massacre of... *muskrats?* The picture didn't make sense, but at least it had edges, and color, and a wisp of possibility.

"What is it?" she asked, reading my hesitation.

"I'm wondering if it's connected to the SUV we saw out there."

"It may be," she said, and left it at that.

"These muskrats...how many were there? Any idea how long they'd been dead?"

A sensible woman might have left the scene as quickly as possible, but not my mother. She liked details, and for that reason, I knew she would give me a startlingly accurate answer. "Maybe thirty or more. Some weren't very old—a few weeks, I'd say. They looked to be in various states of decay."

I could visualize what that meant, so I moved on. "What about Jax?"

She shook her head. "I brought him to the vet right away, but Charlie advised me to put him down. The whole thing just... when a dog finds thirty dead rodents in the woods, you can't take chances." She looked up, her eyes somehow softer in the light. "I'm sorry, Aubrey."

"You did the right thing," I said, even though it twisted my core to say it, as if summoning a whole new depth of grief. My father would have said those exact same words, and then he would have excused himself, and later, alone, he would have cried.

I looked up, determined to finish this distasteful line of questioning. "And then you locked your doors," I said.

"Yes. I also called Jim—again. This time he came right over."

"Of course he did," I muttered. The man had a real hard-on

for my mother that would irritate me until the day I died. She handled it by playing dumb.

"It was just a social call. He didn't come in uniform and he left his gun at home."

"He's such a—"

"Regardless, I escorted him out after about ten minutes. Then I sat in the sunroom and watched the road."

"And?"

"I saw the SUV again. Twice."

"In the driveway?"

"Down the hill, through the trees. Each time, it stopped for about fifteen minutes."

"But you never saw anyone get out?"

"I couldn't say if someone left the vehicle or not. It was too far away."

"When was this?"

"Shortly before you came home."

"But you weren't in the sunroom when I came home."

She nodded, anticipating this. "The phone rang."

"And?"

"I went to answer it. You know the rule around here." My father's rule: always answer the phone in case it's someone who needs help. Everyone in town knew that rule, too. *Which meant...*

"No one was there," I said.

"No, but by then I'd put the pieces together. Whoever was in that SUV wanted to make sure I was home."

"Jesus."

"Aubrey," she scolded, as if the Lord's name in vain had scalded her ears.

"Sorry."

"I was hiding in the old servant's quarters when I heard the glass shatter."

"That was Luke," I said.

She folded her hands and looked me dead in the eyes. "So I've heard."

"He had nothing to do with this," I said, as instinctively as if she'd asked my heart to beat. "In any case, the SUV couldn't have been his. He was with me."

"That hardly proves anything."

"You think *Luke* is behind this?"

She put the mug to her lips, but didn't swallow. "I don't know what to think."

"How could you? We don't even know what 'this' is." I rose from my chair, abandoning the steaming cocoa that infused the room with a dizzying nostalgia. I never asked why my mother professed such loyalty to a beverage that most people associated with cozy nights by the fire and childhood Christmases. A part of me didn't want to know, and another part, a greater part, feared an impersonal, throwaway answer. I didn't covet her secrets anymore—I was content to simply wait them out, like a sentry on a wall, not so much determined as foolishly hopeful.

But that night, with a soft, sudden sigh, she let me in. Not entirely, and not all at once, but enough for me to glimpse a rare part of her. A *broken* part of her, as we both were, in a world without my father.

"He asked me not to do this," she said, and without another word, she lit the kerosene lamp and led the way upstairs.

***

The mill lacked electricity, so we used handheld lamps to navigate the encroaching darkness. My grandfather had fortified the stairs with plaster and stone, but he didn't bother widening them. With our backsides flush against the wall, we had to shimmy sideways up the steps to reach the second floor.

The stairway led into the mill's sole bedroom, a loft with a low, slanted roof and two giant opposing windows. My vampiric mother preferred the couch downstairs because she couldn't stand the abundance of sunlight, which sated the loft from dawn till dusk. In this and many other ways, we disagreed. I thought this room—with its unfiltered light, bold architecture, and delicate shadows—was one of the most beautiful places on earth.

While I admired the splash of moonlight on the east wall, my mother crossed the room and counted each side board from the top corner down. "Here," she said, stopping at what appeared to be number six.

It took a combined effort to pry the plank off the wall, revealing a deep recess that smelled like paper rather than dust, the air dry and clean and almost breathable. I expected a glaze of cobwebs and grime and found none, suggesting recent—and frequent—use.

My mother reached in until her hands could no go farther. With some maneuvering, she pulled out a brown box about a foot square. I did the honors with the lid, although my mother of course knew what to expect. I swallowed a gasp as the kerosene glow fell on the contents.

Paper charts. A dozen of them, at least, stacked one upon the other in no obvious order. Although the presence of these charts in my father's possession did not altogether surprise me, the number of them did. I didn't think there would be more than four.

"I gather this is what you've been looking for," she said.

"I didn't say I was looking for them."

"Well, word got around easily enough."

We counted the charts as we laid them out on the bed: thirteen in all, none containing more than a few pages of notes and lab values. Eight of the names were unknown to me, or at least distantly known. Five were familiar. I set these aside.

"You look perplexed," my mother said.

"I am, a little."

"You thought there would only be four."

I nodded. "Four deaths. Four charts."

"There were others who had similar symptoms. Your father rotated their files for review—he took a few charts home, then exchanged them for others. He didn't want anyone to notice they were missing."

"But these people didn't die."

"No," she said. "There were other differences, too."

She added the eight unknowns to the pile of charts belonging to Kyle, Ryan, Tristan, and Bo. I had their last names now, too: Kyle Kennedy, Ryan Parsons, Tristan Assendorp, and Bo Samson. Bo was the oldest at eleven-years-old.

I would start with these four, but now we had another area of interest: the survivors. Eight here, but many more in the file room. Interestingly, the charts belonging to two of Moira's other children were in this pile.

"Moira's daughters had this?"

"They had something," my mother said. "She brought all three of them into the clinic on a Wednesday morning. I remember because your father came home very late that night—after midnight, in fact. He'd never done that in his life."

With the exception of the rare medical emergency, I couldn't remember a single time in my childhood when my father missed dinner. He was a creature of habit, a devotee to certain rituals, especially when it came to family.

"Did he talk about it with you?"

"Not at first, but by the end of that week, it was obvious he was in over his head. I sat him down and demanded he tell me what was going on."

I shuddered at the thought of my mother *demanding* anything. She usually just had to breathe a certain way and the deed was done. Her students would tell you that—and they did, back when I was in high school. *Your mom is scary.*

"What did he say?"

"He told me about Moira's first visit with her children. They all had what your father described as non-specific symptoms— cough, runny nose, low-grade fever. Bo also had a rash."

"What kind of rash?"

She pulled Bo's chart out of the stack. "I haven't gone through these, but I'm sure your father's documentation is better than my memory."

I doubted that, but his medical lingo might provide some

useful details. I started with the first relevant entry dated Wednesday, July 14th. There were four visits documented between the 14th and the 19th.

HPI: Bo Samson is a healthy 6-year-old boy who presents with a dry cough and a rash. Mom provides the history.

Symptoms started two days ago as a runny nose and progressed to a dry cough. Patient started coughing up scant blood yesterday. Low-grade fevers, temps 100-101 per measurement at home. 101.2 F in the office today. He developed a rash this morning which is pruritic and widespread. Also has areas of desquamation on the forearms and thighs. No recent travel. No reports of tick or insect bites. History positive for sick contacts – two sisters. Both have similar symptoms with the exception of this rather unusual maculopapular rash...

"Do you know what some of those words mean?" my mother asked.

"I do..." I didn't have to explain, though. My father had included several photographs in the chart. As I pulled them out, she turned her head the way she used to do during horror movies.

"My God," she whispered.

The rash had been documented over a period of days: 7/16, 7/17, and 7/18. "Widespread" was putting it mildly; even "desquamation" didn't quite capture the vast blisters on his arms and legs. The boy's skin was an angry, pulsing red— so angry it raged and bled and dissolved into every fold and crevasse of his ravaged body. His eyelids, lips, fingers, toes—all were affected. Nothing had been spared.

But then, on 7/19—the day he died—the fire had clearly begun to recede. His face was pink instead of red. His palms and soles were clear of whatever had plagued him the day before. For lack of a better word, he looked cured.

I read my father's note from 7/19:

Maculopapular rash much improved today despite lack of targeted intervention.

Lab values indicate severe aplastic anemia with multi-organ failure.

Med-Evac contacted AGAIN for immediate transfer to tertiary level of care.

There was no death certificate, which meant Bo Samson must have died en route to the hospital. Luke said an autopsy had been performed on the last boy, which had to be him. The others had died the day before.

Sure enough, a copy of the autopsy report had been stapled to the back of the chart. Official cause of death: *Multi-organ failure in the setting of sepsis.*

Whoever prepared it may as well have written, *No fucking clue what happened here.*

"This autopsy report is useless," I said.

"That's what your father said. He had high hopes they might find an answer, especially since there were other cases. The parents were so distraught they refused any additional autopsies. And you know Moira—she was very vocal about the whole thing."

"About Dad's care?"

"No, no. Not at all. She credited him with saving her daughters. She took Dirk's pick-up and drove all the way to Portland to have a word with the coroner."

"That sounds like Moira."

"I'm not sure Moira ever would have accepted Bo's death without seeing his body on that table. She had the coroner repeat the autopsy with her in the room."

I had seen that grisly process only once, during my second year of medical school. The Y-incision, jagged but somehow clean. Those steel grey floors, reflecting an array of stark, prying lights. And all this with a *mother* in the room? It was too horrible to imagine.

"I just can't believe this happened here," I said.

"No one could. Four deaths in less than twenty-four hours."

"And no answers."

She shook her head as she reached absently for the closest file. "Your father kept very good records, including photographs, as you can see. He ran every test imaginable and paid for them out of his own pocket."

"How much did that cost?"

"For send-outs? Thousands. Tens of thousands. The results are all in there."

"I'm guessing nothing came back positive."

"Oh, a few things came back positive. One of the boys had been exposed to the virus that causes mono. Another had a platelet disorder. But there was no obvious connection between them."

"But they all died of multi-organ failure." The lab tests confirmed as much. Kidney failure. Liver failure. Aplastic anemia indicating bone marrow failure. In the wake of a mysterious infection, their bodies had simply shut down.

Though it turned my stomach, I willed myself to study the photographs, which captured the rash in its subsequent, mystifying stages. The other boys had the same rash, same distribution, with the same pattern of progression. As with Bo, the spidery red blotches had started to clear as they got sicker. Odd. I couldn't think of any disease that behaved this way.

Unless a treatment had been attempted. I sorted through the charts, scanning the Assessment/Plan for each note. Early on, my father had recommended supportive care for symptoms: acetaminophen for fever, hydrocortisone cream and oatmeal baths for itchy skin, humidified air for cough, fluids to stay hydrated. As their conditions worsened, he got desperate: antibiotics, IV steroids, even vaccines. Med-Evac showed up a full *twelve hours* after he'd first contacted them, citing mechanical difficulties. In the end, there was nothing he could prescribe for a dying liver.

I closed the files. It would take hours to comb through every detail. I needed a clear head to do it, not the concussed brain I was working with right now.

"Satisfied?" she asked.

"No." I put each of the charts back in the box. "Not at all. This must have been devastating—and not just to the families of these poor kids, but the whole town. Why wasn't the Department of Health notified? The CDC, even? Something should have been done."

"Something *was* done. Your father notified all the proper authorities, but they looked at Bo's autopsy report and decided not to drive all the way out here for 'a bad case of parvo,' as they called it."

"Parvo doesn't look like this."

"The infectious disease specialists at the CDC were quite convinced."

Parvovirus B19 did cause a rash, and it predominantly affected kids. It could also cause an aplastic crisis consistent with these lab values. Despite this, it was rarely fatal. Fetuses were a different story. But six-year-old kids? And four in a week? Parvo was not the answer.

I put the box back in the wall and helped my mother replace the planks. Dusk had given way to a clear, moonlit night, and the kerosene lamps responded with a dim, but resolute glow. I dug into the chest for a wool sweater, scratchy and oversized and warm.

We made our way back down the narrow stairs. I didn't want to sleep in the loft tonight, not with those ghastly photographs buried in the walls. My mother prepared the couch with white cotton sheets while I took the floor.

As she extinguished the lamps, casting her shadow on the wall, a stray thought came to me. "Mom, what is St. Christopher the patron saint of?"

"Travelers," she said.

"Anything else?"

The last of the lamps went dark.

"The plague."

SIXTEEN

An hour after dawn, with ample light to guide my way, I set off for town armed with my grandfather's shotgun. I hadn't fired a gun in years, but this was bear country, and I'd learned early. Not that bears were my primary concern right now; with every stride, I remembered the squeeze of that man's arm around my neck.

The skies were a clear, chilly blue, wiped clean by the cold front that had moved in overnight. I wore hiking boots to protect my feet and a heavy coat to fend off the chill. The river churned alongside me, drowning out the sound of my footsteps. I kept close to the bank, where the openness of the trees and sky diminished the sensation of being stalked.

After a forty-five minute hike, I climbed the final hill toward Main Street. Callihax flourished on Monday mornings, with deliveries being made, all the porch floors clean and glistening. Employees looked somewhat more chipper than they were three days ago. I entered the clinic from the back and stored the shotgun—locked, but loaded—in my father's office.

The start of the workweek also brought its usual entourage of disgruntled patients to the clinic. Most didn't have appointments. As I'd come to expect, they had waited until business hours to have their urgent-but-not-emergent needs addressed: stomach flu, sprained thumb, full-body hives. I'd pulled the chart on all the patients scheduled for that morning when Corinne materialized before me and said, "Sheldon's not here."

"He's not?"

"Nope."

"You sure?"

She rolled her eyes. "I'm not *stupid*."

"Okay. Sorry." I tried to sound convincing. "Did he call?"

"Nope."

I couldn't go ahead and see a full morning's worth of patients without him, especially after last week's snafu. He would react poorly. Maybe violently.

"I'll call him," I said.

"What should I do about everybody in the waiting room?"

"Let them wait."

Corinne shrugged. "Whatevs."

I dialed Sheldon's number and let it ring until the machine picked up. A second attempt produced the same result.

"Corinne!"

She strolled into my office with her usual sloth-like sway. "What?"

"I need to run over to Sheldon's."

"Now? But there's like ten people out there..."

"I know, but I need to get ahold of Sheldon."

"Can't you just see 'em yourself? Aren't you a doctor?"

"Just tell them I'll be right back, okay? Ten minutes."

"Whatevs," she said again.

I went out the back door to dodge the impatient glares of a dozen patients. Too late, I realized the Rover was nowhere in the vicinity. I'd have to cover the mile to his house on foot. *My poor feet.* Sheldon had encouraged crutches for at least a week, but a part of me wondered if he'd said that to keep me out of work. I gritted my teeth and walked on.

Sheldon lived on the outskirts of town near an abandoned warehouse known to locals as The Boneyard, so named because some kid had discovered a human skeleton there years ago. Unsurprisingly, the house on the property had been vacant for years. The folks of the North Woods were notoriously superstitious, and Sheldon had probably missed the memo.

His Prius was parked out front: baby-blue and polished, as suburban as a car could be, and which would never survive the winter. I peered inside the windows on my way to the front door.

Books on tape. A coffee mug. Spare gloves and a hat. All very practical, not to mention boring. So much for the retired spy theory.

"Sheldon?" I rang the bell and waited. No answer. *"Hello..."*

I tried the door. Locked. Unusual, but maybe habitual for Sheldon. I went around back to try a different door. Circling someone's property in the hopes of getting inside was criminal behavior in the city, but out here, revolving doors were the norm. If you didn't want someone walking in unannounced, you moved. It occurred to me that my mother and I had done just that.

The back door was unlocked. I nudged it open and called out into the empty house. A fragile echo rolled off the papered walls, then died. Somewhere down the hall, a faucet leaked. *Drip-drip-drip.* I stayed by the door. The memory of yesterday's terror pulsed through me.

"Dr. Kline?"

A bowl of fruit languished on the kitchen table. The surface had been wiped down, the dishtowels hung in their proper place. The air smelled faintly of mold and stale coffee, like a forgotten morning.

I surveyed an adjoining room: the dining room, from the looks of it. Once stately, and perhaps even elegant in its heyday, the room had fallen into grievous disrepair. Water damage curdled the faded wallpaper. Warped hardwood lined the floors. The once lavish buffet looked as though it had toppled over at some point, with cracked mirrors, broken handles, and dusty drawers. *Such a shame*, my mother would have said. I had to agree.

As was the case with most of these old houses, a set of service stairs sat just off the kitchen. I kept my back to the wall and the door wide open as I walked that way. Dust particles danced in the scarce slants of light.

"Dr. Kline?" I shouted his name into the stillness. "It's Aubrey."

The whisperings of unease in my ears escalated to a scream. "I'm going to call the police," I said. Again, no answer. I retreated toward the back door, just as a gust of wind slammed it shut.

No no no. My fingers slipped on the lock—twice, three times. The knob wouldn't turn. I used my father's trick and pulled the knob toward me while turning the it with my free hand. The tendons in my wrist splintered with the effort.

Finally, the door gave way. It swung open into the sunshine, and there in the distance, was a shed.

With a black SUV parked inside.

SEVENTEEN

By the time I made it back to clinic, the waiting room had cleared. I stumbled past the empty chairs toward my office, red-faced and gasping. A wheezing seven-year-old on his way out of Room 2 offered me his inhaler.

"Corinne!"

A toilet flushed; the restroom door swung open. Corinne looked at me like I'd sprung three heads. "You look like crap," she said.

"We need to call the police—"

"Here, you need this." She took a comb out of her pocket and placed it in my palm. "Sheldon's in Room 1 with the Wallicke kid."

"Sheldon's *here?*" Funny how everyone called him Sheldon behind his back but always Dr. Kline to his face.

"Yup."

"Are you sure?"

"Uh, yeah." She gave me one of those *duh* looks. "I know what he looks like."

I started towards Room 1. The wise move would have been to sit, and think, and process, but I wasn't feeling very wise right then. The state of total disrepair in that house, the peeling wallpaper, the Boneyard nearby—these details were like splinters in my brain. And the shed. The *SUV.* It all fit—except it didn't. At all.

I barged into Room 1 without knocking. The Wallicke boy sat on the exam room table, swaying his legs to and fro as he admired his brand new dinosaur band-aid. Sheldon patted his knee. "You're good as new," he said, and the boy grinned.

His mother looked my way, which also drew Sheldon's

attention.

"Oh, Dr. Lane. Why, hello."

"Uh. Hi." I remembered the comb. *Too late.* "Can I talk to you for a sec?"

"Certainly." He helped the boy off the table and said good-bye to the boy's mother. She skirted by me, no doubt feeling unsettled by my wild hair and crazy eyes.

Alone in Sheldon's presence, the fear that had rippled through me earlier quickly turned to embarrassment. This man was too benign to be a threat: rosy cheeks, rosy demeanor. Even his voice had that steady, annoying lilt that indicated a perpetual good mood. And he was good with his patients. Very good.

Then there was the obvious: he wasn't *here* when those boys died. I doubted he knew the North Woods even existed a year ago. It was also possible, of course, that the threat to *Get out* had nothing at all to do with those boys—and therefore nothing to do with him. Maybe it was personal. Maybe Jed Walsh's family blamed me for his demise and wanted me gone.

Even the SUV wasn't exactly criminal. And I couldn't say for sure it belonged to Sheldon, when in fact the odds suggested a border-crosser. Moon Pond in the off-season was a natural hideout; for years, it had served as the backdrop for all kinds of seedy activity. Years ago, a few kids built a meth lab in the woods over there. Jim Ranson had put a stop to that with secret cameras and snares. Unorthodox, but it worked.

"First of all," Sheldon said, "I'd like to apologize for my tardiness. My wife caught the same bug and was quite sick this morning."

Wife? I hadn't seen any signs of a sick woman. That house was empty, and utterly devoid of a woman's touch. Paranoia resumed its slow creep into my consciousness.

"I'm sorry to hear that," I said.

"I hope you didn't run all the way over there in your nice doctor outfit." He appraised my mud-splashed pants and boots with a smirk that didn't sit quite right.

"I was worried something might have happened to you," I

said.

"Ah. Well. I'm quite all right." He offered me his handkerchief to wipe the sweat off my brow, which I declined. We sat in silence for a moment, each of us waiting for the other to say something. Eventually I got up and left.

I retreated to my office and changed into scrubs and sneakers. There wasn't much to be done about my hair. I would look like a mess for the rest of the day, but few patients noticed my presence anyway.

***

That night, back at the mill, I lit my kerosene lamp and went to work learning about my patients. And not just their names, but family members, backgrounds, jobs, education, unusual tidbits of information—anything and everything that might elucidate who these people were and what they might be capable of.

My mother joined me after a while. I told her about the SUV in Sheldon's shed, but she wasn't convinced it meant anything. "That man couldn't choke a puppy if he tried," she said.

"Maybe we're underestimating him."

"Maybe you need to consider other possibilities."

I didn't want to talk about Luke again; that was a road to nowhere. "Jim Ranson, then," I said.

"He drives a Chevy."

"Far as we know."

"Aubrey, if that man had a sleek SUV, he'd be the first to flaunt it. You know that."

Okay, so Jim Ranson wasn't the driver, but he might still be involved. For one thing, he didn't like me. For another, he had all kinds of secret liaisons with shady people to generate revenue in barely-legal ways. The muskrats might be related to some such deal, although I couldn't begin to imagine what kind of "deal" involved hydrophilic rodents.

"Jim Ranson told me *you* contacted Sheldon when Dad died," I said. "Is that true?"

If the question took her by surprise, she didn't show it. "Yes."

"Why?"

"Because your father had been in contact with him recently."

"How do you know?"

"I overheard them on the phone."

"You heard their conversations?" I asked. My mother had a real talent for eavesdropping, and secrets didn't last long in the Lane household.

"No," she said. "I respected your father's privacy when it came to his patients."

"So they were discussing patients." *The dead boys?*

"I don't know that for sure."

"So why did you decide to call him after Dad died? Did he *tell* you to contact him?"

"No. I called him because he seemed like a reasonable place to start in terms of a replacement."

"That seems like a stretch."

"It really wasn't. Sheldon Kline was the only name I had, the only doctor your father seemed to have a relationship with—other than you, of course."

"And you'd never met him before."

"No."

"Talked to him?"

"No."

"Did Dad ever talk about him? Like his background, credentials, how they met…"

She shook her head. "They reconnected sometime last year—before that, I'm not sure they talked at all. I don't know where he lived, what he specialized in…for whatever reason, your father said very little about him."

So there was a connection there, but hardly a robust one. If prompted, I suspected Sheldon would say the usual—"old friends, met at a conference, blah blah." Maybe he and my father were indeed old friends intent on keeping their mundane business to themselves, but I didn't think so. I was starting to think they had other, deeper secrets.

"You think Sheldon Kline is involved in this," my mother said. She waited for my reaction, which didn't come quickly because "this" was still indefinable.

"I think he drives an SUV and he hides it in a shed..."

"...And he parked it down the hill, stalked the house, and attacked you."

"Maybe 'attack' is the wrong word."

The kerosene lamp on the kitchen table flickered, then went dark. Somewhere behind us, the bald-faced clock over the oven ticked toward midnight.

"Someone wants me to leave the North Woods," I said. A draft took the flame, made it dance. Slender shadows scattered on the white walls. "I've been warned twice."

The soft lines in her forehead deepened. "When?"

"Once the week I arrived, and again when..." I didn't have to finish the thought; the look on her face told me she already knew. Maybe she'd seen the black scrawl on my bare skin, or maybe she simply sensed it, like she sensed so much else.

"And you think it was the same person?"

"I don't know. Could have been."

"Why?"

"Because I'm a terrible doctor? Because I set the car alarm off the other night? Because Jedediah Walsh died in my office?" I tried to gauge her reaction, but she didn't flinch. "I can think of a hundred reasons."

The second kerosene lamp went harder then the first, spilling a demonic shadow on my mother's face. "Then you should leave," she said.

The actual words didn't startle me, but her assured tone did. "That's your solution?"

"Yes. Now. Tonight." She peered out the window, as if searching for something in the distance. "You're not safe here."

As my mother knew better than most, danger was a lifetime affair in the North Woods. This place was not a respite for the weak; it was a stronghold for survivalists. Isolation, blizzards, grizzlies. Roads that gave way to savage wilderness; rivers that flooded in the span of a sunset. A darkness so absolute it consumed even the hardiest souls who dared challenge it.

No, I had never been safe here, but I'd survived. I had moved to a city of eight million people, and I survived that, too. No matter who or what tried to convince me otherwise, I would leave on my own terms, just as I had done twelve years ago.

"I'm staying," I said.

EIGHTEEN

I didn't feel safe in that Victorian on Lews Hill, and neither did my mother, quite frankly, so we made the mill our temporary home. No one knew about the move—until we figured out who wanted me gone, I thought it best to stay hidden for as long as possible. Every afternoon after the last patient left and the charts had been filed, I hiked through the woods with a shotgun under my coat, using a different path each time.

When the sun went down, I dissected those charts until the photographs developed a nightmarish dimension, projecting faces and eyes and fevers that made sleep impossible. My father was right: the walls did talk, but not as loudly as these photos. Four little boys had come to him seeking care, comfort, and inevitably, a cure. He had failed them.

A year later, he has a heart attack and dies. *A broken heart?* Possible. The back of the charts indicated he had delivered two of the boys—breech births, per the record. He had watched them grow up and thrive and develop personalities. He had given them vaccines and bandaged their skinned knees and set their broken bones. He knew them by name. Kyle. Ryan. Tristan. Bo. I had no doubt he went to each of their funerals.

I spent all day Saturday reviewing their charts for the third time. The progression of illness was almost identical in each case: upper-respiratory symptoms, rash, organ failure, death. For the children who hadn't died—at least the ones I knew about—they had the cough and runny nose and low-grade fever, but never a rash. I wasn't sure if this was significant or not. It was certainly unusual.

The histories provided more detail than anyone could have asked for, but my father had clearly struggled with the

Assessment/Plan. For one of the boys, he had listed *fifty* possibilities. His desperation pulsed on the page.

Parvovirus
Rocky Mountain Spotted Fever
Lyme Disease
Babesia
Dengue Fever
Coxsackie virus
Hanta virus
Lupus
Urticaria
Disseminated Staph
Mononucleosis
Drug reaction
Drug allergy
Hand-foot-and-mouth disease
Herpes zoster
HIV
Eczema
Poison oak
Poison ivy
Poison (??) causing dermatitis
Cocci
Lymphoma
Roseola
Scarlet Fever
Measles
Rubella

The list went on for three pages. Newer ideas were scrawled in the margins. Others had been dated, then crossed out as they were eliminated. Next to each one, he had written lab values and various test results, which either supported or refuted the diagnosis. For one boy, Tristan, he had eventually crossed out every single item on the list. On the fourth page he'd written one word in large, angry scrawl:

VECTOR???

There were thousands of vectors, known and unknown. My favorite medical school professor had defined vectors as the Trojan Horse of the pathogenic world, a vessel for disease that worked best when no one knew what was hiding inside. Ticks, flies, spiders, and on and on—all vectors for thousands of different pathogens. Although in my experience, vectors weren't always the smoking gun: in "classic" zoogenic diseases, such as Lyme disease, the tick bite and/or the tick itself was often never found.

The physical exam could be helpful, or even damn near diagnostic, but the best way to identify the vector was through the history. My father had been very thorough in this regard, going so far as to add multiple pages titled, ADDITIONAL CLINICAL HISTORY. Most of these details came from the boys' parents, although some of it came from siblings and friends. In each case, he had tried to recreate the last healthy weeks of their lives. Where had they gone? What had they done? Any travel? Long hikes through the woods? Any dietary changes? Had they ingested anything unusual?

For all their impressive detail, the histories were also disappointingly mundane. As one would suspect in a place with limited entertainment options, the boys had gone to many of the same places and done many of the same things. June in the North Woods meant freedom from school and lazy afternoons. They had swum in the river and the creek and Moon Pond. All had taken short hikes with their brothers or sisters or parents. They went to sleepovers and birthday parties and Murphy's for ice cream. They ate what their mothers cooked for them. They never traveled more than ten miles outside of town.

My eye hinged on Moon Pond. Luke had mentioned the poor water quality that had delayed its opening last year—or at least what looked to him like poor water quality—but every test had come back negative. Per this report, obtained through some private water testing agency, Moon Pond was cleaner than just about every body of water in America.

The obvious answer was some kind of tick-borne disease. The

symptoms fit. Lyme Disease could cause a rash as well as multi-organ failure, but antibody testing for Lyme had come back negative. *Maybe a false negative?* I looked closer and saw that the tests had been run a second time. Still negative. In fact, all the tests had been run twice. This work-up must have cost my father a fortune.

When the clock downstairs chimed twice, signaling the two o'clock hour, I put the charts aside. Infectious disease was not my specialty; neither was dermatology. I needed to talk to a specialist, or at least someone who knew more about these bizarre diseases than I did.

To my knowledge, there was only one person in town who fit that description.

NINETEEN

I didn't have to wonder too long about how to finagle a meeting with Luke because the next day, his name showed up on the clinic schedule. Under "reason for visit," Corinne had documented, *2 wk f/u – broken nose.*

Sheldon didn't miss a beat. "Perhaps I should see this one. You know the rules about patient-doctor relationships…"

"I'm afraid I don't," I deadpanned.

"Aren't you two, you know…involved?"

"Not even remotely."

"Pardon me for saying so, but I'd consider high school fairly remote in your case."

I wrestled Luke's chart out of his hands. "More so for you, I'd say."

"Touche." He walked away, whistling as he went.

A week had done wonders for Luke's face. The swelling had gone down, restoring the natural proportions of his face. He had a nice face. Handsome. The years had graced his features with a fine masculine edge, which suited him well.

"Mr. Ainsley." I shook his hand with the steadfast formality of a professional. "Hello."

He released my hand faster than people usually do. "Doctor." There would be no jokes or sarcasm today. I wasn't surprised given the nature of our last conversation.

"Your nose looks a lot better."

"It feels better."

"Good." I took the doctor's stool and inched closer to him. There would be no easy way to examine his face without it feeling intimate. Maybe gloves would help. I started to get up, then decided against it. Gloves implied a communicable disease, and I didn't want him to think I was worried about cooties. I washed my hands and resumed my seat on the stool.

"Hold still," I instructed him.

He flinched as I placed my hands on his face. The bones had set nicely.

"Everything okay?" he asked. His voice had improved, too. No longer nasally but husky and deep, like he had a sexy cold.

"Everything's fine. I'm going to remove the sutures."

I used the scissors to snip the fine purple threads, which usually went smoothly but not today, not with him. My hands had developed a tremor in the last five minutes.

"Great. All done." I dropped the scissors in the sharps container and washed my hands again. Luke gently tapped the bridge of his nose.

"Still painful?" I asked.

"Nah. It's fine."

Technically, we were done here. I should leave. He should leave. One of us should have known better.

"How's Lois?" I asked.

"Good. Really good. I got her to go to summer camp with me."

"You go to summer camp?"

"I'm a counselor," he said. "I mean, more than that. I lead the camp. I hire everyone…" A rare blush found his cheeks. "It's a pretty adult job."

"I'm sure it is."

"Anyway, yeah. She likes it. You should come by sometime."

"Yeah." I twisted my face into a smile. "Maybe I will."

"You won't, but that's okay."

I was two long strides from the door, easy enough to say good-bye and slip out, but Luke had never been an easy man to walk away from. I tucked his chart behind my back and leaned against the wall.

"It's not that I'm angry with you—" I started.

"You just don't trust me," he said.

"I do." *Mostly.*

"Did you talk to Jim about what happened?"

"I filed a report." I had waited until the middle of last week to do it, by which time I had watered down most of the key details. Jim Ranson had looked it over with his usual muted enthusiasm.

"What did he say?"

"He said he'd look into it."

"Has he?"

"I don't know. I guess. He didn't seem that motivated."

"I'll talk to him—"

"No." I took a step closer to the door, but stopped there. "It's fine. I may have overreacted to the whole thing."

"But you left your house."

"How did you know that?"

"I drove over there a couple nights ago." He dangled his feet over the exam table like a three-year-old nervously awaiting his shots. "I wanted to apologize."

"For what?"

"For...I dunno. For scaring you. For whatever I did—"

"Like I said, I overreacted. It's fine."

"How is it fine? I don't like all this"—he gestured vaguely to the space between us—"distance."

"Maybe a little distance is the best thing for us."

"Distance is the wrong word then. Animosity, maybe."

The door swung open and Corinne blustered in. "Your next appointment's here—Oh, Luke! Hi! It was so nice seeing you the other night."

"Yeah." He dodged my gaze as he mumbled, "I had fun."

"Me, too! I *love* fireworks."

"Yeah."

"Thanks, Corinne." I shut the door on her face.

"Anyway, we're done here," I said to Luke. "Call with any issues."

"Aubrey—"

"I have patients to see."

A lesser person would have raised an eyebrow at this, but Luke let it go. He climbed off the table and walked toward the door— toward me, as it were.

"Thanks for fixing my nose," he said.

"You're welcome." I barely looked up. His lush summer scent made my head spin.

"Aubrey?"

"What?"

"I can't take this."

"Take what?"

"*This.*" He backed up a step. "You think I'm the enemy."

"I don't know what you're talking about."

"Those boys." His voice had a hushed, somber quality to it. Almost a whisper.

"Those boys died a year ago. I don't see how it's relevant now." Except it was. Of course it was. I just couldn't find the connection between those boys and everything else—if there even *was* a connection—and it made me uneasy.

"Something isn't right in this town," he said.

"It just feels that way because my father's gone. New people. A new way of doing things—"

"It's not that." He looked at me with deep-set worry in his eyes, and my unease, deep but dispensable just a moment go, began to pulse. "I didn't go to Moon Pond last night to see the fireworks."

"To see Corinne, then?"

"She's not my type." His cool tone startled me. "I went because I couldn't shake the feeling that something happened there."

In another minute, Corinne or even Sheldon would barge in here and start asking questions. *What's taking so long? Are you not aware of the doctor-patient code of conduct?*
I decided to let them; this was more important.

"Moon Pond opened on the 11th last year," he said. "Those boys started dying a week later."

"Coincidence."

"Maybe."

"All the tests were negative. I saw a copy of the report."

"How?"

I'd walked right into that one. "My father had it."

"Where?"

"Does it matter?"

"No," he said. "I guess it doesn't."

He made another aborted attempt to pinch his nose. In the room next door, a baby wailed. Sheldon's voice rang out in the chaos as he tried to get the kid to calm down. Not surprisingly, he seemed oblivious to my absence.

"Luke, what do you want from me?"

"Same as you. Answers."

"To a tragedy that happened a year ago?"

"That's part of it."

I knew the other part; had known it since the call came on that rainy Tuesday morning in the hospital cafeteria. Luke had been there when death swept through this town. He was there when my father died. He *knew* that whatever had killed those boys hadn't entirely moved on.

"You said it looked like a heart attack," I said, almost a whisper.

"I thought it was."

"What changed your mind?"

He looked up. I met those silver-grey eyes, and with it, that haunted, spiraling sensation of falling into him. I remembered the very first time I felt this way, not as a teenager but as a small child, on a bleak, moonless night in November. It was Thanksgiving night, and despite my mother's obsessive planning, she'd forgotten to buy cranberry sauce for the dinner. She sent my father down to the corner store, and I went along with him because he could never say no to me, not even then —especially then. He parked the car, tapped my forehead in that affectionate, teasing way he sometimes did, and said, "Wait here, my little troublemaker." And I did. I waited for about three minutes, at which point a fox emerged from the tree line, and I climbed out of the car to investigate.

Foxes make a strange sound, a kind of robotic, mechanized bark, though I didn't know it at the time. I would never forget hearing that sound as that sly, scared little fox barked at me. It startled me to the core, a kind of nightmarish scream that could only mean an impending attack—such was my four-year-old logic. I ran into the woods.

I hadn't run far, but it didn't matter. A crazed sprint in darkness had rendered me lost, hopelessly lost. There was no moonlight to differentiate the shadows from the trees, just stars —pretty and twinkling, but meaningless to a child who didn't understand north and south and east and west. I remembered my father's strict instructions to "stay put" should I ever lose my way in these woods, but I panicked. I wandered farther in. Deeper. I kept thinking Main Street or the river or someone's house would simply appear.

Anyone who says the night has no soul has never lived in a deep forest. The darkness started to mock me, with its icy, howling winds and a strange sense of forever. For the first few years of my life, I had shunned nightlights and other such crutches; I'd always enjoyed the peaceful privacy that came after sundown. Everything changed that night, a betrayal of the most natural, inevitable order. I sat down and covered my ears and hummed, and cried, and rocked myself to-and-fro, dead leaves crunching under my shins.

I didn't hear voices or see flashlights. I don't remember anything except those grey eyes, soft and sad and familiar, belonging to six-year-old Luke Ainsley. He found me huddled under an aspen tree a hundred feet from the river. When my father asked him how he knew where to look—I was nowhere near where everyone else had focused their search—he said, "I just knew, Dr. Lane."

I just knew. Just like he knew my father hadn't died the way Jim Ranson said he did. Like he knew something wasn't right in this town, and it hadn't been in over a year.

"We need to figure out what killed those boys," I said, deciding then and there that although many of these people didn't *like* me, the hardened folk of Callihax didn't turn on outsiders without a good reason. They had accepted my father, who had been new to this town; they had forgiven Luke, who had returned. They might want me to leave, but they wouldn't threaten me. As I'd somehow come to forget, Callihax had been founded on the rigid principles of the antebellum North.

"Okay," Luke said. "I agree, but why?"

"Because someone doesn't want us to."

***

After clinic, we met at Gargoyle's Pub, which wasn't exactly private, but the men who wiled away the hours in that place cared about two things: liquor and beer. I had traded my white coat for a tank top and jeans, which made me feel clean, if not quite attractive. I found Luke sitting in the booth under the dart board.

His gaze found mine as I slid into the booth. A pitcher of beer and two glasses had already been served. I poured myself a pint because what the hell.

"I wasn't sure you'd want to show your face in this establishment," he said, which was a bit of an old joke. As the doctor's daughter, I used to make a big stink about the dangers of alcohol to anyone who would listen. That didn't buy me too many popularity points.

"Probably a poor decision on my part."

"Probably."

He held up his glass. "Cheers to poor decisions."

"Cheers."

We drank a little too much, a little too fast. There was no real conversation going on—just a general "feeling out" process. The more he drank, the more his eyes roamed. Neck. Collarbone. Shoulders. I wasn't wearing much of a shirt, that was for sure.

"How was summer camp today?" I asked.

"The usual. A few fights. A stubbed toe. One girl lost an earring."

"Sounds serious."

"A popsicle did the trick."

"I bet."

"Busy day in clinic?"

"Not for me. I mostly just take notes."

"I bet your notes are stellar, though."

His smirk made me smile. "They are, actually. Unfortunately no one reads them but me."

"I'll read them."

"Thanks, but I'm not looking for a critique partner."

He finished off his pint and poured another. I could tell by the rhythmic tapping of his feet that he was nervous. Anxious, even. He palmed his skull with his hand as he gazed into the amber void of his drink.

"I really don't know where to start," he said.

"You don't think my father had a heart attack." I downed the last of my beer and set it aside. Now we were even, at least in terms of booze. "How's that?"

The tapping stopped. "I'm not sure what to think."

"Okay, let's start with my father's sudden death and those four boys. Is there a connection?"

"I'm not sure there is, except for the obvious."

"He treated them."

"Yes."

"In fact, he treated a number of kids that summer."

"The ones who were sick but survived," he said. "You know about them?"

"I know enough." I poured my second glass and gestured to the waitress for another pitcher. The playful gleam in Luke's eyes told me he accepted the challenge.

"Here's my theory. Let's say Doc figured out what happened to those boys—or maybe he was close. Maybe he'd hit on something big."

"How *big* do things get out here, though? This isn't exactly Washington DC."

"Well, that's a hole in the theory."

"One of many."

"Agreed." He took a swig. I matched it.

"Also, this all happened a year ago. Why wait so long to..." I couldn't quite say the word *murder* in reference to my own father.

"He spent all year trying to figure out what killed those boys. Maybe he wasn't a threat until now."

"A threat to whom? I can't think of anyone in town who might be capable of this. And when I say 'this,' I mean a mysterious disease targeting children. It's too sophisticated."

"And sinister," he agreed. "People here look after their own."

"True." To be honest, I had forgotten just how much this was true.

"Has anyone moved to town recently?"

He stared at the table. We both reached for our glasses at the same time.

"Other than me," I said.

"Just Sheldon Kline."

"No one else?"

"The Placketts moved into the old farmhouse on Route 22, but that was eight months ago."

"Who are they?"

"A family. Two kids. Both in summer camp. Very polite."

"How about their parents?"

"Never met the father, but Mom seems normal."

"Isn't that kind of strange?"

"I wouldn't say so. Plenty of folks keep to themselves around here."

The Placketts. I might have to give them a ring about those sports-physicals..."Anyone else?"

"Not that I can think of."

"What about Corinne?"

"She's been here longer than the Placketts."

I pondered this for a moment. "Have you ever, you know..."

"Have I ever what?"

"Well, she's very attractive."

"Not as attractive as you," he said. The utter lack of hesitation in his response brought a lump to my throat.

"Anyway, I think the answer is in the history," I said. "We need to find the vector."

For the thousandth time, I thought of those massive black letters swarming that blank page. My father must have spent hours and days and weeks and months searching for it.

"Could be tough," he said. Luke was right, of course; my father had had one huge advantage in that he had actually *seen* the patients. Chart review was just that—chart review. Like trying to tell a story second-hand.

"I know," I said. "Maybe impossible."

"No bite marks on the skin?"

"No, nothing like that. The physical exam wasn't helpful."

"The boys who died had a rash, though."

"Yes, but..." I restrained myself from launching into the finer details of those photographs. For some reason that had to do with my father's lifelong devotion to patient privacy, I balked at the prospect of sharing those grisly files with Luke.

"But what?"

"I'm not sure what the rash tells us."

"It tells us a lot! Come on, you're a doctor. Rashes are identifiable."

"Not this rash."

He gave me a searching look. "You've seen the photographs."

No sense in lying now. "I have."

"Well, that helps. The history should be there."

I shook my head. "Those charts shouldn't even exist, Luke. They should have been sent to the CDC."

"So you're telling me you've broken some confidentiality laws."

"Absolutely."

"You seem upset," he said with a smirk.

"Look, I got curious. That's it. I should never have even mentioned this to you."

The waitress came by to refill our salty snacks. Popcorn. Peanuts. Pretzels. We waited until she left to resume the conversation.

"Did you, ah…did you ever work with muskrats?" I asked.

"Muskrats?"

"In your lab."

"No," he said. "Why?"

"This is going to sound strange…"

He set the popcorn aside and waited for me to go on.

"My mother said someone buried thirty muskrats in the woods near Moon Pond."

He looked at me for a beat, his stare so intense it made me wonder if I had pretzel on my face. "That's the strangest thing I've heard in a while."

"I know."

"I haven't seen a muskrat around here since Calvin Copes brought one in for show-and-tell in second grade."

"Me neither. I was thinking…"

"Lab rats," he finished.

I nodded. "Crazy?"

"Pretty crazy, for a few reasons. One, no one uses muskrats for experiments. Two, I can't imagine anyone in this town doing animal testing."

"Well, you're the virologist," I said, laughing nervously. Too nervously. He lifted an eyebrow, and despite my best intentions, I broke out in a cold sweat.

He sipped his beer. "Wasn't me," he said.

"I didn't mean to suggest—"

"I know," he said, but I worried he didn't.

"Maybe she got it wrong."

"Your mother? Not possible." He took another long pull from the glass. "You'd need quite a bit of infrastructure to do any kind of animal testing around here. A lab, to start. Freezers, refrigerators, all kinds of supplies and materials. It wouldn't be easy."

"But doable."

"Anything's doable."

I chewed thoughtfully on a pretzel. "How about Sheldon?"

"What about him?"

"Maybe he built himself a big lab in the Boneyard."

He laughed, but something in his eyes flashed with doubt. "Now that's ambitious."

"I think we should check it out."

"You mean like Nancy Drew style?"

I rolled my eyes. "I'll just drive by. Scope it out."

"You do remember the Boneyard, right? Bones. Bodies…"

"I'm not nine anymore."

"Well, *I* for one am still scared," he teased.

The waitress swung by with more beer. I waved her off, noticing then that it was almost eight. Thirty minutes till sunset.

"We have to go," I said.

His teasing smile faded, and I wondered if he could see the disappointment on my face, too. Even so, he knew, maybe better than anyone, that I wouldn't be walking home in the dark.

He dropped a twenty on the table and escorted me out.

TWENTY

In my haste to get back to the mill before nightfall, we made plans to meet again on Saturday. I also had three beers in me and was in no condition to ponder medical mysteries. Luke offered me his jacket and a walk home. Sober, I might have refused. Tipsy, and therefore easily disoriented, I accepted with embarrassing enthusiasm.

I hoped the booze wouldn't slow us down—or get us lost. I trusted Luke's sense of direction, but these woods had been the downfall of many after dark.

We took the usual path down to the river and went south from there. I ignored the dull ache in my feet, determined to limp right along at Luke's easy pace.

"So what happened at Moon Pond last night?" I asked.

"Fireworks. Lawn games. The ceremonial cannonball."

"Who did the cannonball this year?"

"Maggie."

"Seriously?"

"No," he laughed. "I keep holding out hope, though."

"Were the fireworks good?"

"Not bad. You remember. Nothing's changed."

I did remember. Fireworks were a point of pride in Callihax, a testament to the many veterans who had lived and died here. Jim Ranson spent fifty-percent of the town's budget on a thirty-minute fireworks show. To his credit, each year brought something a little different—new fireworks, music, an entertaining snafu. My seventeenth and last year, though, was the most memorable. I'd had my first real kiss under that red-green sky.

I tripped and nearly fell as the memory swam in front of me.

Luke got his hand under my arm and caught me before my knees hit the dirt.

"You okay?"

"Fine." I pulled my arm away, yet the memory intensified. That night, Luke had chosen a spot on Banden Hill, away from the crowd but not entirely separate from it. From where we sat, we could still hear the *oohs* and *ahhs* of young children; the distant drone of patriotic music. He had wrapped his arms around my waist, his lips teasing my hair as he whispered, *I can't watch the fireworks like this...*

I stumbled a second time. Luke caught me again, but this time I didn't pull away, and he didn't let go.

He kissed me on the mouth: soft, sweet. A little brazen. He didn't go for more. Maybe it was the uncertain look on my face or maybe it was the rush of painful memories. Good-byes. Letting go. A decade removed from the lovers we'd once been. The *people* we'd once been.

His sad smile broke my fragile heart all over again. "To poor decisions," he said.

And we walked on.

***

The race to get to the mill in daylight turned frantic when it occurred to me that Luke had no idea where we were going. I had never taken him here before. In fact, aside from my mother and me, no one knew this place even existed.

"Are we close?" he asked.

"Just a little farther."

For the first time, I detected worry in his voice: *how am I ever going to find my way back?* It wasn't a simple matter of following the river. The river that flowed through town twisted and bent and diverged a hundred times between here and there. I knew the landmarks, but Luke didn't. My beer-addled brain had failed to consider how difficult it would be for him to navigate alone—and in the dark. Impossible, really.

I found the last two landmarks and then, finally, the mill—nestled in a grove of trees, a kerosene lamp hanging from the eaves. Luke stopped to admire it for a moment.

"Wow," he said.

"Come on."

We found my mother slicing apples in the kitchen. If she was surprised to see company, she didn't show it. "You're late," she said. "Busy day?"

"Not too bad."

"I made a stew for dinner if you'd like some."

"I would love some," Luke said.

"Have as much as you like," she said. "I'll never eat it and Aubrey won't consume something that doesn't fall straight from the heavens or sprout from an angel's butt or however she describes it—"

"Mom, that's not true."

"Are you a vegetarian?" Luke asked.

"No."

"A vegan?"

"No."

"A Whole Foods enthusiast?"

"Definitely not." Somehow that seemed the worst of the three, albeit the most accurate. I sat down and helped myself to a hunk of stew. I had long ago stopped asking what my mother put in her summer, winter, and Christmas stews.

Luke reached for the salt—

"I wouldn't do that if I were you," I said.

My mother finished with her apple slicing and joined us at the table. Not a speck of food or juice on her apron, and her fingernails sparkled. No wonder she sighed when she saw my white coat at the end of a long day.

"How nice of Aubrey to bring you out here," she said to Luke.

I stared at my stew. A bizarre comment, but not out of bounds for my mother.

Luke hadn't missed the subtle judgment in her tone. "I didn't even know this place was out here," he said.

"No one does." She spooned a tiny morsel into her mouth while keeping her gaze fixed on the man at her table. "We've tried hard to keep it that way."

"I see." He looked at me, but I was too busy glaring at my mother to acknowledge him.

"You won't be able to leave, you know," she said.

"Uh oh," he said, but the joke fell flat.

She nudged the salt in my direction. "It's too dangerous to hike these parts of the woods at night. We're too far from town."

"I could probably make it."

"Probably?" I gave him a sharp look.

"Fifty-fifty," he admitted.

My mother watched me shove the salt back in her direction. She responded with a thin smile—angry in ways that could not be defined; satisfied in ways that made my stomach roil. "Then you'll just have to stay here," she said.

***

While Luke was in the bathroom, I took my mother aside. "You're angry," I said, my voice hushed. Shaky. The prospect of balancing three degrees of tension in an enclosed space had torn my reserve to shreds.

"Of course I'm angry. This place is too small for you, me, and your ex-boyfriend."

"That's not why, though."

She shrugged, although for her, it was more a twitch of the shoulders. "The fewer people who know about what's upstairs, the better."

"I wasn't going to show him the files."

Her face betrayed a flicker of surprise. "So why did you bring him here?"

"Because we had a few beers and I didn't trust myself to walk back alone."

"I see."

"Why don't you trust him?"

"I don't trust anyone." She reached into the linen closet for clean sheets. "Not even you."

"That's hardly news to me."

"I would be disappointed if you told me everything."

"Rest easy, then."

She allowed the mildest of smiles, which endeared me to her more than I thought it would. She put the clean sheets in my arms. "For the bed upstairs."

"Where will I sleep?"

"Not on the couch with me, that's for sure."

She walked away as Luke came back inside. He must have used the outdoor shower, too, because his hair was wet. No shirt, either, but he had a towel wrapped around his shoulders. Pants still on, thank God.

I ran upstairs before he could comment on the fresh sheets. The ones on the bed had endured only a few nights' of restless sleep on my part, but my mother had instilled in me a hotel-mentality when it came to hospitality. I stripped the bed and tucked the fitted sheet under the mattress. Then the other sheet, blankets, and Gran's afghan. Never underestimate the utility of layers in the North Woods.

He didn't come upstairs, not that I ever expected him to. I shimmied back down the stairs and found him in the kitchen, drinking a tall glass of water. My mother had disappeared into her nook, the only corner of privacy in the mill. For better or worse, she would stay out of sight until morning.

"Thirsty?" I asked.

"I forgot about your mom's love affair with salt."

"It's gotten more intense with age."

Love affair? Intense? I tried to focus on something other than the wet, shimmering skin under his towel. "Will Maggie be worried that you didn't come home?"

"Maggie doesn't give a damn. And Lois isn't home tonight."

"She isn't?"

He shook his head. "Sleepover at the Placketts. Just her and their little girl. She seemed excited about it."

"I always cried at sleepovers."

He smiled. "Why? The ol' hand in ice water trick?"

"I liked my own bed."

"Ah." He poured another glass and handed it to me. "Understandable."

"Speaking of which, this house doesn't have a whole lot of options. I'm sorry..."

"It's fine. I'm good with the floor."

"My mother would decapitate me if she found you asleep on the floor."

"Yikes. Would hate to see that."

"So you've got the bed upstairs. I made it up for you."

"Where does that leave you?"

Could I trust myself to share a bed with him? Not really. But it was either that or the cold stone floors—or outside.

"How big is that bed?" he asked.

"Not all that big."

He washed his empty glass, dried it, and put it in the rack. His gaze drifted to the window, to the infinite sprawl beyond the glass. The balmy night air hummed with the promise of thunder.

"I can walk back," he said.

"*Now?* It's pitch black out there."

"I can't put you in this position." He clarified: "Put *us* in this position."

I thought of the way he'd kissed me earlier, a testing of the waters. He had tasted lush; familiar. The subtle restraint with which he'd done it left me wanting more, but there couldn't *be* more. There never would be again.

"It's one night," I said. "We'll survive it."

"The last thing I want to do is make you uncomfortable."

"I'm comfortable."

I sent him upstairs while I took my turn in the outhouse —essentially a toilet built into the ground with no sink, no mirror, no vanity. A hose hooked up to the back wall served as the "shower." The mill was very much a summertime retreat, especially for those who prioritized hygiene. I wasn't trying to look fantastic—this was the middle of the woods, for Chrissakes —but I could not sleep two feet away from Luke Ainsley without feeling clean.

I undressed, turned on the hose, and endured sixty-seconds of an ice-cold spray. A spritz of shampoo and a brutal rinse with crusty soap and the ordeal was over.

I grabbed one of the tiny towels and ran up the path before the night, total and absolute, could swallow me whole. I didn't dare look into the woods. Instead, I willed myself to look straight ahead, toward the kerosene lamps; toward humanity.

My mother remained out-of-sight, having removed herself from our little drama. *Consider it a lesson learned,* I thought. The towel barely skimmed the top of my thighs.

I hoped Luke had done me the favor of already going to bed— or at least pretending to be asleep. The stairs betrayed my climb to the second floor, a series of creaks and groans that sparked my nerves. The flicker of the kerosene lamp danced on the wood stairs.

The loft was dark except for the moonlight that fell in steep slants on the walls. Luke lay facing the west window, his body so close to the edge of the bed he risked falling off. I couldn't see his face, but the unevenness of his breathing told me he was wide awake.

I exchanged the towel for shorts and a threadbare t-shirt. He was breathing faster now, but he didn't dare move. Didn't say a word.

This was such a bad idea. I hadn't thought so the first time. He was eighteen; I was seventeen. Too young, my practical, birth-control wielding father would have said. Too sinful, per my mother. And maybe we were, indeed we were, but in a place as remote as this it was easy to feel as though the world revolved around you, only you, and loving Luke was my axis. Losing my virginity to him had never been a decision—it was simply part of our story, part of *us.* It had happened as naturally and inevitably as the turn of the seasons.

I exhaled with the memory, wondering not for the first time if he even remembered that night. Maybe I was more emotionally fragile than I liked to believe.

The mattress creaked with my weight as I slipped under the covers, which smelled like summer and soap and him. I pushed the soft linens below my waist and rolled onto my side. Neither of us was side sleepers. This was going to be a long night.

He never said a word, but somehow, some time later, he touched me or maybe I touched him; and our bodies came together, his arm around my waist, my head on his chest; as new as the first time, as familiar as the last.

***

Luke left at dawn before the reality of what we'd done could settle on him. On *us*. After the door closed downstairs, I went to the kitchen and poured myself a glass of water. It had stormed overnight, and the wet, woodsy air crackled with electricity.

I thought my mother might wake up early just to torture me, but she was still sound asleep on the couch. Maybe she hadn't heard anything. Sure.

The hike to clinic seemed to go on for an extra five miles thanks to the incessant chatter of my own thoughts. I tried to remember the sequence of events the night before—Who initiated it? Why didn't I say anything? Why didn't *he*?—but it was all a blur. A surreal, spectacular, devastating blur. It hadn't even been that one time. Three times in, what, eight hours? *Three times.* And not a single word spoken between us.

A release. That's all it had been. Two sex-starved exes in the middle of nowhere with slim pickings in terms of potential mates. Luke had ended an engagement to someone named Anna —a year ago? Less? I tried not to think about her; about them. Whatever their history was, it had been a long time since my last relationship. Summer didn't help matters. Hormones always went beserk in the summer. *Wasn't I too old for hormones?*

By the time I walked into town, I had decided that yes, I was too old for hormones, but a part of me was still seventeen—and ten, and six, and four.

A part of me still loved him.

***

Morning clinic ended with the wearying presence of Ophelia Sinclair. The first three hours of the day had not gone well. Tommy Hess called me a "mute turd." Hayden Michelsson sneezed in my face and seemed to relish it. Then there was the whoopie cushion on my office chair. Sheldon got quite the kick out of that one.

While the boss took a bathroom break, I handled Ophelia Sinclair's intake vitals in Room 1. Her vendetta against pregnancy had not abated in the least.

"I feel like a cruise ship," she said.

"You look great, Ophelia." She did not, in fact—her ankles had ballooned to twice their normal size, acne had taken over, and her maternity clothes didn't fit anymore, but sometimes lies had their place. "How do you feel?"

"Like I said. A cruise ship."

"All right."

"Like I'm gonna sink at any minute."

"Cruise ships don't often sink."

"Well you would know, huh?" She took a gander at my pencil skirt and silk blouse. Maybe it was time to ditch the LA wardrobe, even though it gave me confidence. *Used* to give me confidence. Here, I felt like a privileged phony.

"I didn't mean it like that—"

"Anyway, this one does."

Having exhausted our pleasant chit-chat, I rubbed some goo onto her belly and used the ultrasound machine to find her baby's heartbeat. Ophelia always smiled when she heard the steady thrum, only to start complaining again as soon as the exam ended.

"Sounds perfect," I said.

"Sounds like a bunch of static to me."

I put the stirrups back in their proper place and helped her off the table.

"Hey, I got a question," she said.

"Yes?" I waited for Sheldon to barge in and tell me he intended to repeat my exam, which happened with all the pregnant women except Ophelia. The reason for this was unclear— he didn't like her? Recoiled at her baby-as-parasite references? Fortunately, Ophelia didn't seem to notice or care that the "real doctor" never evaluated her.

"Well, I got my own daycare service, as you probably know."

"I didn't know, actually." I stifled a groan as the image of Ophelia caring for other people's children warped my mind.

"It's down on Rhubarb Road. Anyway, do I need to worry about that summer bug going around?"

"Summer bug?"

"Yeah. You know, that nasty cold half the kids have. Except it's not a cold 'cause it's hot out. See what I mean?"

A strange shiver caught my spine as I said, "Yes, I see what you mean."

"So do I gotta worry?"

"No, I wouldn't worry."

"Then I won't." She ambled toward the door. No "thank you." No "see you next week." Her lack of courtesies didn't grate on me as it sometimes did. My mind was on other things.

After she left, I went back out to the waiting room. No one there. The noon slot was open today, and the next appointment wasn't until 1:30.

Corinne had just started on a salad when I walked into the break room—which, in fact, was a fully-functional kitchen. It had a stove, oven, and two fridges. One was for food, the other for biological specimens. The storage freezers and incubators were in the basement.

"Did anybody call with an urgent appointment?" I asked.

"Uh…" She spooned a clump of raisins into her mouth. "Nope."

"Anybody call the office asking about cold symptoms?"

"It's July."

Just answer my question. "Anybody?"

"Yeah, I mean, a couple people, but I told 'em to come in if they really wanted to."

"Did you tell Sheldon about it?"

"Of course."

She didn't tell me, though. She never told me.

"What did he say?"

"He said kids get colds. Big deal." She let her fork dangle. "Why?"

"Just curious is all."

"Whatevs."

**

We saw four patients that afternoon—one with a toothache, two with sore knees, and a diabetic who had yet to grasp the concept of insulin. "I don't do needles, sweetie," he'd said to me. I said, "How about dialysis? Do you do that?" A little harsh, but he got the message.

There was no one else. No children. No one showing signs of a "summer bug," which unlike SARS, or Ebola, or Babesiosis, sounded like a benign, pleasant cold. Maybe sleeping so close to those files had made me paranoid through some sort of sleep-induced osmosis. Maybe it wasn't the files at all; maybe it was Luke.

Thursday was much the same: no sick kids. Not so much as a stomach ache.

Then came Friday.

TWENTY-ONE

A torrential rain arrived just in time for the weekend. With a gray dawn on the horizon, I hiked down to the road in galoshes and rain gear and took the Rover from there. I hoped everyone with a non-emergent medical issue used the miserable weather as an excuse to stay indoors. Fridays were always chaotic as people tried to be seen before the weekend, and I didn't want chaos today. I wanted calm.

I turned onto Main Street at half-past seven. At first glance, everything looked deserted, a wet, gloomy wasteland stretching from Murphy's soda fountain to St. Rita's churchyard. There were no dog-walkers strolling the sidewalks; no cars parked along the curb.

Then I saw the clinic.

Two lonesome figures stood on the front stoop. Both were huddled under a green-and-white umbrella on the sidewalk, and they turned at the sound of the Rover's approach. My breath caught when I saw Luke waving at me. Lois stared at the ground beneath her feet.

I parked out front to let them in. All fears of an awkward conversation vanished when I saw the look on Luke's face. He had that glazed look of the sleepless, his eyes dark with worry. Lois looked tired, but not sick.

"I know we're early," he said. "I would have called, but I figured we'd just come down."

"Room 1's clean," I said. "Go right in and I'll be there in a second."

I grabbed my stethoscope from my office and called Sheldon, who picked up on the second ring. "Hello?"

"Dr. Kline? It's Aubrey. Luke Ainsley is here with his niece."

"For an appointment?"

"No, it's an urgent issue."

"What kind of issue?"

"I don't know yet. I just roomed them—"

"Well find out, for goodness sakes. You shouldn't be talking to me if the poor girl's in anaphylactic shock."

"Right. Sorry." The familiar heat of shame rushed my cheeks. *Another check in the Aubrey-is-incompetent column.*

"I'll be there in fifteen minutes," he said.

Fifteen minutes. I could keep the peace for fifteen minutes.

They were waiting for me in Room 1—Luke on one of the chairs and Lois on the doctor's stool. She offered it up when I walked in.

"No, no, it's fine. You go ahead," I said.

She sat back down and proceeded to spin round-and-round on the stool, her feet kicked out in front of her. Luke held out a hand to catch her in case she fell.

"What's going on?" I asked.

He spoke in a falsely casual tone, undoubtedly for Lois' benefit. "Have you heard about the summer bug?"

The nerves in my stomach turned to stone. "Yes."

"Most of the kids at camp have it. Runny nose, cough. It started the day after..." He looked at Lois. "It started a couple days ago."

"We've had a few calls about it."

"It was worse over the winter—every little sneeze sent people into a panic. Your dad was seeing patients on the weekends."

"How do you know?"

"Because I was one of them," he said with a wan smile.

"No one's come in, though."

"Maybe the collective paranoia in this town's run its course. I don't know."

"So why are you here?"

"Because I'm more paranoid than most people." He slowed Lois' spinning stool to a stop. She wiped her nose with the back of her wrist, which came away shiny and wet.

Thin, clear, normal mucus. No blood. Experience told me this was a garden-variety cold, something I'd seen a hundred times. "Does she have any other symptoms? Fevers? Chills?"

"No. Just a runny nose." He gave me a sheepish look as he realized what this must have looked like. "I knew I overreacted."

"I wouldn't say that. It's always better to be on the safe side."

"It's exactly what the other kids have. Just a runny nose."

"No cough?"

"Not that I've seen."

"Well, let's see what Sheldon says."

"What do *you* think?" he asked.

In all my years of residency training, I had never been asked this question by anyone other than my superiors. In spite of my best attempts to give my own impression, patients always wanted to know what the attending thought. Some would politely nod along to whatever I had to say. Others would blatantly ignore me. I was always just the trainee; a woman of wasted words.

Now I understand the comfort in that position. Until now, no one cared what I had to say because my impression didn't matter. Someone else was making the decisions. Someone else was going to take responsibility if something went wrong.

What if I said Lois was fine, and she wasn't fine? What if I overreacted and subjected her to a hundred painful, expensive, useless tests? Such were the decisions we made every day—well, Sheldon made. I bit my lip and said, "I'm not sure."

"You must have an idea, though."

"I don't want to be wrong."

"Isn't that part of being a doctor?" His easy demeanor had morphed into something more intense. My face flushed with the sudden inquisition.

"I'm not really a doctor."

"Yes you *are*. Jesus, Aubrey. Your diploma's on the wall out there."

"Why are you antagonizing me?"

"Because I want you to act like the smart, capable, confident woman you are. Make a decision. Tell me that Lois is okay or not okay so we can go home."

Tears stung my eyes. The humiliation was almost unbearable. "I think I hear Sheldon's car—"

"Aubrey, wait—"

I ran out the door before Luke could follow. Sheldon was humming a tune as he walked in. "Oh, hello," he chirped.

"They're in Room 1."

"Have you examined her?"

"No."

"Why not?"

"Why should I? You're the doctor."

The smile on his face lost its luster in a way that both surprised and moved me. He looked disappointed—in me, or in that comment, I couldn't tell.

"Well, let's go in, shall we?"

"I think I'll sit this one out."

"No, I think you'll join me."

"Dr. Kline—"

He cut me off with a robust knock on the door to Room 1. We found Luke and Lois standing by the window, admiring the tulips outside the corner store. "Ah, the lovely Ainsley duo," Sheldon said. "Such a pleasure to see you on this fine Friday morn."

"Hi, Doctor," Luke said, with barely a glance in my direction.

"I hear little Lois is the patient here today." Sheldon scooped Lois up and onto the exam table. Most children either laughed or screamed when he did this, but not Lois. She kept a straight face the entire time.

"Now, then. What's the matter, my dear?"

"She doesn't, ah…" Luke gave me a helpless look.

"She's a very good listener," I said. "But she'd rather you do the talking."

Sheldon gave her a warm smile. "I see. Well. I see you have a runny nose."

Lois nodded as she wiped her face again. "Here, have a tissue, dear." He put a fresh Kleenex in her hands. "Now blow."

She blew. Having mastered the discreet act of analyzing someone else's mucus, Sheldon gave it a cursory glance and threw it away.

"Do you hurt anywhere?" he asked.

She shook her head.

"Coughing?"

Again, no.

"Belly ache?"

No.

"Do you feel sick, sweetheart?"

She waited a beat, then nodded. I could see that her answer had surprised him.

"Where?"

She spread her arms wide, as if preparing for a curtsy.

"Everywhere?"

She nodded.

"But it doesn't hurt?"

No.

Sheldon frowned as he thought this over. "Dr. Lane, may I borrow your stethoscope?"

I handed it over. He placed its bell against Lois' back, then prompted her to take a series of deep breaths as he listened to her lungs. From there, he examined her heart, and then her abdomen. He mashed on her belly and tapped on her knees. He looked in her ears, mouth, and eyes. Unlike most physicians in the twenty-first century, we didn't have the advantage of CT scanners and MRI machines to tell us what might be going on inside the body. We had our eyes and ears and a worn-out stethoscope. Callihax was not for the insecure.

When this was done, he asked me to help undress her. I pulled Lois' summer dress over her shoulders, and together, we inspected every inch of her porcelain skin. At every turn, with every bend of her body, I dreaded the telltale splotches that would give it all away.

"Find anything?" Luke asked.

"Not a thing." Sheldon gestured for me to put the girl's clothes back on. "Hearts and lungs sound clear. Eyes and ears look good. Except for a runny nose, her exam is completely normal."

"Any rash?"

Sheldon didn't answer right away. "Not that my old eyes could see," he said.

He sold it with a smile, but that moment of hesitation was enough to confirm what I'd long suspected: Sheldon knew about the boys. The rash. He knew it all.

But how? *Why?* Had someone mentioned it to him? It seemed like a strange subject to mention in passing. *Doctor, I'm not sure if you've heard, but four boys got a rash last summer and died...*

"Are you sure?" Luke asked.

"Quite sure," Sheldon said. "In any case, I wouldn't worry. You know what they say about colds."

"What's that?"

"Two days coming, two days here, two days going." Sheldon offered Lois a sticker: a butterfly or a bus. She chose the bus.

"This is only the first day," he said.

"Then it may get a little worse before it gets better. You'll see."

Luke helped Lois with her raincoat. "So that's it?" he asked.

"That's it." Sheldon beamed with enough wattage to power a lighthouse. "You take care now."

Sheldon stepped out while Luke wrestled with Lois' raincoat. The wise, Harvard-educated doctor wasn't worried. *So why was I worried?* I let the door close behind Sheldon, leaving the three of us alone again.

"How many kids at the camp are sick?" I asked.

Luke frowned. "It's just a cold, Aubrey. You heard him. I feel like an idiot for wasting your time."

"I'm curious. How many?"

"I dunno. Twenty?"

"*Twenty?*" I'd been expecting five or six. "Out of how many?"

"Fifty-five kids."

"How old?"

"Mostly the younger ones. First and second-grade." He finally managed to match Lois' right and left arms to the correct sleeves. He gave up on the hood when she swatted him away.

"Boys or girls?"

"Both." He took Lois by the hand. "Look, we're late for camp. Lois has swim class first-thing and it's her favorite, so we gotta go—"

"Can I come by the camp this afternoon?"

"Why?"

"To just…I dunno. See what's going on."

"You mean surreptitiously examine twenty kids?" His laugh made me wince. "No way, Aubrey. Forget it."

"This is how it started last year, right?"

"Aubrey—"

"Yes or no?"

"It's a cold."

"The first boy got sick on July 14th."

"Let it go."

"What if we miss something?"

"You weren't here last year. It's not the same."

"Then tell me how it's different."

He sat Lois on the edge of the table and tried to get her shoes on. I nudged him away and eased them onto her feet. Lois tied the laces herself.

"The kids were sicker," he said. "Fevers. Throwing up. It didn't look like a cold." He averted my gaze as he lifted Lois off the exam table. "I remember what it was like last year. I remember every detail."

"Luke, I'm sorry—"

"Don't be. I didn't lose a child." He let Lois smack the sticker on his forehead. "But I can tell you no one wants to relive what happened with tests and mass hysteria and all the rest. Sheldon cleared her. It's fine. Just a cold."

Luke carried Lois out of the room, her bare, skinny legs dangling past his waist. She looked at me over his shoulders, and our eyes met, and held, and I knew in that moment she desperately wanted to tell me something. I thought of the way she spread her arms wide when Sheldon asked her where she felt sick. *Everywhere.*

Luke was right: I couldn't barge into summer camp and examine fifty kids. Tomorrow, though, I wouldn't have to—because tomorrow was Saturday. And I knew where the town went on hot summer Saturdays.

Moon Pond.

TWENTY-TWO

I played the part for my daytime excursion to Callihax's version of a beach with a swimsuit, cover-up, and sunglasses. My tote contained a dog-eared novel and a towel that had nurtured dust mites for fifteen years. The weather, thankfully, had cooperated. Brilliant blue skies, with a soft, sultry heat that often came in the wake of heavy rains.

Mr. Parsons was lifting the barricade as I made the final push down the path to Moon Pond. "Good mornin'," he said. "Hopin' to beat the rush?"

"Just wanted to get a good shady spot."

"I hear ya. I'd try the south side. Gonna be a hot one."

I tilted my head toward the sky. Hot, indeed, with a blazing orange sun. A stream of sweat made a slow run between my shoulder blades.

"Don't be afraid to wear some sunscreen," I said.

"Surely will," he said, which meant he would do no such thing. With indomitable cheer, he tipped his baseball cap as I walked off. Well, at least he had that.

Just ahead, Moon Pond welcomed me in all its lush, early-morning glory. Maple and aspen trees leaned over the water like overprotective parents. Wildflowers peppered the grass, which was maintained not by lawnmowers but the footfalls of running children. And the sky—there were no words for a sky as clear and blue and endless as the one overhead.

I chose a spot in full view of most of the water and its surrounding shore. It didn't matter where I sat; no one would question my reasons for being here since it was hot, and sunny, and summer. Moon Pond was Callihax's most reliable form of warm-weather entertainment. And if Luke showed up, well—I looked the part of a weekend warrior.

The first families started showing up at nine. I recognized most of them, though only a few said hello. One grandmotherly-type took one look at my two-piece and snorted. So much for wearing my most "conservative" suit.

The best spots on the grass were gone by ten. By eleven, you could hardly *see* the grass. In a town of 432 people, this didn't translate to a mob scene—but it was close. I estimated a hundred people either sitting on beach towels, wolfing down sandwiches, or testing the water.

I abandoned my novel with its sexy-man-cover—my mother did surprise me at times—and ambled over to the water's edge. A brother and sister raced past me and dove in with a messy splash. *Cold.* Freakishly cold. I wasn't the only wimp; no one over the age of twelve had ventured in. I waded in, feeling the icy burn as it crept up my legs. A school of fish swam between my ankles as if I were part of the natural landscape. Pale grey stones massaged the soles of my healing feet. Moon Pond looked exactly as it had a week before: pristine.

"Nice suit," came a voice behind me.

Moira smirked as she looked me over.

"Thanks," I said.

"A little cold for you?" She gestured to the water.

I recoiled from Kyla and Francine's splash as they sprinted past me. "Maybe. What's your excuse?"

"You know how many kids pee in there?"

I didn't, but Moira seemed anxious to educate me.

"All of 'em."

"Urine is sterile."

"Huh?"

"Never mind."

Francine trudged out of the water, looking hurt while Kyla pointed and laughed. Moira brushed the strands of wet hair out of her youngest daughter's face. "Don't let her tease you like that, Francie. Come on now."

"My bathing suit *droops*." She pointed to her butt. The fabric had indeed started to sag.

Moira laughed. "Get used to it, sweetheart." She gave Francine a little love tap to coax her back into the water.

"Where's Sammy?" I asked.

"Home with his Grandpop."

"Oh."

"Why?"

I swear, Moira was more my mother's child than I was; she had a sixth sense that put dogs to shame. Maybe we'd been switched at birth. "I just thought he'd probably like it here."

"He does." She chewed on a piece of grass as she waited me out. "I'm gonna take him tomorrow, when it's less crowded. He don't really know how to swim yet."

"I see." I couldn't deny the logic in that. "How's your dad?"

"The same."

As much as I wanted to know about these kids' father, I didn't dare ask. Moira would volunteer the information if she wanted to—which meant I would never, ever know.

"Sammy ain't sick, if that's what you're wondering."

I choked on a breath. "I'm sorry?"

"You heard about the summer bug goin' around."

"We had a few calls."

"And you're here to scope out the scene?"

"No, I'm here to relax on a Saturday."

Moira Samson would dominate every staring contest until the end of time. Conceding defeat, I looked toward the trees. For a while we said nothing at all.

"I'm guessing you heard about Bo," she said.

Looking up, I saw that her gaze had noticeably softened. "I can't imagine what you must have gone through," I said.

"Nothing like losing a child." She yelled at Kyla to take it easy on her little sister, then asked me, "You want kids?"

I thought a moment before answering honestly with, "I don't know."

She waded in a little deeper. The cold didn't seem to faze her as it did me and every other adult on the shore. "I know what people say 'bout us," she said. "Country hicks, no interest in education or whatever, having kids we can't afford."

"Who says that?"

"You. People like you. Anybody with a college degree, pretty much."

"I don't judge—"

"Of course you do." We watched Francine attempt a few strokes of butterfly. Kyla laughed, and Francine told her to "Cool it!"

"I never said a word to you, Moira."

"Which is part of your problem. You're too subdued."

"Subdued?"

"In your job. You can't do that job if people don't believe every word out of your mouth, even if it ain't true."

"Thanks for the advice," I muttered.

"Your dad was a good doctor. Real good."

I stared at the surface, remembering my very first trip to Moon Pond. My father had packed us a lunch and bought me a new suit and told me to pick a spot, the *best* spot. "This is our day," he had said. We stayed from dawn till dusk. I didn't want to leave.

Now he was gone. What would he have given for one more day at this place? One more day with his daughter, twenty-five years older but in some ways, just the same?

"He tried to save Bo," she said. "He did everything he could."

Her voice ached with the memory, with grief. Moira was no different than any other mother—both immune to and comforted by the passage of time. We watched her girls splash and laugh and play the games that children play when the world belongs to them.

"Have you seen the file?" she asked.

How she knew—or even sensed—such things, I would never know. "Yes."

"Those fuckers botched the autopsy."

"How do you know?"

"I was there. I saw what they did. Assholes already had their minds made up."

"About what?"

"The diagnosis."

"Parvo?"

She snorted. "Parvo my foot. All four of my kids had Parvo three years ago."

"My dad diagnosed them?"

"Nah. I knew the slapped cheeks when I saw 'em. Me and my brothers had it as kids."

Moira was correct on that front: Parvovirus B19 manifested as a facial rash that looked like slapped cheeks. I had seen it a few times in residency, but not as often as my medical school professors led us to believe.

"Did you mention this to my dad?"

"'Course I did. I told him about every goddamn snort and sniffle my kids had since birth. He said if they already had Parvo, they'd be immune."

"But the coroner told you it was Parvo…"

"Yeah. B19. Same virus he had three years ago." She gave me a sideways glance. "In other words, total bullshit."

"So you think it was something else."

"Your dad thought so, too. We tried to get those big honchos at the CDC to look into it, but they read the report and decided hell, it's practically a third-world country up here, so no big deal if four kids die. Blame it on 'limited access to healthcare.'"

"Why are you telling me this?"

The girls bounded out of the water and ran for shore. Francine doubled-back and wrapped her arms around Moira's thighs. "I *told* her, Mama!"

"Good. Now go get the sunscreen so I can lather you up again."

"Okay!" She ran off again.

"Fat chance of that happening," she said, which made us both smile.

We started back toward her beach towel, sprawled out on the grass. I doubted Moira wanted me to sit with her—no one in town wanted to be associated with me, to be honest—but she waved me over. "Sit down," she said. "Have a sandwich."

She had packed about ten of them. I unwrapped a delicious peanut-butter-and-jelly while Moira slathered Francine in sunscreen.

"Damn Welsh skin," she said. "We all burn up like a fireball."

"Fireball," Francine giggled.

"Time for lunch," Moira commanded. Both girls sat quietly as she unwrapped their sandwiches and opened two bottles of juice. Francine reached in the bag for a cookie.

"Nah-uh," Moira said. "Healthy stuff first."

"Okay, Mama."

I watched, spellbound, as Moira doted on her little girls. Maybe "doted" was the wrong word—but how she loved them. In high school, Moira Samson was the bad girl that put all the bad boys to shame. Pranks and parties and cat fights in the parking lot. She toyed with all the guys—popular, nerdy, athletic, dumb, smart, naïve. Whatever. She played them all and she played them beautifully. When she got pregnant senior year, I figured someone had finally played her. Now I wasn't so sure.

"You're a good mother," I said.

The turkey sandwich she had unwrapped languished on her right knee as she considered this. "Thanks," she said.

After the girls had wolfed down their sandwiches, Moira rewarded them with a cookie. Kyla wanted to go back in the water, so naturally Francine did, too.

"Let the food digest, for Chrissakes," Moira said. "Give it fifteen minutes."

"That's like *forever*," Kyla whined. Moira distributed extra cookies to placate them, although I sensed that if she hadn't, they would have waited anyway.

"Small battles," she said to me.

I sat with the girls as they adhered to Moira's strict timeline. Francine showed me her friendship bracelets. Kyla told me about narwahls.

At or around the fifteen-minute mark, Moira set them loose again. The sun smoldered overhead, which had inspired a few more brave children to test the water. There were maybe ten in there now. I couldn't imagine any kind of hysteria surrounding this place. It all felt so peaceful. Idyllic. Innocent. I had yet to see a child with so much as a sniffle, much less a rash.

Moira had drifted to a rare, preoccupied silence. If she noticed my presence, she didn't say so.

"Anyway, I should go." I stood up and brushed the grass off my butt. "Thanks for lunch." A few heads swiveled for a look at my "skimpy suit." Apparently the cover-up didn't cover enough.

"I love my kids," Moira said. Her blue eyes blazed in the high-noon sun. "I'd do anything for them."

The last hour had convinced me of that. No, the last three weeks. Maybe the last twenty-nine years. Moira Samson would defend her ilk to the death, and anyone who knew her growing up would have said the same.

"I failed Bo," she said. "Will couldn't handle it."

"Will?"

"My husband. You remember him."

Will Rienne was technically my cousin, but my mother had been estranged from Will's father for years. Although we lived in the same town, our families existed worlds apart. We never saw each other at family gatherings. Never said hello in church. My mother's animosity toward her only brother had trickled down from parents to children, such that Will and I behaved like strangers. We barely even talked.

"I didn't realize you married him."

"Married him on my eighteenth birthday. Had four kids with him." She put the empty juice boxes back in the cooler. "It's a shame you never really knew him."

"Are you still…?"

"He died last year." She spoke the next word softly: "Suicide."

I didn't have to ask her to put it together—not that she would have, anyway. The sequence of events spoke for itself.

"I'm sorry," I said.

"I love my kids." She wiped her eyes as she watched her little girls hold their own against the twins that had splashed me earlier. "I would do anything to protect them."

There was vengeance in those eyes. Vengeance and anger and the fierce maternal resolve that had carried her through the suicide of her husband; the death of her son.

"So would I," I said, meaning it in more ways than she would ever know.

TWENTY-THREE

The echoing agony of Moira's loss followed me home, a shadow at my heels. She had moved on from Bo's death, but she hadn't let go. Not even close.

That night, I dove into the files again. For the next four hours, I focused on the sick children; the survivors. Luke was right: their symptoms had been more severe than the illness Ophelia had described. Low-grade fevers. A hacking cough. In some cases, my father had noted "profound pallor" on exam. This suggested anemia, which again, could be consistent with Parvovirus. But no rash. None of the sick children—even those with a spectrum of nasty symptoms that mirrored the fatal cases—had ever developed a rash. It was the only real discrepancy in their history and exam.

Then I reviewed the lab tests. Renal failure. Liver failure. Severe anemia. These tests were well documented because they were cheap, easy, and could be performed here, in the clinic. All had been repeated several times in each of the deceased, and at least once in the other cases. None of the surviving kids showed any signs of organ failure—they had never gotten that sick. The two that were anemic had recovered without a transfusion or any other intervention.

I took a closer look at the antibody testing. These tests were pricey—thousands of dollars for some of the rarer diseases my father had sent out for. Because it was difficult—if not impossible—to *see* a virus under the microscope, the fastest way to test for viral infection in a live patient was through immunoassays. PCR testing was the gold standard. These tests had been run at three different academic centers in the Northeast.

In Bo's case, a viral culture had also been performed post-mortem. The technique was fairly complicated and involved using primary and continuous cell lines to replicate the virus until a cytotoxic—cell killing—effect could be seen. Luke would know far more about this process than I did, but I gathered from the testing report that viral culture was useful for cases in which the differential diagnosis was very broad. Antibodies were then used in a separate schema of testing to identify the specific virus.

Interestingly—or not, if you asked Moira—PCR testing had confirmed infection with Parvovirus B19 in all four deceased subjects. Both IgM and IgG antibodies were positive, which explained why the coroner and every other infectious disease specialist had latched onto Parvo as the cause of death. IgM antibodies were only present during the acute phase of a disease —in this case, up to 120 days after infection. Beyond that, IgM was undetectable. IgG, on the other hand, was present for life and indicated either a chronic disease state or exposure to the virus at some time in the past.

But 120 days? That meant the boys could have contracted Parvo up to four months before these tests were run. That was plenty of time for the virus to come and go and have nothing to do with the disease that had actually killed them.

The specialists hadn't thought so. I looked at the coroner's report in Bo's file:

Primary cause of death: Multi-organ failure secondary to Parvovirus B19

Secondary cause of death: Severe anemia

No mention of the rash, but then again, rashes themselves didn't kill people. I wondered, though, why no one had commented on its atypical appearance and unusual course. The rash had started to resolve—then boom, multi-organ failure and death. Maybe the coroner and whoever else reviewed these cases didn't comment on it because they didn't know what the hell it meant.

I wondered if Luke would talk to me after that uncomfortable encounter at the clinic yesterday. Which, of course, had followed that other encounter in the bedroom. Instinct told me no, he wouldn't want to revisit this. Not after the scare he'd had with Lois.

I extinguished the kerosene lamps some time after two.

At three, the phone rang.

***

The phone sailed off the bedside table in my mad rush to answer it. "Hello?" I said, yanking it up by its cord.

"Aubrey? It's Luke."

"Luke?" His voice didn't sound right. "Are you okay? What's the matter?"

"It's Lois. I just…"

"Hey, it's okay. Take a breath. What's wrong?"

"She's worse."

"Worse how?"

"She has a fever now. A cough." His words were tumbling over each other. "Shit. I don't know, Aubrey. I know Sheldon said she'd get worse before she got better, but this…" The sound of Lois' coughing filled the background. "I can't stop thinking about what happened last year. I can't—"

"It's okay. Bring her down to the clinic. I'll be there in ten minutes."

"Thanks."

My mother appeared around the corner as I hung up. "He should have listened to Sheldon," she said.

"Mom, he's scared. I'll just talk to him."

"He doesn't understand children like parents do. That girl needs her mother—"

"Well, she's not around."

"Of course she's not around. She died three years ago."

I stopped at the door. "What did you say?"

"You heard me."

"How?"

"Perhaps you should ask Luke about that."

I wasn't sure what to make of the edge in her voice: an accusation? A challenge? Even during my volatile teen years, she had never identified Luke as an enemy. I was surprised to hear her turn on him so quickly.

"It doesn't matter," I said.

"He didn't tell you, though, didn't he? About why he came back here?"

I wrestled on a pair of shoes, using the twisted shoelaces to distract myself from my mother's questions. Ten minutes to get to the clinic. I had already wasted two.

"Aubrey—"

"I have to go."

She stood between me and the door. "Ellen Ainsley overdosed three years ago while Luke was doing his PhD in Boston. He was the one who found her."

I didn't want to hear this, not from her. I hated how the people in this town betrayed one another's secrets, the kind of exchange that always ended in hurt, and suspicion, and in my case, denial. "Why are you telling me this?"

"Because *he* didn't."

I gave up on the laces and shoved my feet into the shoes. "It doesn't matter," I said.

"Of course it matters. You left town to get your degree. Luke left for reasons unknown to anyone—your father thought it had something to do with the way you broke his heart—"

"It wasn't like that."

"Then how was it, exactly?"

I broke his heart by leaving and he broke mine by staying. *That's* how it was. People expected some great drama, but really, our relationship had ended in silence and tears, a summer romance that ran its course. At least, that's what I told myself. The truth was that I replayed the last days of our doomed relationship over and over in my mind *for years*, and not just during idle hours at work, or on a date with a smooth-talking lawyer, or in my apartment late at night. I dreamed about it, too.

The end. No matter what I did, no matter how much time passed, I couldn't seem to forget the end.

"Aubrey?"

"I'm leaving."

"You should at least talk to him—"

"I *have* talked to him. He didn't want to talk about Ellen. I'm sure he has his reasons." I couldn't think of what they were, though. Shame? Loyalty? Luke had never been one to lay his emotions bare, but he wasn't a liar, either.

"Well, whatever happened, he's not the same."

"*No one's* the same. I'm not the same. You're not the same." I stood up, meeting her at precisely eye-level because were precisely the same height. Like looking into the eyes of my future self.

After a moment, she stepped aside and let me pass.

He's not the same.

I wondered about those four words until my heart rejected them.

***

We convened in Room 1. Lois had the sleepy-eyed look of a child who belonged in bed. Her head lolled on Luke's shoulder as he lay her down on the exam table.

"Did you call Sheldon?" he asked.

"Not yet." I had learned my lesson last time. Examine first, call second. Unless it was a true emergency, in which case every sensible patient in town called him at home. I never even heard about those calls.

I repeated Sheldon's exam with obsessive thoroughness. Lungs. Heart. Abdomen. Eyes, ears, nose, mouth, throat. Except for the occasional wheeze on expiration, there was nothing worrisome on this part of her exam. Taken together, her history and physical still looked and sounded like a cold.

"Did you check her skin?" I asked.

"Just her arms, legs, and back."

I lifted Lois' shirt over her head. Her arms, shoulders, back, and torso were unremarkable, except for the swimsuit lines that revealed a mild sunburn. She had skinned her right knee, but aside from that, her legs looked normal, too.

"I don't see anything unusual."

"Okay," he sighed—with relief, mostly, but there was doubt there, too. "I guess we'll just have to wait this out, then."

I brushed Lois' white-blond hair out of her eyes. "Lois? Hey." Her eyes fluttered open. "Do you feel sick anywhere?"

She nodded.

"Everywhere?"

She nodded again.

"Worse than before?"

She shrugged. *If only she could tell us what was going on.* Pediatrics was often a guessing game, even more so out here. Without any specifics to go on and no diagnostic machines at our disposal, I felt helpless. Sheldon made his decisions based on intuition, knowledge, and years of experience. Some way or another, I would have to learn to do the same.

"It's just a cold," I said.

"You still think so?"

"I think so."

Luke hoisted her into his arms. As Lois dozed against his chest, he swept her fine blond hair over her shoulder, revealing the smooth expanse of her neck.

A silent scream rolled through me.

On the nape of her neck was a red, angry rash.

TWENTY-FOUR

"Aubrey?" Luke was shouting now. "*Aubrey.*"

"I'll call Sheldon."

Lois stirred in his arms. He whispered something in her ear, which soothed her back to sleep. When he spoke again, his voice was hushed. "Aubrey, tell me what's going on—"

"I saw a rash."

His arms tensed around Lois' little body. "Where?"

"On her neck."

He swept the hair away again and caught a glimpse of the quarter-size rash that had taken root at her hairline. It looked like a tiny hand, with red, blunted fingers that reached toward the collar of her shirt.

"Jesus," he breathed.

"Stay here."

I ran down the hall to the office phone. Sheldon picked up on the fifth ring.

"Hello?" He sounded as though his mouth had been stuffed with cotton.

"Dr. Kline? This is Aubrey."

"Ah, Dr. Lane. Why in God's name are you calling me at this hour?"

"I'm at the clinic."

I heard a mattress creak as he sat up in bed. "With whom?"

"Luke and Lois."

"Again?"

"Yes." Best to lay out all the cards now. "She has a rash."

The mattress creaked again as he stood up. I failed to hear any garbled murmurings from a bed partner, which again made me wonder about his supposed wife. "I'll be there as soon as possible," he said.

Luke had abandoned the ominous confines of Room 1 and sat on the desk in my office. Lois slept soundly in his arms.

"It's probably nothing," I said.

"What if it's not? What if..."

I took his hand, a gesture that didn't heal so much as soothe. I had held the hands of hundreds, maybe thousands of patients. It was different for us; I knew that. But his breathing slowed and somehow, he relaxed.

Less than ten minutes after my phone call, Sheldon blustered in with the loud, windy force of a nor'easter.

"Dr. Lane! Where are you—"

"In here." I called him into my office.

Sheldon frowned. "Room 1," he said.

We migrated to the exam room en masse. Sheldon turned on all the lights and rummaged around in the drawers for a solid minute.

"Ah ha." He held up a glass slide. "Let's have a look, then."

Luke held Lois' hair while Sheldon inspected the area of interest, using the glass slide as a pressure point. He lay it flush against the rash and pressed down. The area of redness turned white, which was consistent with a viral exanthem—a fancy name for a childhood rash.

"What time is it?" he asked me.

"Almost four."

"On a Sunday."

We all knew what time it was, what day of the week it was. Just as we knew many hours it would take for a copter to get here, how many miles to the nearest hospital. The hysteria those propeller blades would cause if 430 people heard them whirring in the night. And for what? A little girl with a rash so common it didn't even have a name. As my father once said, viral exanthems are as much a part of childhood as skinned elbows and ear infections.

Sheldon put his hands on his knees and got to his feet. In that moment, he looked older than his sixty-some years. Decades older.

"Draw some blood," he said. "I've got some calls to make."

***

Lois was an unusual seven-year-old in a number of ways, but she screamed and cried like any other kid when I drew her blood. Sheldon hadn't specified the tests he wanted, but I figured the more blood the better. That way I wouldn't have to stick her twice.

"I should call Maggie," Luke said.

"Why? Is she waiting up for you?"

He shook his head. "He told me not to bring her in. Said I was a hypochondriac."

"You are, you know."

"Sheldon looked worried."

I thought so, too, but didn't say so. Luke was inches from his breaking point. I had never seen such blanket terror in his eyes.

"He's just being cautious."

"And you?" He touched my arm as I withdrew the needle from Lois' skin. "Are you worried?"

If Luke panicked, Lois would sense his fear, and the shred of restraint that remained in this situation would unravel. Sheldon had been calm. *I* could be calm.

"I'm not worried," I said, which was a lie, and if Lois' rash wasn't just a rash, and the worst possible outcome became reality, Luke would hate me for it. But right now, I didn't know. I couldn't turn his world upside down until I knew for sure.

"So this is just routine?"

"We always do more tests when a patient comes back to clinic for the same issue."

He seemed to accept this for what it was: a massive generalization. We did more tests not so much to reconsider a diagnosis, but to placate worried parents. *Is that what Sheldon was doing now?* Or was he genuinely concerned that this was something he couldn't handle?

"Any idea who he's calling?" Luke asked.

"I'll go see."

I started toward the reception area, but the muffled drone of Sheldon's voice made me hesitate. The doors to the exam rooms were exceptionally made—yet another testament to my father's devotion to privacy—but the reception area, not so much. Important calls were never made from the reception area.

I held my breath and inched closer. Sheldon's tone was caustic rather than jovial, as if a stranger were behind that door. Bits and pieces of his conversation permeated the silence:

"Yes, a seven-year-old female…working on obtaining samples now…first documented rash, but I haven't seen any other cases…Ground transportation is a no-go with Route 81 flooded…Then you *get* me a back-up plan. *Now.*"

He slammed the phone down. I backtracked into Room 4 across the hall. From here, I could see the street.

And there, at the end of the block, was Sheldon's SUV.

Ground transport. Where, though? And more importantly, who was authorizing this?

Sheldon's footfalls echoed through the corridor as he returned to Room 1. I had left Lois' blood on ice, as he'd requested. We would have to call in the technician—Bobby Cain, a retired vet—to run the lab tests.

"Dr. Lane!" He bellowed.

I stole a moment of calm in front of the mirror. My reflection revealed a tired girl in an oversized white coat, sweat glazing my forehead. My hair hadn't been brushed since the night before, and the sunburn on my cheeks had done nothing to dampen the circles under my eyes. *Look the part,* my father said on my medical school graduation. *The rest will fall into place.* I didn't look the part of a confident doctor; I looked scared.

I found Sheldon labeling the samples while Lois dozed on Luke's shoulder. The clock on the wall showed quarter-till-five. Just an hour till dawn, but that didn't mean much on a Sunday. The town was closed except for church services at nine. Everyone would be out and about, roaming Main Street, privy to whatever drama was about to unfold here.

"We need to run these," Sheldon said. "Do it stat."

"Dr. Kline, I honestly don't know how to run the samples—"

"I can do it," Luke said.

Sheldon looked skeptical.

"I used to work in a lab," Luke said. "In grad school."

"Dr. Lane, go with him," Sheldon said. "I'll watch Lois."

"I can watch Lois," I said.

Sheldon gave me a look that made me pause. *He doesn't trust me.* "These are human specimens, Aubrey." *Aubrey.* The façade was gone. "You need to be there."

"Let's all go, then."

The animated tone of this conversation had roused Lois somewhat. She tugged on Luke's sleeve and pointed to the bathroom.

"Aubrey's right," Luke said. "She should probably stay with me."

"Fine," Sheldon huffed. "We all go downstairs."

TWENTY-FIVE

The cellar smelled like old leather thanks to Edwin Coggeshall, the house's former owner and ambassador of the famed Coggeshall saddles. The hooks and hides and various other tools had long since been removed, but the odor remained. Lodged in the stone walls, embedded in the concrete floors, the heady smell of leather reminded me of yet another turn in Callihax's history.

In its modern state, the cellar housed three miniature labs —chemistry, hematology, and microbiology. Each "lab" had its own fridge and freezer, where we stored the samples. "Chemistry" entailed tests like sodium, potassium, and creatinine, which measured kidney function. "Hematology" meant blood counts and smears. The patients on coumadin had their blood drawn every few weeks, and over time, they acquired their own shelf in the fridge. There were fourteen such patients in Callihax.

The microbiology lab sat apart from the others. Confined in glass walls, the micro lab processed a variety of specimens— blood, urine, semen, other fluids. A sample from each specimen was streaked on plates or slides, depending on the test we'd ordered. Then Bobby stuck it in an incubator and watched it grow. Some of the incubators smelled sweet (pseudomonas); others, like fresh-baked bread (yeast). Then there were the organisms left to grow in room air, because although bacteria preferred warmer temperatures, they could grow in anything. Bobby had left three of these out over the weekend, including the nastiness sampled from Mr. Wilhelm's necrotic toe. That petri dish had flourished.

Luke navigated the lab with ease. Sheldon wanted eighteen

tests on Lois' blood, most of which could be run simultaneously. While these tests were cooking, Sheldon dabbed a drop of blood on a slide and looked at the smear under the microscope.

I knew what he was looking for: hemalyzed, or burst, cells, which indicated a major problem in the bloodstream; and reticulocytes, which meant the marrow was working hard to create new cells. Both indicated that a virulent bug may have penetrated Lois' bone marrow.

"Have a look," Sheldon said to me.

A perfect sample, with perfect cells. No indication that something was amiss.

"Looks normal," I said.

"Indeed."

We waited thirty minutes for Lois' eighteen blood tests to generate a final result. When the timer finally sounded, Sheldon put on his reading glasses and scanned the numbers. I looked over his shoulder. *All normal.*

He removed his glasses and pondered the blood sitting on the shelf. The digital clock inched toward six. A new day was upon us.

"I have one more call to make," he said. "Wait here."

With brisk strides that, again, suggested a whole new man, he took the stairs two at a time. The weight of his footfalls shook dust from the banisters.

Luke gave me a searching look. "Were the tests...?"

"Normal," I said.

"Then why did he look so worried?"

Because he read the files, I thought. I had no idea how, since those charts were sitting in a hidden compartment in a remote mill, but he had. He also knew the organ failure didn't set in until after the rash had begun to clear. If Lois had what we both feared, any testing at this stage was meaningless.

I didn't tell Luke this. Maybe he knew. Maybe he worried about asking questions in front of Lois, who didn't speak but listened better than most.

And so, we waited.

And waited.

The digital clocked chimed with the passing of the hour. Seven o'clock.

"It's been a while," Luke said.

Devoid of windows, the cellar imposed upon its inhabitants a very timeless, disorienting effect. I tried to picture Main Street at this hour on a Sunday morning. Father Meade would be inside St. Rita's, readying the church for Mass in much the same way I did at clinic every morning. The especially devout were probably already out front, saying their "pre-prayers" before Father Meade opened the doors. My father used to wonder about that bunch.

"Maybe we should go back upstairs," he said.

I pictured Sheldon—this new, duplicitous Sheldon—laying in wait by the door. Despite every attempt to recreate and/or legitimize that phone conversation in my head, I couldn't make sense of it. My father never discussed evacuation options with anyone but the dispatcher. It was *his* call to Med-Evac someone —no one else's. The accepting physician might give him a hard time, but in the end, the transfer happened if he wanted it to happen. Sheldon had the same power. *So why the negotiation?*

"Why don't you two wait here," I said. "I'll see what he's up to."

"Shouldn't we be calling Med-Evac?"

"I'll find out."

Luke nodded, but his eyes told me to hurry. Upstairs, the clinic was quiet, subdued. No ringing phones or crying babies. None of the weighty anticipation that came with weekday mornings. The air was crisper; cooler. On days like this, the break room felt like a kitchen, the exam rooms like vacant rooms of a house. I trespassed through the halls and into the reception area, expecting at every turn to hear Sheldon's voice.

The first floor was deserted. Silent, too. No voices. No staccato hum of an ancient air-conditioner that should have been replaced five years ago. No sign of Sheldon whatsoever.

I was on my way back to the basement when the floorboards creaked overhead. Probably just the house's old bones, as Gran used to say. Then I saw the door to the second-floor stairwell, which I always locked for safety precautions. Someone had left it open.

Every step groaned with my weight, betraying my ascent. Halfway up the stairs, I heard the muffled lilt of Sheldon's voice —again, behind a door. Not the file room, which was all the way down the hall, but closer. Very close. Had to be my father's office, right there at the top of the stairs. No one but me had been in there since he died. No one had any reason to go in there.

My mind went to the shotgun in the downstairs closet. Locked, of course, with the keys in my office, but still reachable in less than thirty seconds. Then again, what would Sheldon think—or do—if I barged in there with guns literally blazing? Was he armed? Would he shoot me first? *Had I completely lost my mind?*

Forget the shotgun. I ran up the stairs and barged right in, finding Sheldon by the window with a cell phone to his ear. And not just any cell phone, but a piece of decidedly advanced technology that belonged in a science fiction movie. It also appeared to be fully functional.

Sheldon whirled around. "I'll call you back," he said into the phone.

"Who was that?" I demanded.

"What are you doing up here? I told you to wait—"

"We waited. For an hour." I left the door behind me wide open. "I think I deserve to know what's going on."

"I think you know what's going on," he said.

He started walking toward me. I took two steps back. "Stop," I said.

The intense look in his eyes flickered with confusion. He held up his hands. "I'm not going to hurt you."

"I'm not sure I believe you after what you did to me in my own house."

His stone-walled expression gave nothing away. He took another step. I stood my ground, even though every bone in my body raged at me to run. Run and scream and get help. Someone on Main Street would react to a screaming woman. *Right?* Maybe they wouldn't react to a screaming Aubrey Lane.

"Stay there," I said.

He came closer, hands still held high. "You're in danger, Aubrey. I tried to warn you."

"I don't believe that either."

"My telling you to get out of this town wasn't a threat. It was sound advice."

"You don't think being stalked in the woods and knocked unconscious qualifies as a threat?"

He finally stopped. For a moment, we simply stared at each other, the kind of tense assessment that determines what happens next. He looked different—younger, maybe. More capable in some ways and less in others. This wasn't the Sheldon Kline who put dinosaur band-aids on little boys' knees.

"Who are you?" I asked.

He glanced at the scene outside the window. Sunday mornings started early in Callihax, especially in summer. The sun brought everything to life, a daily rebirth after hours of absolute night. The town hummed with it.

When he met my eyes again, his expression was inscrutable. "Sheldon Kline, board-certified internist."

"Who told you about those boys?"

He picked up the St. Christopher statue and studied it for a moment. A faint smile crossed his features as he did so.

"I always enjoyed the story of St. Christopher," he said. "I'm Jewish, mind you, but my wife was Catholic." He looked at me again. "Do you know the story?"

I did, but Sheldon didn't seem particularly interested in my answer.

"Christopher was seven-and-a-half feet tall—a scary bastard. Ugly, too. People feared him. In fact, Christopher himself was driven by fear, which he equated with power. He followed the king because people feared the king, and then he followed devil because the king feared the devil. When he discovered that the devil feared Christ, he endeavored to serve Christ, the most powerful figure of all.

"But Christopher struggled with prayer and fasting and the common habits of the devout. He went to a hermit for advice, who thought Christopher might be well-suited for carrying people across the wild river that had claimed many lives. A terrible, job, as it turned out. Dangerous and exhausting. But this giant of a man kept at it, until one day a child asked if Christopher would be so kind as to carry him across."

He set the statue on my father's desk and went on, "Christopher welcomed the task. The child was so small, unlike the many grown men he had carried on his shoulders. But as they crossed, the river swelled and the child grew heavier and heavier. Christopher thought they would surely drown. He told the boy, 'I do not think the whole world could have been as heavy on my shoulders as you were.' And the boy said—"

"You had on your shoulders not only the whole world but Him who made it."

He smiled. "So you know it," he said.

"My father loved that story."

"I'm not surprised. A doctor in a town as remote as this bears a similar weight on his shoulders. He shepherds his patients across a river of sickness and doubt, knowing that if he stumbles, there is no surgeon or MRI scanner to save him."

"Something tells me you didn't come here to shepherd his patients across that river," I said.

"I didn't come here to drown them, if that's what you're implying."

He was right, of course: my father had welcomed the task of carrying the people of Callihax on his bare shoulders. For the past few weeks, Sheldon had done the same. *So if Sheldon was the enemy, what did that make me?*

"Lois is going to die," he said.

The anger in my chest diffused in a great, painful rush. "How do you—"

"I read the files. The *copied* files." He gestured for me to sit down, but I opted to stand. "I know your father held onto the originals, but I don't know where they are. I imagine you've seen them." He left no room for questions, nor even a lie. He *knew* I'd seen them. In that moment, he seemed to know everything.

"Who are you?" I asked again.

"A board-certified internist, like I said, but also FBI."

He said this with stone-faced authority, which might have reassured the TV-obsessed masses, but not me. Sheldon Kline was portly and red-faced and had a chuckle better suited for Christmas parties than drug-raids. In short, he didn't look the part at all.

"I don't believe you."

"Then I've done my job," he said. "I'm undercover."

"An undercover doctor?"

"Well, no, not exactly. I'm an undercover agent with a useful background. In any case, here." He handed me his cell phone. "Feel free to call my supervisor."

I saw the most recent contact number on the display—a 202 area code. Washington, D.C. He could have faked the number, but the phone itself? No. It must have been some sort of satellite phone; the nearest cell tower was a hundred miles away.

"The FBI sent you to medical school? Somehow I doubt a government agency would invest so much time and money in that kind of cover."

"They don't. I joined the FBI late in life, my dear. Life circumstances, as it were."

I thought of the way he'd referred to his wife in past tense. The empty house. The distinctly masculine, dusty smell in the hallways. No telltale sign of a woman's cooking. No love in that house; just loneliness.

"So who sent you here?"

"Your father, albeit indirectly. Your mother made the call, but that was merely convenience—a nice tidbit for my cover. I would have come regardless."

"I don't understand."

"Your father contacted just about every government agency under the sun last summer. CDC, FDA, FBI, even CIA. He was convinced those boys' deaths were a part of some wild conspiracy."

"And you ignored him."

"Of course. It's tragic, but children die. In remote areas with limited access to healthcare, they die more often. This is a risk people take living out here."

"So what changed?"

"Your father kept excellent records, which entertained a consultant down at the CDC in Atlanta. He read through the cases. Performed a vast literature search. Spoke to several specialists in-house. He ran a lot of the same tests your father paid for out-of-pocket, which all confirmed the same thing."

"Parvo."

"Yes. IgM and IgG antibodies to B19, which confirmed recent infection and satisfied just about everyone involved in the case. Limited access to healthcare plus positive antibody testing plus a clinical history consistent with that particular virus essentially closed the book on the mystery."

"Except it didn't."

He nodded. "The intern at the CDC wasn't satisfied. He prepared a thirty-page report on the North Woods Exanthem, as he called it."

Exanthem was an exotic name for a common ailment, but it sounded ominous coming from him. "And his report made it to the higher-ups?"

"Hardly," he said. "It languished in a stack of paperwork on somebody's desk." He saw my reaction and said, "Such is life at a large federal agency. Too much paperwork to keep track of."

"Like medicine."

"Exactly like medicine. In any case, the file eventually died. Until a month ago."

"What happened a month ago?"

He waited a beat, then said, "Are you familiar with a little island country by the name of Nauru?"

"No," I said.

"It's the second-smallest country by population in the world, with some 9,000 residents. By last census, in any case. The number is much smaller now."

Sheldon's voice took on a darker tone as he went on, "In March of this year, the children of Naura started dying. It happened quickly—ten dead the first week, fifty the next, three-hundred by Day 14."

Three-hundred children. The sheer volume implicit in that number made my heart clench. Almost the entire population of Callihax, and a tremendous tally no matter who was counting. My head swam with the horror of it.

"For children who developed the exanthem, mortality was 98%. There were others who developed symptoms—cough, rhinorrhea, low-grade fever—but all of those patients survived. Very similar pattern to the cases here. Identical, really."

"Cause of death?"

"Multi-organ failure. Rapid, irreversible organ failure. By the time Naura officials realized what was going on—although, let's be honest, no one knew what the fuck was going on—it was too late for experimental treatments. Seven-hundred-twenty-one children died."

It was too tremendous to process. Too horrific. *Over seven-hundred children.* The deaths of four boys had devastated this community; I could only imagine what 721 could do.

"What about adults?"

"No reported cases in anyone over the age of sixteen. Our best infectious disease specialists had no explanation for this."

"Was it Parvo?"

He shook a finger at me. "You're getting ahead of me here."

"Well?"

"With few exceptions, the entire population tested positive for Parvo antibodies. IgM and IgG, exactly as was the case here."

I frowned. I'd expected a negative result—something that would finally and indisputably dismiss the Parvo theory. The photographs didn't fit, and the pattern and severity of the exanthem looked nothing like those classic "slapped cheeks." Moira, too, had seemed convinced the Parvo explanation was bogus—not that she was an expert in the matter, but her conviction made it difficult to ignore.

"We can dismiss four lethal cases of Parvo," Sheldon said, "but not 700."

"So they resurrected the file?"

He nodded. "And me."

"What do you mean?"

"I'd retired a year earlier. I was getting too old for the whole undercover-spy routine. It used to be Big Pharma manipulating numbers. Then it became terrorists and biological warfare— high stakes, sophisticated networks. My job was suddenly very risky."

"Seems like part of the deal when you sign up for undercover work."

"Not for an old fart like me. I could never have predicted where it would go."

I didn't entirely believe this. Sheldon had demonstrated his talent for playing the charismatic old-school doctor, but he wasn't naïve. He made decisions with authority. Navigated small-town politics with ease. He knew what he was doing.

"So what, then? The feds paid you big money to come here?"

"The feds don't incentivize people with money. I came because I had a vested interest in the case." He looked at the St. Christopher statue with its chipped plaster and faded colors. I wondered what he was thinking about: His wife? The impossible burden on his shoulders? On mine? Maybe he had come here with the intention of carrying these people to safer shores—and now, with Lois, he knew we had failed.

"Which is what?"

"I spoke to your father numerous times. He believed wholeheartedly that something sinister had happened here—a targeted attack, if you will."

"In Callihax," I said, still skeptical.

"I knew he was right when the Naura cases turned up. I told him to bury the files, wait for the FBI to investigate."

"And he did that."

"Yes."

"And a week later he was dead."

He studied my eyes, seemed to sense the challenge there.

"We were too late," he said, with a weariness that told me he probably blamed himself—at least in part—for my father's death.

"So you came here to do what? Find his murderer?"

"I came here to validate your father's theory and to give these people answers. And yes, I came to find the person or persons who killed four children."

"Using Parvo," I said, testing him.

"Parvo is transmitted by respiratory droplets—you know that."

"So you don't believe it was Parvo that killed those people."

"No," he said. "I don't." He walked toward me, hands at his sides. I twitched with the urge to back away, but the details he had provided were too sophisticated to be a lie. I didn't completely trust him, but I didn't fear him, either.

"What's your theory, then?"

"Well," he said. "I can tell you the CDC believes Naura was an act of biological warfare. Not targeted, per se. Naura has few, if any, political enemies. More of a practice run."

"*Terrorism?*" The word tasted like a bitter pill.

"Yes."

"Why, though? Why would anyone target children?"

"It's beyond my pay grade to figure that out."

"And you think the North Woods Exanthem was, what? A practice practice-run?"

"Something like that."

"But who could possibly be capable of something like this? You've met everyone in this town—close to it, anyway. You've probably investigated them, too." This thought gave me pause, because his investigation had no doubt included me. Maybe even *focused* on me.

"I have," he said.

"And?"

"And there are only four people in a two-hundred mile radius with an advanced degree in the biological sciences." He ticked us off with his fingers. "Your father, of course, is deceased. That leaves you, me…"

He didn't have to say it. I already knew.

Luke.

"Doesn't prove anything," I said.

He responded to this with a slight shrug, then said, "Your mother found the muskrats—quite a find, in fact. I knew they were out there. I'd found another dump site down by the river a week earlier, which confirmed active animal testing somewhere nearby. I thought it might lead me to the source."

"That's why you were parked out by Moon Pond…"

"Yes," he said. "You don't just round up some rodents in the woods for testing. You order them from specific companies, and those companies have records. I was chasing a lead—a bit of a Hail Mary, but worth it to try. Turns out *no one* breeds muskrats for biological testing. I never found a supplier."

"What does that prove?"

"Essentially nothing. My guess is someone wanted muskrats for some reason, but that someone bred them under the radar."

"Why muskrats?"

"Not a clue."

"Okay, let's say the muskrats are part of some elaborate experiment. Why would a terrorist stick around the North Woods? It doesn't make any sense."

"It makes plenty of sense." He paused. "It makes crucial sense."

"How so?"

"For one thing, to monitor outcomes after the initial outbreak. This is a contained environment. Whoever launched the 'study' would want to keep it that way."

I tried to picture any one of Callihax's 432 souls—of which nearly 100 were children—orchestrating such a tremendous undertaking. Impossible. I knew these people. I knew their families. I'd been to their weddings and funerals and baptisms. I knew their hopes, their fears, their dreams; I knew who had stayed in the North Woods because the outside world terrified them, and who had stayed because it rejected them.

No, it wasn't possible. Callihax had its share of evil—every corner of the world did—but not like this. The scope was too tremendous, the target too personal.

"Here," he said. "Have a look at this."

He tipped the statue on its side. Carved into its base were four tick marks—each labeled by date, which happened to be July of last year. The dates each of the four boys had died.

In two days, maybe three, there would be a fifth.

And if Sheldon was right about the Naura connection, there might, someday soon, be a hundred. A thousand.

I recalled Moira's words over Jed Walsh's dead body: *Too late for that.* And I was, then. But Lois—*no.* Lois' body hadn't failed her yet. *I* hadn't failed her yet.

I respected Sheldon Kline, but this time, I would prove him wrong.

TWENTY-SIX

The sound of creaking hinges broke the silence. Sheldon put the figurine back on the sill and sidestepped me toward the door. We listened.

Footsteps. Two floors down, climbing the stairs from the basement.

"Did you have to *choke* me?" I whispered.

"I knew you weren't equipped to handle the mess you were walking into."

The footsteps stopped somewhere below us. Luke called my name in the silence: "Aubrey? Are you still here? Hello?"

Sheldon put a stiff hand on my shoulder. "Have you shown him the files?"

"No, but he's not—"

"Don't. Don't tell him where they are, or even that they exist."

Failed on that count. Sheldon frowned as he registered the look on my face. "It doesn't matter," he said. "Just don't mention them again."

"That could be a bit of a challenge now that Lois is sick."

"Of course it will. The real challenge here is keeping the people in this town under control. Hysteria will not help us. In fact, it could be dangerous. Mortally dangerous."

"How so?"

"Let's worry about that if it happens. For now, we need to reassure Luke that Lois is going to be fine."

"He knows you're worried about her."

"Then I'll work on my acting skills. Emphasize the normal lab values. It's a small rash—could be anything."

"But it's not."

"I don't know yet. You and I must work on the assumption

that this is NWE."

"NWE?"

"North Woods Exanthem."

Even though I had long feared these woods, I was having a hard time associating it with a deadly virus. "All right."

"We have a little time. Two days before the rash clears." He left the foregone conclusion unspoken: *And she dies.*

"That's it? We can't evacuate her? Take her to the CDC—"

"The CDC won't take her. And I've got strict instructions to keep the infected as far away from Med-Evac as possible, for reasons you can probably imagine."

Infectivity. Viral spread. Devastation and death and all the rest. Callihax was a natural quarantine. Which meant Lois would die here no matter what we did, and Sheldon was not about to change that. Maybe he had called someone on his satellite phone to confirm his plans with the higher-ups. Maybe this theory about a "terrorist" was all a ruse to impose quarantine and isolation on 431 innocent people.

Luke had resumed his path toward the reception area. The stairwell was right next to Corinne's desk. He would come upstairs next.

"So what's your plan?" I asked.

"We've got to document every case that comes through the door, but we must do it quietly." He dropped his voice to a whisper as Luke walked the halls. "Your job is to prevent a panic, and that starts with Luke. Go talk him down."

"This town is already on edge."

"Then we keep it there. Do not go over. I'll find some way to evacuate Lois safely."

I wanted to believe him. I *needed* to believe him.

The trouble was, I didn't.

TWENTY-SEVEN

With Sheldon's admonishment ringing in my ears, I went back downstairs to find Luke. "Where's Lois?" I asked him.

"Asleep in Room 1." He pinched his healing nose with his thumb and forefinger. "I think I'm on the verge of a meltdown."

"Try not to worry," I said, remembering Sheldon's instructions. *Prevent a panic.* The false reassurances caused me physical pain, but Luke was too distraught to notice.

"I don't know anymore," he said. "After last year…"

"I know. Everyone's anxious."

"Maybe me more than most."

"You're worried about her. That's understandable."

"I told you I was lousy at parenting. Or uncle-ing, I guess." He looked like one of those parents on the first day of kindergarten, when moms and dads stood at the door and either sobbed, made false promises, or bribed their kids with chocolate. Luke had just established himself as a member of the first group.

"You did the right thing. Come on, let's go home."

"Where's Sheldon?"

"Calling somebody he knows in Boston." At least this was partially true.

"To ask about Lois?"

"To get some perspective on things."

"Do you think he knows what happened here last year?"

We walked into Room 1 to find Lois curled up in a fetal position on the exam table. I lay a soothing hand on her forehead. "I think he knows the gist," I said.

"Shouldn't we call the CDC, then? Or at least the people your father contacted—"

"And what? Wait for them to save the day like last year?"

"Maybe they know more now."

"We have all the results, Luke. I saw them in the chart."

"I ran additional tests. Water samples, air samples, even pet samples. Did you find those reports?"

"Yes," I said.

"Well, we should look at them again. Maybe there's an answer in there somewhere."

"I think we should head home," I said softly. "Let Lois get some rest. You, too."

He sagged onto the windowsill, such that the blinds behind him crinkled and bent. He seemed not to notice. I leaned on the sink and folded my arms, as uncomfortable and tense and tired as I'd ever been. Lois slept on, oblivious. The three of us, disparate yet connected, bound by truths and lies and strange silences. I thought of that moment in the cafeteria and wondered how *this* could possibly have come of *that*.

"Luke, I need a favor."

He looked up with world-weary eyes. Oh, his eyes. Fraught with mystery, tinged with longing. I saw myself in those eyes.

"Anything," he said.

"I need you to act like everything's okay."

He searched my face for a beat. "That's quite a request."

"We can't afford a panic."

"And what about Lois? What happens to *her*?" He brushed Lois' hair out of her sleeping face. "What if we're wasting time?"

"Luke, you heard what Sheldon said—"

"I don't believe him." His gaze cut through me. "And neither do you, I can tell."

His voice caught in his throat as he lifted Lois off the table. She stirred, but never opened her eyes. I wanted to reach out and touch her. Touch *them*. But there was a distance between us now, a chasm of hurt, sadness, and mistrust.

I followed him out the door and into the hallway, and beyond that, into the spectacular sunshine of a summer morning. If it weren't for the shadow of events to come, I might have followed him anywhere.

"Luke, wait."

He opened the backseat of his BMW and eased Lois inside. "I appreciate all you've done for us," he said. "I mean that."

"You have to understand—"

"I do understand." He belted her in and closed the door. "I do."

His eyes had gone a deep, skylit blue, as if the promise of a new day had roused him. Although this resurgence eased some of my fears, it also ignited new ones. "What are you going to do?"

"Take her home, like you said."

He got in the car, his right hand finding the gear shift as he set his gaze on the road ahead.

I gripped the open window frame. "Luke, what are you doing?"

"Nothing."

"Stop lying to me."

He smiled a wry, painful smile. "I think we crossed that line a long time ago, don't you?"

"Luke—"

"You would do the same."

As he said this, his eyes found mine with the innocence and loss and regret of the boy who let me go twelve years earlier. He had done it then with thinly-veiled sorrow. He did it now with absolute conviction.

Then he put the gear in first and disappeared in a haze of gravel and dust.

TWENTY-EIGHT

Sheldon found me standing in the middle of the street. "What happened?" he asked.

The instinct to lie had vanished with Luke. "I think he's taking her out of the Woods."

"What did you tell him?"

"Exactly what you told me to tell him."

"Well, he won't get far. Road's flooded."

I watched the cloud of dust settle back into place. Luke knew these roads—and the side roads, and trails, and everything in between. Sheldon had sorely underestimated Luke's knowledge of the terrain.

"And if he does?"

"Then he does. We have other things to worry about."

"Aren't you worried about containment?"

He started back toward the clinic. "We open for business tomorrow as usual. Keep the town calm and happy."

"And Lois?"

"I'm working on it, Aubrey. You have to trust me."

I hurried after him. "What makes you think I'm just going to drop everything and blindly follow you?"

"Because you've done it so far."

I stiffened my shoulders, a poor defense against such a lashing blow. My father would have hung his head and said, "I raised you better than that." Or at least he would have thought it.

"Well I'm demanding answers now," I said.

"And you'll have them. But logistics first. Let's get the clinic prepped in case there's an outbreak. We need to be prepared for that."

I held my ground on the front stoop. "Is there a cure?

Something that might have been developed since the Naura outbreak? Tell me that."

"Dr. Lane—"

"Enough with the formalities and all your other bullshit. *Is there a cure?*"

He stopped, exhaled, and turned around. His ruddy cheeks looked pale; almost sickly. His pale blue eyes radiated the cold, heartless truth. Then he pointed to his SUV across the street.

"Let's go," he barked.

"No."

"No? Fine. Stay here and watch it all unfold. Just like you did with Jedediah Walsh."

"I'm not going anywhere until you tell me the truth."

He didn't flinch, barely even breathed. But I saw a foreign emotion flicker in his eyes: not quite respect, but something close.

"No," he said. "There is no known cure."

And we drove off into the woods.

***

I thought my newfound knowledge of Sheldon Kline's identity might somehow lift the gloom that surrounded his house, but there it stood in all its unsightly horror, the windows black with shadows and depth. Sheldon pulled the SUV into the shed and left the door open.

We waded through the overgrown yard to the front door. Potted plants rotted on the stoop. A ravaged bird's nest languished in a state of decay on the sidewalk.

Sheldon ignored all this and led the way inside. Again, I was struck by the interior's heartlessness, as if the house held a grudge for its years of abandonment. The tables and chairs and sofas were mere set-pieces in an adult-sized dollhouse. The air smelled like damp July heat. The floorboards creaked not with use, but with stiffness and rot.

I was thinking of ways to leave unnoticed when Sheldon

stopped at the door to the basement. "Wait here," he said.

He yanked on the string dangling from the overhead bulb, which cast the stairs in a foul yellow glow. When the gloom had swallowed him completely, I retreated toward the kitchen, the most open room in the house. The windows, though grimy, at least afforded a view of the outside world, which had just now gone overcast. So much for a glorious summer Sunday.

Sheldon's footfalls pounded the stairs on his way back up. He locked the cellar door behind him and pocketed the key.

"Here." He handed me an iPad.

"What's this?"

"A protocol. You wanted to know the plan? Here it is."

The screen flashed on, a display of color and technology I'd almost forgotten in the weeks since my escape from LA. My fingers danced across the screen. There were three files on the desktop: NWE, Naura, and I/Q Protocol.

I clicked on the I/Q protocol.

The first line definitely set the tone:

As issued by Executive Order of the President authorizing quarantine and/or authorization for known infectious diseases that are causing, or have the potential to cause, a pandemic.

I scanned the list of diseases: tuberculosis, plague, viral hemorrhagic fevers, yellow fever, SARS…

"NWE isn't on this list," I said.

"It will be."

"And then what?"

"Then we get the federal and state governments to enforce isolation and quarantine." He pulled up a different file: the Naura file. This one was quite official-looking, with graphs, extensive citations, and high-resolution photographs. In short, nothing like my father's homemade assembly of charts in walls of my grandfather's mill. The CDC had clearly spent significant time and resources on the Naura file.

"See this graph?"

The statistics were striking. Numbers of cases had been compared against numbers of deaths, with only a slim margin between them. The bottom line: NWE carried an extremely high mortality rate.

"That's what happens when you fail to contain an outbreak."

"And you're convinced Lois is about to cause an outbreak?"

"I'm saying Lois is one person. *One* life. What if she gets to Bangor, or Portland, or Boston? What if Lois infects someone everywhere she goes?"

"The virus doesn't behave that way. You know that. It's right here in the file. No airborne transmission. Vector unknown."

"Viruses mutate," he said. "That's what they do."

"I'm not so sure Lois is a threat to national security right now."

"Then you're naïve."

"Call the CDC, then! If you're so convinced she's about to unleash a plague on the world, why is it just you and me up here? Why not call in the National Guard?"

He swiped the iPad from my hands and started for the stairs.

"Where are you going?" I asked.

"Filling in for the National Guard," he said.

"Dr. Kline—"

"Go babysit the clinic. If someone comes by, let them in. Document an exam. Adults, kids, whoever. If you see somebody with a rash, you keep them calm; say it's absolutely nothing to worry about. I'll be there as soon as I can."

"But it's Sunday—"

"Then say a few prayers while you're there," he said. "This town's going to need them."

***

What Sheldon didn't understand was that hanging an OPEN FOR BUSINESS sign in the clinic window on a Sunday afternoon would incite a panic as surely as a fire or a bomb threat. So I put a lawn chair on the sidewalk, propped the clinic door open, and pretended to clean. A deep, bone-crunching clean, with fans and mops and all manners of bleach.

Sunday's foot traffic dissipated in the hours after the church service. All the stores and dining establishments were closed in deference to God. No parades or festivals on this particular weekend. A game of stickball had gotten underway in the empty lot across the street, but otherwise, pedestrians were scarce. I was ready to call Sheldon with this reassuring update when Moira Samson poked her head in the door.

"I saw your lawn chair out front," she said. "You workin' on a Sunday?"

"Just cleaning," I said.

She had all three of her kids in tow, two of whom looked like the picture of health. Sammy had a runny nose he couldn't keep up with.

"I thought you had Ellie Ruskin do your cleaning."

"Ellie's, ah...away." *Stupid.* People in this town never went away—and if they did, everyone knew about it.

"You're a lousy liar," she said.

With Moira, I had to be careful. She read people as if their thoughts were printed on their foreheads. It wouldn't take much for her to blow this whole thing open.

"Hi, girls," I said.

"Hi!" Francine squealed. Kyla gave me one of those too-cool-for-school waves.

I bent down to say hello to Moira's youngest. "And how are *you*, Sammy?"

"He's got the bug." Moira scooped him into her arms. He looked at me with weepy red eyes, which Moira dabbed with her sleeve. His skin looked clear on a cursory glance, but I didn't dare look very hard. She would notice my roaming eyes.

"That's too bad," I said. "I hope he feels better."

"You wanna take a look at him?"

"Oh, well, I'm sure it's just like you said—"

"Take a look," she said, and passed him to me. The look in her eyes made me wonder if this was some kind of challenge; a test to debunk the "cleaning" pretense. But I couldn't imagine what it would accomplish. Moira would surely know if her boy had a rash.

I took him into Room 2, the cleanest of the bunch. Sammy permitted and even cooperated with my exam, but he looked tired. Disengaged. He took the lollipop I offered him, but he never brought it to his mouth. Moira ended up throwing it away.

I recalled meeting him for the first time three weeks ago and asking myself the same question that came to me then: sick or not sick?

Back then, the answer had been *not really*. Today, it was more like *maybe*.

I took my time with his skin exam: not just legs but feet, ankles, knees, groin. Same for his arms and hands and elbows and shoulders. I asked Moira to take off his shirt, not just roll it up. If she knew what was going on, I couldn't tell by the look on her face.

I waited while Moira turned her son around in her lap. She smoothed the hair on his head and rubbed his legs to calm him. I leaned in close to examine his back, his shoulder blades...

His neck.

TWENTY-NINE

There was nothing there.

No rash. Not even a sunburn. His skin was pristine.

"See?" Moira said. "Nothing. I don't know what the hell's going on here—"

"Nothing's going on."

"Uh huh. Except you lyin' to me."

She took Kyla and Francine by the hand and knocked over the trashcan in her haste to leave. "I thought you were starting to get what it means to live in this town."

"Moira—"

"Seriously. We protect our own here. You and Sheldon...I dunno what's going on there, but seems to me you're covering your own asses."

"Moira, please." I scrambled to block the door. "Just sit down a minute."

"I told you what I went through a year ago with Bo. I *trusted* you."

"I know, and I'm sorry—"

"Sorry?" She barked a laugh. "Lemme guess. You're sorry that my son died. You're sorry Will died. You're sorry for all the shitty luck I've had 'cause *Moira, you're a good mother*." Her sarcasm stung like a slap across the face.

"We're just being safe. As safe as we can—"

"Safe? For who? You and that sly fuck?" She covered Francine's ears and breathed out a sigh. "Don't repeat that, baby girl."

Francine nodded.

"Sheldon told me to keep the clinic open today as a precaution," I said.

"Because of Lois."

"You heard about Lois?"

"Everybody knows about Lois."

"Knows what, exactly?"

"Whatever there is to know," she said. Her voice was taut; controlled. Maybe Ms. Ainsley had talked about Lois at church? It didn't matter. Sheldon had underestimated the power of small-town gossip.

"Luke drove her out of town," I said. "To get help. I swear to you she's the only patient we've had with a rash—"

"Does she have what Bo had?"

Sheldon would expect me to say *No, definitely not, just a virus. Poison oak. Dry skin.* Something along those lines. And Moira would believe me, not because I had the power or authority to convince her, but because she wanted to believe me.

"Yes," I said.

Moira's stare seared through me. I could almost see her walls —forged over a lifetime; shaken last year; rebuilt higher than ever—crumble around her. She took a breath that rattled in her chest and caught somewhere deep in her throat.

"Jesus," she whispered.

"But we have reason to believe the kids who were sick last year have immunity."

"Sammy wasn't sick last year."

"What?" I had somehow forgotten this small detail, but it came back to me then like a blow to the gut.

"He was fine. Healthy. He wasn't..." She faltered on the last part. Sammy whimpered against her neck.

"Sheldon is talking with the CDC right now, in case anything happens—"

"He's fine," she said, as dignified and sure and stoic as she could manage. But I glimpsed the doubt in her eyes, the reflection of fear in those pools of blue.

She took her girls by the hands and whisked them out the door.

THIRTY

Sheldon called every hour to inquire about new cases. Each time, he sounded winded, like he was climbing a hill. I wondered what the I/Q protocol really entailed—fences? Armed guards? I tried calling Jim Ranson, but he never answered the phone on Sundays, and today was no exception. If I went to track him down myself, that left the town with no doctor, even if that "doctor" was me. My only play was to stay at the clinic.

As the sun set over the western ridge, I wondered about Luke and Lois. Luke's plan was heroic, in a sense, but not very practical. Moira knew better than to venture out of these woods without a destination or plan. I could see it in her eyes: *if Sammy has what Bo had, then it's already too late.*

It was this sentiment in Moira's reaction—the fear, the denial, the whisper of despair—that sent me upstairs into the file room. I had some 1,900 charts at my disposal and eight hours to sort through them all. The answer had to be here. Maybe not a cure, nor even an identifiable virus, but *something*. Sheldon could do all the isolation and quarantine he wanted. I wanted to know why. How. *What.* I wanted to give the real enemy—this virus, or pathogen, or whatever it was—a face and a name.

I made it through 37 charts before exhaustion took over. Some time later, I woke with a start to the distant sound of knocking. I stepped over a pile of manila folders and orphan papers and scrambled down the stairs. Sheldon said he would be back at seven. By my watch, it was just past six.

The knocking became a fury. I remembered my shotgun in the closet, locked and loaded. My rule in LA was never to answer the door for someone who showed up announced; that's what cell phones were for. No one in Callihax had a cell phone (with the exception of Sheldon's superphone, or whatever that was), but we certainly had a landline. I would have heard it ringing from the file room.

"Hello?" I called out. "Who's there?"

The knocking fell silent.

"Aubrey? It's Luke."

I exhaled a breath that had been causing me physical pain. "I'm here," I called out.

"Can you open up? I came right here, I need help—"

I opened the door to find Luke standing on the stoop, his niece cradled in his arms. They were both soaking wet, saturated with sweat and rain judging by the flush in Luke's cheeks. Lightning flashed in the distance, the remnant of a downpour.

Luke lay Lois on the table in Room 1 while I rounded up some blankets and pillows. I removed her wet clothes: socks then pants then shirt. Her teeth chattered in the silence.

The rash was everywhere. Neck, shoulders, back. Its red, knubby fingers had morphed into tentacles, reaching for the clear, smooth expanse of her skin. I didn't have to do blood tests to know what would happen when that angry fire consumed her.

Luke started to cry. Not the weepy, loud sobbing I'd heard in exam rooms just like this—*You can't hear the heartbeat? Why? What does that mean?*— but a subdued, soundless display of defeat. The tears on his face landed on his hands, splayed on his legs in the palm-up, defenseless position of a man who had run out of options. He looked at me with that same, helpless wonder.

"What happened?" I asked.

He was shivering—from cold or grief or shock, I couldn't tell. His gaze fell once more to his hands. "I don't...I tried..."

I helped him with his clothes, too: shirt, pants, socks. When he was down to his boxers, I wrapped a blanket around his shoulders. Even though I'd turned the radiators as high as they would go, it was another five minutes before he stopped shivering.

"Luke?"

"We made it to the river, and Sheldon was right—the road's flooded." The blanket fell from his shoulders as he buried his head in his hands. "I tried a different route. The old logging trail by Harrick's place…" He sucked in a breath. "The tires blew out."

"You got a flat? In the Beamer?"

"No," he said. "I took the Subaru; better suited for rough terrain. Both tires blew out. I knew right away I'd driven over something."

My mouth went dry. "You drove over what?"

"I got out and saw nails. And not just some lame kid job—professional, camouflaged nails. Enough to stop a tanker if it rolled through there."

"Could Harrick have done it?"

Luke shook his head. "Harrick had a stroke two years back. Lives with a little old nurse named Sally. Last I heard, Harrick can't use his left side and Sally bakes pies for breakfast, lunch, and dinner. They aren't the type to do this."

"So someone put them there intentionally."

"There, and everywhere. I fixed the flats as best I could and tried a third route. Barely a route at all—more like a gap in the trees that connects with another road.

"And the tires blew out again."

He nodded. "Never even saw them." He seemed to think about something for a beat. "And it wasn't just that. I sensed a presence out there. I know you must think I've totally lost it, but I swear, somebody knew we'd try to leave. I got Lois and hiked back to town."

Sheldon. His protocols. Isolation and quarantine. He wasn't worried about Luke and Lois because he knew they'd never make it out of these woods.

"It was Sheldon," I said. "He has quarantine protocols…"

"I figured as much. It was almost too easy."

"Harrick's place is a good ten miles from here." Ten miles may as well have been a hundred in these woods. At night, a thousand. "You hiked all this way?"

The look in his eyes told me that he had.

"We should drive over to Jim's place and drag him over here." He shook his head.

"What?"

"I don't trust Jim."

"You don't trust him? Luke, he's the closest thing to a policeman we've got—"

He grasped my arm and drew me close. "I don't trust anyone after what I saw out there."

"Do you trust me?" I asked.

He held my gaze for a fraction of forever. The world had brought us together again, only to pull us apart, inch by agonizing inch. Trust took years to earn; moments to lose. I wondered if that moment was about to come and go.

"I need you to save her," he said. "I need you to do that." A non-answer. Maybe the kinder answer.

"I'll call Med-Evac."

I ran up to my father's office, where all the emergency calls were made. The radio looked as though it hadn't been used in months—dusty, inert. I flipped the switch—

Nothing.

No power. No sign of functionality whatsoever.

I flipped it three more times. Pressed other buttons to see if it would kickstart an accessory circuit. My father had taught me how to use this machine the same way a barber taught his son how to cut hair—*If it's* me *who needs a copter, you're going to know how to use this.* I remembered every detail, but more than that, I remembered standing here with my father as a teenager, awed by this indestructible connection to the outside world. *Almost as reliable as your mother's carrier pigeons*, he'd said.

But not today. Today, the radio was inexplicably, indisputably dead.

I tried the landline phone.

No dial tone.

I pulled the drapes aside and saw a misty grey dawn, with fat black clouds on the horizon. The phones had survived storms far worse than this. It was barely raining—just a soft, steady drizzle, pattering the hoods of the cars parked outside.

I found Luke at Lois' side, his hand on her forehead. There was no need for me to do the same. I could feel her fever from here. "Luke…"

He knew from the tone of my voice what was coming next. "You couldn't reach anyone."

"The radio's down."

"*Down?*"

"Phones, too." I hated the idea as much as he did, but we had no choice. "We need to find Jim."

***

As predicted, Jim Ranson failed to answer his door. We went inside anyway—roaming the halls, calling his name. Unlike Sheldon's house, Jim's had that cluttered, lived-in feel. I stepped over tools and boxes and old magazines.

"He's not here," Luke finally said.

We left a note on his fridge: *COME TO CLINIC ASAP.* Maybe he'd notice it while making that slop he called coffee.

"Sheldon said he'd be at the clinic by seven," I said. The cuckoo clock on Jim's wall showed ten-after-seven. "Let's see if he's there."

"You *trust* Sheldon after what he did?"

"What choice do we have?"

I didn't like it either, but we were running out of options. At least Sheldon grasped the gravity of what was happening. He knew how quickly a placid crowd could turn into a mob.

The absence of Sheldon's SUV out front was the first worrying sign. We checked every room in the old leathermaker's house: basement, exam rooms, offices, reception area, chart room. The clinic was deserted.

"He was supposed to meet you here at seven?" Luke asked.

"That's what we said."

"To do what, exactly?"

"Enforce federal protocols, if necessary."

"You mean quarantine."

I nodded.

"And what? Watch more kids die?" He looked and sounded angrier than I'd ever seen him. "So Sheldon and whoever the hell he works for quarantine Callihax. You know what that means? Blood draws. Test subjects. All-out panic with nothing but a bunch of dead kids to show for it. Same as last year, Aubrey, just 'more official,' to make Sheldon feel better."

"How do you know—"

"Because I *know*, Aubrey. I've seen how the WHO operates. Mass hysteria ensues. And in the end, people die anyway. We don't need the CDC. We need a cure."

"*There is no cure.*"

Luke took a step back, his rage diffusing in the space of seconds. His nervous thumbs were quiet. He rubbed his temples and closed his eyes.

"Everything has a cure," he said.

"You know that's not true. HIV, Hepatitis, malaria." I followed him downstairs, into the lab. "Ebola. Cancer."

He threw open the glass doors to the microbiology lab. "The *common cold*, Luke. Think about what you're saying."

"Just because we haven't figured it out yet doesn't mean a cure doesn't exist."

He sat at the hood, where Bobby Cain cultured the samples and did his daily work. Luke settled right in; I had no trouble believing he'd spent three years in a lab.

"Your father knew the answer was here. In those blood samples; in their histories. He couldn't see it but he knew it was there. I think he called me because he needed another set of eyes. He was *close*, Aubrey. He had to be."

"You'll torture yourself if you think like that."

"A virologist has to think like that. How else could we devote our lives to something 40,000 times smaller than the width of a human hair?"

"Insanity?"

He almost smiled. "Something like that."

"We need a clue. Something to point us in the right direction."

"You have the files. The photographs."

Whatever my reasoning had been for keeping them from Luke no longer mattered. He was right; we needed clues. We needed a vector.

"Sheldon has another file that may help us," I said.

"What kind of file?"

"The Naura outbreak."

He nodded slowly as a memory took shape. "I heard about it."

"You did?"

He studied his knuckles for a beat. "I'm on some, ah, list-serves for virus enthusiasts."

"Oh. Right."

"There weren't many details. Hundreds of victims, all kids... wait a minute. There's a connection?"

"Sheldon certainly think so."

"That doesn't make it random, though. That makes it..."

"Terrorism."

He paced the room with Lois in his arms. His eyes pulsed with an almost manic energy.

"Are you thinking what I'm thinking?" he asked.

"We need that file."

***

On our way out, I put a sign in the window under my father's hand-painted one: *CLINIC CLOSED*. I had to write it on a scrap of printer paper because no such thing had ever adorned that window. Even on my father's worst days—as he liked to remind me, doctors get sick like everybody else—he left the doors and phone lines open. If someone needed him in a true emergency, he would be there.

I wondered if he had been tempted to close the clinic last year, especially with everyone congregating in the same place. He must have worried about other people getting sick, only to be rebuked by the CDC, WHO; the entire federal government. No one had come to *his* aid. Every door he tried to open for the sake of his patients had stayed closed.

Not this year. I wouldn't waste time with those doors.

I would break them down.

THIRTY-ONE

With Lois asleep in the backseat, we pulled up to Sheldon's house under the cover of overcast skies. There were no lights on in the windows, no screens to ventilate the dead air inside. The doors to the shed were closed, but fresh tire tracks suggested recent use.

"You stay with Lois," I said.

Luke looked skyward at the crumbling eaves. "I'm not sure this is a great idea."

"What choice do we have?"

"Are you sure the file is even in there?"

"It's on his iPad."

He shook his head. "Sheldon wants to quarantine the town. Okay, fine. I get that. But you know who else would want to keep this thing contained?"

The possibility of Sheldon-the-terrorist had crossed my mind, but he knew too much. He had *shared* too much. In any case, he'd had ample opportunity to kill me, which would have been far easier than showing me an I/Q protocol.

"It's not him," I said.

"Did you ever see any I.D.? Did you call anyone at the FBI? Anything?"

"No," I admitted.

"You just took him at his word?"

"It's not him," I said again.

The hollowness of that statement gnawed at me, but it also propelled me closer to the house. With each step, dead leaves from seasons past crunched underfoot. A loon drawled in the distance, the sound fading as I reached the front door.

I resisted the urge to look back at Luke, who would try again to talk me out of this. He would try a hundred times. But Lois would die without an answer—and soon. Forty-eight hours, best case. So he stayed by the car and I pushed open the door.

It opened with no resistance, the hinges slick and silent. Rotted floorboards announced my presence to the rodents and whatever else lived here. As I rounded the corner into the kitchen, the open cellar door caught my eye. *Ignore it.*

The dining room occupied the northwest corner of the house, where light was scarce and darkness reigned. The drapes had all been drawn, the furniture layered in dust. An ancient chandelier loomed over a vast dining room table.

Behind the table sat the buffet—a rustic, ruined oak, with cracked mirrors in the paneling. Fingerprints cut through the dust like brushes of paint on a white wall—fluid and seemingly haphazard, yet purposeful in their pattern.

I glanced over my shoulder. *Nothing there.* No movement. No stray shadows. Only a breath of stale air, tinged with something sickly-sweet.

I opened the buffet drawers as quietly as its age and construction would allow. The rollers had long since given way to a grating friction of wood on wood. The sound bellowed through the empty halls, lingering in the silence.

No iPad, but close enough. The box that sat in the well of the bottom drawer had the word CONFIDENTIAL stamped on the lid. I reached in and grabbed it. Rather than risk another sound-byte by closing the drawer, I left it open. Sheldon would know it was missing regardless—just as he would know who had taken it.

I left that ghastly room and walked into the kitchen. That smell—*what in God's name was that smell?*—intensified as I passed the table, the oven, the fridge...and finally, the cellar door. Still open. Still dark as pitch down those stairs.

Ignore it.

On another day, in another life, I would have. In LA, my mantra was always *keep walking*. Even though the hospital boasted security and shuttles and the ubiquitous presence of the LAPD, there were often late nights or early mornings when I ended up walking through that parking garage alone. If tail lights came on, I walked faster. If someone called out to me for the time, or directions, or money, I pretended not to hear.

Such practices were not ingrained in me; they had been acquired over a period of years. When I left Callihax at seventeen, I'd never even *seen* a parking garage. I had grown up in a town of minimal crime and neighborly good will. Jim Ranson had never investigated a murder or rape or even an aggravated assault, and neither had the sheriffs before him. The instincts to run or hide or fight back had never taken root in me the way they did for most children, at least not in response to a human threat.

Now, those instincts clashed. As a child, I would have turned on the light and raced down the stairs and checked to make sure no one was down there. As a woman who had seen the bloody consequences of so many things—shootings, muggings, rapes— I hesitated.

A grungy string dangled from the light-bulb over the stairs. I had to lean quite a ways forward to reach it. The smell became a stench. *Leaveleaveleave.*

I lost my balance for a moment and yanked on the string. A dismal yellow light swept the stairs, the walls, the shallows of the darkness down below—

And cast its eerie glow on the body of Sheldon Kline.

THIRTY-TWO

It took a moment for my eyes to adjust to the gloom. Whatever or whomever Sheldon had been running from, he hadn't gotten far. He had died such that his left hand looked as though it was reaching for me, and maybe it had been, before the blow to his head had ended it all. He had dropped a bottle of vinegar, which explained the smell.

There wasn't much blood. Just a ribbon of red that started at the crowd of his skull and trickled past his right ear. I didn't stoop down for a better look. I didn't *need* to look. The fuzzy white hair and ruddy arms and squat frame clearly belonged to the man who lived in this house.   Out of habit, I checked for a pulse. His skin was cool to the touch, his neck veins plump with dead, pooled blood. Then I ran. Frantic strides carried me through the hallway, kitchen, foyer, porch. I stumbled off the front stoop, my foot slipping on the moss that had claimed it.

Luke caught me on the front lawn. "Start the car," I said. The box of papers felt like lead in my arms.

"What happened—"

"Just go." I put the box in the foot-well and jumped into the passenger seat. As Luke started the car, I stared at house's front door, swaying in the house's natural draft. The dark interior gaped at us like an open mouth.

Luke floored the accelerator and peeled out of there at breakneck speed. *Thirty...forty...fifty.* Fifty on dirt roads felt supersonic.

The Boneyard flew past us, after which the scenery settled into its usual monotone of trees, skies, and underbrush. Luke kept his hands wrapped, vice-like, around the wheel. Neither of us spoke until we hit paved roads.

"Is Sheldon…" he started.

I shook my head.

"How?"

I glanced in the rearview mirror at Lois, now wide awake in the backseat. Her cheeks had gone a vicious, blistering red.

"It didn't look like a heart attack," I said.

"You sure?"

"I'm sure."

We were a mile from Main Street. Three minutes until we pulled into town; 180 seconds to face the unknown. A mob? A *murderer?* What if there was more than one?

"Turn here," I said.

"Why?"

"Just do it."

We swerved onto Burnstyle Road, which circumvented Main Street by looping around the school. From here, we could drive undetected to the mill—or at least within a half-mile of it. The last stretch would have to be on foot.

"We need the police," he said.

"*What* police?"

"Maybe Jim's home now."

"Or maybe he was at Sheldon's place before we got there."

"Jim?" He shook his head. "No. No way."

"I'm just saying it's possible."

"Anything's possible, Aubrey. That doesn't make it sensible."

"Then who's *your* prime suspect?"

He let his hands fall to the bottom of the wheel. Luke had always preferred to ponder the world in a relaxed, almost dreamlike state. Today's circumstances weren't exactly conducive to those methods, but he was trying. "Are you sure he was…you know—"

"He was dead."

His hands returned to the ten-two position. Although something told me he didn't mean to do it, the speedometer jerked toward sixty.

"We'll call Jim from the mill," I said. "Figure out a plan from there."

"Did you see anyone?" He checked the side-view mirror for the third time. "Is there a chance someone could be following us?"

"I didn't see or hear anyone."

"You sure? Because those old houses have a dozen ways in."

"I'm sure."

We drove on. The road turned narrow, then treacherous, then impassable. Luke parked in a grove of trees forty yards off the beaten path, its red frame glinting in the peaked morning light. We didn't have time for camouflage; I hoped the depth of forest and underbrush would provide enough cover from any passersby.

Luke carried Lois while I forged the trail through the woods, using familiar landmarks to guide my way: marked trees, languishing vines, a smattering of wildflowers. We didn't dare look up or around or behind us, nor did we pay much attention to the ambient chatter of the wilderness. There was nowhere to go but forward.

As the thatched roof of the mill came into view, a shadow darted across our path. Luke tucked Lois into his chest and crouched down. "Did you see that?" he whispered.

I wasn't sure what I'd seen, but in these woods, it was often impossible to distinguish the real from the imagined. We knelt beside a tree until a soft tap on my shoulder wrenched my heart out of my throat. "What the—"

"Aubrey?" My mother stepped into plain sight, looking wet and harried. She must have been hiking for at least an hour. "What's going on?"

"We need to get inside."

"Why? What's happened—" Her voice gave way when she saw Lois. "Oh dear Lord," she said, as solemn as a nun in church. Apparently the gossip hadn't made it this far.

We set up camp in the kitchen, with my father's files as the centerpiece. Fourteen of them and now, the Naura file. My mother helped Luke get Lois settled with blankets, pillows, and of course, cocoa. Luke kissed the girl's temple as he lay her down on the couch.

"I'm assuming you called Med-Evac," my mother said to me.

"The radio's down."

"That's impossible. It has too many failsafes to break."

"I don't think it broke," I said.

She folded her slender fingers and waited for me to go on. While Luke hummed Lois to sleep, I told my mother about the blocked roads and the scene in Sheldon's basement.

"And you came *here?*" Her nostrils flared in a rare demonstration of her masterfully-latent temper. "If you found a man murdered in his own home, we need to call for help."

"You don't understand. Jim wasn't home. The phones are down. The roads are out." I watched while stirrings of unease dawned on her face. "There *is* no help. We're on our own out here."

"What about Lois? That girl needs more than what we can offer her."

"I know that." I glanced at the 200-page file on the Naura outbreak. It would take days—no, weeks—to go through everything. We had hours.

"What is all this?" she asked.

After Lois had finally drifted to a restless, shivery sleep, Luke came over to join us. He stood at the head of the table, a commanding presence that cast a long shadow. He spread the pages until the kitchen table was a storm of white.

"The cure," he said. "It's in there somewhere."

***

We gave ourselves an hour. One hour to find the connection between Naura and NWE; one hour to save Lois. Luke and I both knew the consequences of spending all day here while Callihax spiraled into a panic. After the hour was up—cure or no cure— we would drive back into town and warn the masses about what was coming.

This, too, took planning. We couldn't just show up at the clinic and start screaming bloody murder—or "plague," for that matter. We had to be careful. Deliberate. Although some would claim that a rogue border-crosser had killed Sheldon, I knew he had been targeted. Someone had silenced him—just as someone had silenced my father.

After fifty-five minutes, we were nowhere. The case reports from Naura were barely organized. Photographs misplaced and undated. Hundreds of dead children with no obvious connection except for the fact they lived in the same *country*.

I focused on one photograph in particular, its edges crisp, the colors clear, handled only briefly by whoever had put this file together. A little girl and her mother sat together at a picnic bench, squeezed in tight, feasting on popsicles. The pair reminded me of the mother and daughter I'd seen weeks ago at the hospital cafeteria, two worlds apart, but both circling tragedy. The Naura mother hadn't known it yet; the LA mother had been living it for some time.

I was about to re-file it when my eye caught the background of the photo, a crowded array of slides and pools and laughing children. It looked hot; sweat and summer hot.

It looked like a water park.

"You mentioned water testing," I said to Luke. "Was it just Moon Pond?"

"No, the drinking water was also tested." Luke slid a 15-page report my way. "Negative results, but Sheldon seemed pretty convinced this was the source."

The photograph wouldn't let go. There was something there. Something *big*.

"In any case, it doesn't fit the pattern," he said. "A contaminated water supply would have killed everyone. Only 15% of the Naura population ever developed symptoms."

He saw me studying the photo: the water, the kids, the numbers...

It fit. *Finally something fit.*

"What is it?" he asked.

A cautious pause. I didn't want to be wrong about this.

"Aubrey?"

"Well, like you said, water is the perfect medium for all kinds of pathogens—bacteria, especially. Parasites. Amoebas."

"There was no evidence of parasites on Bo's autopsy, which is pretty definitive. Parasites are easier to see under the scope."

"I know, but..."

"But what?"

"Let's say it *is* the water supply—just not that water supply. Let's take Callihax, for example. What's the most controlled aquatic environment in town?"

"Moon Pond. But that's a dead end."

"Is it? Let's forget the negative testing. You said yourself we can't test for every virus under the sun. There are what, thousands?"

"Five-thousand described, millions known."

"And of those 5,000, how many prefer water?"

He gave me a skeptical look. "A water-borne virus?"

"It's possible, isn't it?"

"It is, but it's hard to test large bodies of water." He shook his head. "Maybe we're chasing nothing. Maybe it was a virulent case of Parvo all along."

"Or...what if Parvo was the vector? The Trojan horse intended to dupe everybody into *thinking* it was Parvo, when in fact Parvo was just a cover."

I looked at the laughing girl in the photo. "Take a look at this picture." I slid it closer to Luke.

"It's a happy-looking kid," he said.

"Yes, but where was it taken?"

"Hm." He pried it off the table and inspected the details. "Looks like an amusement park."

"Really? You wear swim trunks to an amusement park?"

A blitz of realization crossed his face. "It's a water park."

"A contained environment."

"With its own water supply."

"Exactly."

He let this stew for a moment. "Do you think they tested the water park?"

"There's no record of it in this file. I already checked."

"When?"

"In the last ten minutes."

"You realized this ten minutes ago?"

"That photo's been trying to tell me something."

His smile warmed my thrumming heart. "Wow."

"I'm not saying the mystery is solved—"

"No, this is it. This is the connection between the two outbreaks—which proves it was deliberate, targeted, and waterborne."

He pressed his thumbs to his temples and disappeared once more into his thoughts. Eyes closed; thinking hard. He used to do this when he was deciding what flavor ice cream to order while Mr. Murphy tapped the counter.

"Luke?"

"You're right. *Parvo* is the vector." He slammed the table with his fist so hard it elicited a polite yelp from my mother in the other room. "Parvovirus requires actively dividing cells to replicate, which explains why it likes kids."

"Which means..."

We both said it at the same time: a *supervirus.*

"Yes. Two viruses in one. Combined genetic material." He grabbed my hands like we'd just won something huge—a house, the lottery, an entire planet. "Like Spanish flu. Rare, but doable. Technology has evolved such that we're able to create a more stable virus that doesn't break down when the genes mix. The problem is..."

"It's a target for bioterrorists."

"Yes. Huge target. Our lab funding was drying up because no one in academia wanted to be associated with terrorism."

"Okay, but we still don't know what the other pathogen is."

"Actually..." He waited for me to start breathing again. "I think I do know."

"How?"

"Two things. First, the muskrats." He looked at my mother, watched her nod—slowly, thoughtfully. "Muskrats aren't very popular in the lab for obvious reasons. But for a virus that thrives in water, not a bad choice. In fact, I remember a crackpot PI who talked about using muskrats for study. So I'm thinking those unfortunate muskrats were used for some kind of viral testing—probably to measure burden of disease."

"Meaning how much virus it takes to be pathogenic," my mother said, again from the other room.

I raised an eyebrow at her medical lingo.

"I asked your father a lot of questions over the years," she explained.

Luke smiled, and for the first time in a long while, my mother did, too. "Second of all, there are only a few viruses stable enough to use for genetic recombination. From that pool of potentials, you narrow it down based on viruses that can survive —or even thrive—in water. A supervirus is useless if it dies in transit."

"Go on..."

"Ever heard of polyomaviruses?"

"Only in passing. They aren't clinically significant."

"Polyoma loves water. More common in childhood. Has the potential to cause skin cancer—maybe a nasty rash, if engineered correctly."

"Hm."

"It fits," he said.

"It does seem to fit," I said. Even my mother looked intrigued —dare I say hopeful. She hadn't left Lois' side since we'd started sorting through the files.

"I know what you're going to say next," he said.

"Is there a cure?"

"For a supervirus?" He shook his head, and everything about him—his voice, his excitement, his lean, rugged frame—seemed to deflate in the span of a breath. "Not that we can develop in an hour."

We looked across the room at Lois, her lazy blonde curls wet with fever; her small fists tucked under her chin. A cup of now-room-temperature cocoa sat untouched on the coffee table.

"What if there was, though?"

He turned back around, his interest sparked—but not yet ignited. I waited a beat before continuing: "I heard an infectious disease specialist talk last year. He was using antibiotics on certain viral infections to see if they had any effect."

"Antibiotics for a virus? That's like sacrilege in virology."

"I know, but for certain viruses..." I remembered bits and pieces of that lecture, delivered in a dark room after a thirty-hour shift. I kept drifting off to sleep as this man—this lunatic, I thought at the time—talked about viruses and vaccines and antibiotics and broadening our horizons. There were only a few known viruses for which antibiotics seemed to work. Maybe even just one, per my hazy memory.

Polyomaviruses.

Luke held my gaze for a long moment, his eyes ablaze. When I finally spoke, my voice seemed to find him in a deep, distant, magnificent place; a place of hope, and possibility.

"Luke, I think we can save her."

THIRTY-THREE

Fluoroquinolones.

The answer was fluoroquinolones: levofloxacin, ciprofloxacin, moxifloxacin...there were a number of them. Some worked better than others, depending on the indication for use. I didn't know which ones my father stocked in the clinic pharmacy, but my guess was the best and the cheapest, which meant levaquin and cipro. Not the safest medication in kids, which explained why my father had never blindly tried it in the cases last year, but the risk/benefit analysis in this situation swung heavily in its favor. It was our best and only shot.

With my mother's guidance through the woods, we made it to Luke's car in record time. The camouflage remained undisturbed, but that was a small comfort. I had the unsettling feeling that something—maybe everything—would change when we arrived in town.

My mother sat in the back with Lois, while Luke drove and I navigated. He handled those backcountry roads with intense, focused control. We had a plan now. *Hope.* I could see it in his eyes.

The sky had gone nearly black with thunder by the time we turned onto Main Street. Most of the shops looked open, but empty. I saw the sign in the clinic window: CLINIC CLOSED. That hadn't deterred the group of people standing out front.

"Is it safe to go inside?" my mother asked.

"We don't have a choice," I said.

Luke parked the car out back. It didn't matter. There was nowhere to hide in a crowded clinic, and whoever had killed Sheldon would know exactly where to find us.

"We all go," Luke said. "Safety in numbers."

We approached the front door as a group of four. The rain whipped us from all sides, a battering assault on our faces. Luke tucked Lois under his coat as we hurried up to the building.

There were two families in line: the Samsons, including Moira and her three children; and another family-of-four I didn't recognize. All soaked to the bone, all with pale, scared faces. Moira wielded a pair of umbrellas between them, but it didn't do much against a horizontal rain. I looked at the other family: a set of parents and two children. One of the girls pulled her hood back.

My first thought was *sick*. Sick like Lois. Her plump cheeks were a fiery red, her eyelids just starting to blister. I couldn't tell if the weepy wetness of her face was from the scourge on her skin or the trail of her tears.

Jocie Plackett. The name came to me in a thrust of memory, the tentative little girl standing knee-deep in the still, clear waters of Moon Pond.

And Michael Plackett: also sick, very sick. He leaned on his father for support, who probably hadn't carried his son in years. Michael looked about ten; Jocie eight.

I ushered all of them inside. Luke helped me room the Placketts into 2 and Moira into 4. My mother took Lois to Room 3.

Luke and I convened in my office to catch our breaths and make a plan.

"Did you see the Placketts?" I asked.

He nodded. "It makes sense, in a way. They weren't here last year. But Sammy..."

"Sammy didn't swim last year. He was too young." I remembered Moira telling me she planned to take him swimming when the Pond was less crowded. She must have kept her word.

"Aubrey?"

"It's okay," I said, forcing a breath into my lungs. "It's okay. We can help her this time. I'll try the pharmacy; you check the basement."

"What's down there?"

"Overstock. Sometimes expired meds. We'll use whatever we have."

"Your dad keeps expired meds?"

"An expired med is better than no med," I said.

"Okay. Anything else I should grab?"

"IV's. Saline. Tylenol. I'll be in Room 3. Lois gets treated first because she's the sickest. I haven't evaluated Sammy yet—but that's how we'll do it."

"How do you tell who's the sickest?"

Experience, I thought, but it's not like I had that in spades. "I'll make that decision."

We dispersed—Luke to the basement, me to Room 4. I couldn't let Moira sit in that exam room thinking she was about to lose another member of her family.

I entered without knocking. "Moira?"

She sat in the chair by the window, clutching her children as if they were her last tie to humanity. Kyla looked stone-faced, like her mother. Francine was crying. Sammy was either asleep or unconscious, his cheeks and eyes and ears rimmed red.

"Moira," I said again, but she barely looked up.

I took the doctor's stool that occupied the small space between us. She didn't comment on it this time.

"I think we can treat this, Moira. We're getting the medication now—"

"Sammy's the nicest kid I got," she said with a half-sob, half-smile. "He loves those lollipops. Red, he says. Not cherry. He don't understand flavors yet."

I grasped Moira's hands, a gesture of compassion and humanity and *You're fine. It's fine. You're okay now.* A month ago, she would have laughed at that sentiment coming from me. Then again, a month ago, I never would have done it.

"I can't lose another baby," she whispered.

"You won't," I said, and something in her stirred; came alive again.

Hope.

***

After doing what I could to calm the Placketts, I raced upstairs to find the antibiotics. The storm had swallowed the light of day, and the clinic looked like a tomb.

The power was down. No lights, no automated switches. I used the key to gain entry to the file room, and from there, the pharmacy. Neither room had a window, so I had to use a flashlight to meander between the shelves in darkness. The controlled medications required a key-code for entry into the drawer. It was the only electronic mechanism in the whole building.

Fortunately, antibiotics weren't a controlled medication. I found dozens of them in bottles of all shapes and sizes on the *Kill Bugs Shelf*, as my father had dubbed it. Organized alphabetically, the fluoroquinolones should have been easy to find.

Should have been. There was nothing in the small space dedicated to ciprofloxacin. No levofloxacin, either. That was odd. These medications went fast in the winter, but winter had ended months ago. My father would have re-stocked his supply in the spring.

I tried other shelves. Maybe his eccentric sense of organization had gotten the best of him. Maybe he stocked medications wherever there was space.

The closer I looked, the less that seemed to be the case. All the medications were meticulously categorized and alphabetized, exactly as he had done for years. He had taken great care with this room. *Make a mistake on that prescription pad and you can kill somebody*, he said to me on the eve of my intern year. He had put those words into practice, never once making a prescription error in his long career.

I was on my way back to the antibiotics shelf when the hinges creaked, and a soft draft of incoming air teased my ankles.

The door clicked closed.

"Luke?"

I flashed the light on the cabinet in front of me, the only one with an electronic keypad. Opioids. Sedatives. I tapped out the code.

"Luke?" I called out a second time.

Footsteps.

Some instinctive defensive urge kicked in, and I reached into the drawer and fumbled with a syringe. Any vial would do, but the one that ended up in my hands was Fentanyl. A hundred times stronger than morphine; deadly in miniscule doses.

I drew it up.

"Who's there?"

The footsteps stopped. I shined the flashlight on the opposite wall, but the beam failed to penetrate the shelves. I was cornered. Two shelves on either side; a wall at my back. No windows. The door was on the opposite side of the room, an impossible distance to cover at any reasonable speed in the dark. I'd trip on a box or glass or—

A white light with the power of a highbeam found my face. I dropped the flashlight but not the syringe. *Don't drop the syringe.*

"Hi, Aubrey."

Her voice had lost its fake, chirpy lilt. No dangling bracelets. No *whatevs* drawling from her lip-glossed lips.

She shifted the light two inches to the left, which gave my eyes the chance to adjust to the sight of a shotgun-wielding Corinne.

"You left this in the closet," she said, waving the gun.

"What are you doing?"

"Didn't think a secretary had the brains for something like this, did you?" Her high-pitched, shrieky voice pierced my ears. "Well, I'm not a secretary. But I looked the part, and that's what they needed."

I thought, *Who's 'they'?* Instead, I said, "Can you put the gun down?"

"I don't think so."

I kept my hands behind my back, using my hips to shield the frantic activity going on back there. The needle was still capped. *Shit.* "What are you doing?"

She shrugged, but the rigidness of the gesture suggested nerves. "I think you've figured most of it out."

"You're a terrorist?"

She snorted. "I'm a trained virologist, just like your boyfriend —except he's a high school bio teacher, and I work for a very sophisticated, very highly-trained group of likeminded individuals."

"Terrorists," I said again.

"That's a really simplistic way of looking at it."

"Sorry," I sneered. No matter what she was, I had to give her credit for two years of hard-earned deception. She had befriended people who, by their nature, resisted other people— my father, included. My father most of all.

"Callihax was the perfect place to launch a pilot study," she said. "Contained environment. Total isolation. No one had a clue what was going on—even your father. Talk about lax security measures."

"I'm not sure what you were expecting in a town of 400 people."

"That's just it. No one expects anything up here. Moon Pond was the perfect incubator for a supervirus. Of course, mortality depended on burden of disease—little kids tend to swallow more water, so, you know..."

"Kids? Little *kids* were your targets?"

Her thin smile iced over. "You don't understand, Aubrey. You doctors never do. Look at healthcare the way it is today. Look at the *population*. You infect people that deserve to die and spare the rest."

"That's called eugenics."

"Exactly. Eugenics and biological warfare go hand-in-hand. You should know that your father played an important part in it. He thought that dinkly little swamp was the problem from the very beginning."

"And you killed him for it."

"As I said, lax security measures. He drank a bad batch of coffee and died."

I imagined her tainting my father's beloved habit with whatever poison she liked best. The sick sadness in my gut reared up like a tidal wave. "And Sheldon?"

"Sheldon was an FBI guy who got in way over his head."

"He said he was commissioned by them to come up here."

She rolled her eyes. "Uh-huh. He did some freelance for the CDC and got interested in this little outbreak. He never figured out what the vector was, but *quarantine*—oh, he was all about quarantine and isolation. Which worked out fine for me—easier to 'contain' the situation, if you know what I mean."

She set the high-powered flashlight on the shelf and produced two white bottles from her pocket. "Looking for these?"

"I don't know what you're talking about."

"Of course you do. Come *on*, Aubrey. Relish your little victory here. You were right about the fluoroquinolones—what good is a supervirus without a 'miracle cure' to manipulate the masses? Polyoma was the perfect bug."

I wasn't relishing anything at the moment, not with a shotgun aimed at my face. I watched her dump the bottles in the utility sink and crush the pills with the butt of the shotgun. The she turned on the faucet. "Sorry. I think that was the last of your levo/cipro stash."

She raised the barrel again. "Oh, and Luke's dead. Sorry about that, too."

My knees buckled, but she interpreted this as a charge.

"Don't," she said.

"Why not? You've killed everyone I care about. You terrorized a defenseless town. I'm the failure everyone expected me to be."

She peered at me down the sight of the barrel. There was no hesitation in the way she held that gun. No nervous jitters. Just a cold, calculating control.

"You wanted to prove yourself, didn't you?" I said. "Like me. You volunteered. You wanted to be a part of something big."

"I'm not incompetent like you."

"I won't argue with that. But now what? You start shooting people in little Callihax, Maine, and people will notice. That's not sophisticated. It's desperate."

"Do I look desperate?" She tightened her grip on the shotgun.

"Put the gun down. Let's talk this through."

"I'm not stupid, Aubrey."

"You think I want to go back to LA with four dead kids on my conscience? You're right, Corinne. I hate it here. I'm *nothing* here. My career ended before it even began."

"Because you couldn't make a decision to save your life."

"Well, I'm making one now."

She kept the barrel aimed at my head. "Like I said, I'm not stupid."

"We're just two people having a conversation."

"Doesn't feel like it."

"I help you, you help me. I save your career, you save mine."

Something in her stare gave way, not so much sympathy as curiosity. "How?" she asked.

"I can't talk with that gun in my face."

"Don't care."

"*Look* at me." I gave her a moment to look at what could generously be described as my thin, harried, non-threatening presence. "You're really that afraid of me?"

I had read her correctly. She eased the gun downward.

In the space of a fractionated second, I made my move. The syringe behind my back came out in a wide arc, up and in, finding the soft flesh of her neck before she could even scream. Was it a lethal dose? Possibly. Probably. I didn't care.

The fentanyl took effect in seconds. She sagged in my arms, unconscious before she hit the floor. I looped the shotgun over my shoulder and dragged her out the door, down the stairs. One thing we had plenty of was surgical tape. I bound her ankles and wrists and left her in the downstairs office. Then I forgot about her, because there were others who needed me. Luke. Lois. Sammy. Moira. Ophelia. Jocie and Michael.

This town—*my* town—needed me.

THIRTY-FOUR

Moira had a new fire in her eyes when I found her in the hallway. "The cellar," she said. "I heard somethin' down there." We started walking that way in a hurry.

"Is Sammy okay?"

"He's with Kyla. She can watch him."

"How about the others? The Placketts?"

"All fine. What the hell happened up there?"

"Corinne tried to kill me."

"The secretary?"

I might have smiled if the circumstances were different. "It's a long story."

"I never trusted that bitch..." she muttered.

The cellar door was closed, the lock jammed. I yanked on it until my knuckles ached.

"Here, let me." Moira nudged me out of the way and kicked the door down. No fuss. No mess. Her boot hit the door and it disintegrated.

I called Luke's name, which echoed back at me. The blinking red lights of the incubator pierced the murky darkness. I decided this would be my last trip into a cellar for a while.

"Luke!"

Moira grabbed a flashlight and swept the stairs with it. I braced myself for the sight of another body, but there was only empty space, dusty and dank. The equipment down here ran on a separate generator, and the fridges whirred in the silence.

The *micro lab*. Luke would have gone there to look for the overstock.

The glass walls had been shattered, a spectacular array of broken glass that covered the walls, the shelves, the fridges and freezers. Some of the larger shards reflected the yellow beam of Moira's flashlight. Others were rimmed in a dark, curdling liquid...

Luke had collapsed with his back against the incubator, his legs splayed out on the concrete floors. I wasn't sure which had taken the hit first: the glass walls, or Luke. Whatever had happened here, it had transpired quickly and messily. Blood on the walls, floor, everywhere. *His* blood.

I inhaled; processed; reacted. The memory of Jedediah Walsh flashed in front of my eyes, then faded. I could do this. I *would* do this.

Airway. Breathing. Circulation.

Breathe.

I pushed the glass away and knelt next to him. He had a pulse. Thready, but it was there. Breathing shallow and fast, his body starved for oxygen. *Where was all the blood coming from?* Abdomen. *How fast?* Fast. *How much?* Too much.

"We need saline," I said to Moira. "As many bags as you can handle. Blood, too. O-negative. Do you understand what that means?"

She nodded. "What else?"

"An IV kit with a big bore. As big as you can find. Look for 14-gauge on the package."

"Is he gonna make it?"

"I don't know."

The wound was deep, oozing thick, black blood from a jagged slice in the skin. The glass had probably nicked his liver and maybe more. I shoved my hands against his abdomen with the full force of my weight. Pressure wouldn't save him, but it would buy him time. He needed a copter like the kids upstairs.

I didn't realize he was speaking until his left hand grabbed my arm. "Aubrey," he heaved.

"You're fine," I said, forcing a smile that came from a place of total despair. "You're okay."

"I'm glad you think so." When he tried to inhale, his face paled with the effort, and in that moment, he looked like he might never take a breath ever again.

"I do," I said. "I'm not going to let you die."

He tried to move his arm again, but it flopped at his side. He tried a third time.

Then I saw it—a clear bag, no larger than my hand, connected to a piece of tubing. The label on the front read, *Levofloxacin.* Expired one month ago, but still a perfectly good antibiotic. My mother knew how to place an IV. She could administer a dose to each of those four children. Not enough to cure the disease, but we could get more. We could turn things around...

"Luke." I tried to shake him awake. "*Luke.*"

Moira found me trying to rouse him with a sternal rub. I hooked up the IV and poured blood into him—one pint, two, three...as many as we had. Saline, too.

I put the antibiotics in Moira's hand. "Take this," I said. "Tell my mother to hook it up, get it running. There's enough there for each child."

"What is this?"

"Something Luke was willing to die for."

For a moment, I wasn't sure what Moira would do. I wouldn't have blamed her for taking the antibiotics and doing whatever had to be done to save Sammy, to salvage every minute she possibly could. Instead, she bent down, put her hands under Luke's ankles, and told me to grab his arms. "We can carry him," she said. "Up we go."

Broken glass crunched underfoot as we stole through the basement. The bags of blood and saline rested in Luke's lap while we took the stairs one by one, slow and steady. Amazing what adrenaline could do. We carried all 200 pounds of him as if he weighed nothing at all.

My mother had taken charge of the ground floor, but she wasn't alone; Jim Ranson had materialized in the waiting room with plastic toys at his feet, a pistol in one hand, and a handcuffed Corinne in the other. "At your service," he said to me, as serious as I'd ever heard him. "Just sorry I couldn't be here earlier."

With Jim's help, we lay Luke on the waiting room chairs, using lampshades to hang the blood. I squeezed the bags, tried to run it faster. His heart thrummed in the silence, some 150 beats a minute to keep up with the demand. *It won't be enough.*

A small, but strong hand found my shoulder. My mother knelt down in front of me, a calming presence in a swarm of chaos. She waited until I looked up.

"It's going to work," she said.

I nodded, not quite believing her but wanting to believe her. Over her shoulder, the Placketts and the Samson kids had gathered in the waiting room, and it roused me somehow.

"The dose...for the antibiotics. It's just a guess—"

"I've got everything together in Room 4," she said, and in that moment, I relished her even, unshakable tone. "Don't worry about us. You need to get Luke out of these woods—"

"I can't save him," I said, hating the truth in those words. My voice trembled, then broke. "There's no way out of here."

"What do you mean?" Moira asked.

"The roads are blocked."

"Then you try another," my mother said.

"Luke *did* try. We're stranded."

Moira and my mother shared a look, an entire conversation transpiring in the silence. At last my mother said, "We aren't stranded." Moira nodded.

She took a paper towel off the reception desk and scrawled a makeshift map that looked like hieroglyphics. Then she handed it to me.

"See this here? It's Rubin's place on Bowtie Hill. Do you remember that old road down to Cagey's quarry?"

I vaguely remembered it, but vague would have to do. "Yes," I said.

"You take that north, all the way to Carlton's Creek. From there, turn left until you can't go anymore."

"What's there?"

"The narrowest crossing in these parts. You'll have to ford it."

Ford the river? That sounded like something out of Oregon

Trail: treacherous, unrealistic, and almost always deadly. My games had always ended on a river.

"Mom—"

"You know who lives on the other side, don't you?"

I nodded as the distant memory of my mother's family took shape in my mind. Will, Jacqueline, and my uncle, a man whose face I didn't remember, but the sheer brutality of his frame had stuck with me. Ademar Rienne.

"They won't remember me."

"They will," my mother said. "Family always remembers."

Moira nodded. It occurred to me then that we were family, too; Will's death hadn't changed that. "Ademar'll get you to St. Georges across the border," she said.

"That's two hours away."

"Not if Ademar takes you." She took the map my mother had drawn and placed it in my bloodied hand. "You did this, Aubrey. You fought for my boy; you gave us hope, something we never had last year. This town thanks you for that. *I* thank you for that."

Maybe it wasn't about promises. *Your cancer will go away. You won't have any side effects to this terrible drug. You will one day be young and healthy and whole again.* Moira knew I couldn't promise her anything. I couldn't promise *anyone* anything. Because as a doctor, I wasn't playing God. I was doing my best, fumbling around in the dark, making decisions that sometimes turned out to be the wrong ones.

And maybe that was okay. I thought about these woods, about the scope and shadow of a forest that knew no bounds. Twelve million acres of aspen and pine and uninhabited nature. We might not make it. In medicine, I had that thought a lot, but you tried anyway. You always tried.

Moira helped me lift Luke off the chairs—as did my mother, and Jim Ranson, and then, somehow, the entire town. They stood outside in the pouring rain, soaked but ready. I would never know how word had reached them. Moira, maybe. My mother, perhaps. I wondered if in some way, these private, devoted souls had simply sensed a neighbor in need.

Dirk Samson emerged from the masses and lifted Luke into the cab of his truck. "Rienne's place," Moira said.

I climbed into the cab, holding the bags of blood in one arm and Luke in the other. I sang soft songs in his ear because he missed that about me, and in some small way, I missed that about myself; and I prayed to St. Christopher, the patron saint of travelers, because he had taken us this far.

When it came time to cross the river, I would carry him. With the people of the North Woods behind me, I felt as though I could carry the world.

THIRTY-FIVE

Dirk Samson drove like he lived: with utter, wild abandon. There was a rifle slung over the front seat and a crucifix hanging from the rearview mirror. The interior smelled like sawdust and years, a lot of years, maybe more years than I'd been alive. His Ford pick-up reminded me of those blown-out cars in post-apocalyptic movies.

The trees didn't exactly part for Dirk Samson, but he navigated roads I never knew existed. Not roads so much as dirt trails, scarred over by snow, and wind, and decades of disuse. We passed the occasional cabin, but never a house. Certainly no signs pointing the way. I tried not to think about what would happen if he made a wrong turn.

The blood loss had taken its toll on Luke. Six bags of blood gone already, and almost as much saline. His blood pressure was probably in the toilet, which would have sounded the alarms and sent everything into a controlled panic in my hospital's ICU. The silence of Dirk's Ford provided a false sense of calm.

As this thought crossed my mind, Dirk slammed on the brakes just in time to avoid a hulking moose. It moseyed on into the woods, but Dirk didn't start the engine up again.

"We're here," he said, which looked like *nowhere*. The rainy haze made the forest indistinct; limitless. Dirk helped me lift Luke out of the backseat, but I didn't know where he intended to go from here. I couldn't see more than fifteen feet in front of me.

"River's down this way," he said.

A wiry one-fifty and not an ounce more, Dirk loaded Luke over his shoulder as if the guy weighed nothing at all. I carried two bags of saline knowing that if we ran out, Luke would die.

The river announced its presence right with a sudden spray of rushing water. In a downpour as heavy as the one these Maine skies had unleashed, I couldn't even see the opposite shore. It could have been twenty feet; it could have been two-hundred. Dirk carried Luke by the shoulders while I took his ankles. He was dead weight, but the water would do the rest.

"This is where we cross," he said. "Careful now."

The water was frigid, a slap of ice against my bare skin. Feet, ankles, knees, waist...we waded into the current until the water very nearly touched my chin. Dirk never stumbled; never faltered. He walked with the current in the ways his ancestors had surely done, as ingrained in him as the instinct to breathe. I coughed and choked and walked on my tip-toes to stay above the surface, and all the while, I thought of my father.

With the water rushing into my eyes, nose, and mouth, I fought for bits and pieces of air. With Luke's life literally in our hands, Dirk couldn't afford to worry about me—he just had to trust me, as I trusted him. We never fought the current, even though it fought us. We walked on. Step by step, until the river released us on the other side. I fell forward and got right up again, spitting water until the irony taste of blood laced my tongue.

A few more steps, and my legs gave out. A massive hand landed on my shoulder, followed by a voice I hadn't heard in twenty years.

"Aubrey Rienne," he said. "All grown up and lookin' like your mother."

I looked up into the coal-grey eyes of Ademar Rienne. He wasn't large so much as tremendous, a man so solidly built he could easily be mistaken for a bear, even in daylight. He shook Dirk's hand, loaded Luke onto his bulky shoulders, and gave me room to get back on my feet and climb the hill to his truck—no, his horse.

***

Ademar Rienne had three horses—all brute, massive

stallions, who knew these woods better than any man who had ever lived here. We made the Canadian border in just over an hour, a journey that should have taken three in the best of circumstances. I started to ask about passports, but Ademar held up a hand.

Sirens. Still a ways off, but coming closer. We were nearly there.

We tied up the horses and trekked a quarter-mile more through dense underbrush. I insisted on bearing part of Luke's weight, even though Ademar didn't need my help. He needed to know I was here. Fighting for Luke. Willing him to survive.

"There." Ademar pointed through the trees. A lone ambulance awaited us on the shoulder of a narrow road—a Canadian road, with signs in French instead of English.

We ran the last stretch, soaking wet and drenched in mud, like three ghouls. The paramedics intercepted us with shouts and orders, all uttered in a language I hadn't spoken since childhood. But somehow, as if summoning the depths of my subconscious, I understood.

Airway...

Breathing...

Circulation...

Large puncture wound to right upper quadrant...

Hypovolemic shock...

Initiate massive transfusion protocol...

As the paramedics loaded Luke into the ambulance, Ademar stood back—hands in his pockets, his reddish hair slick with sweat and rain.

"Ademar—"

"Don't thank me," he said. "Just come 'round sometime."

"I will," I said.

With a final, grateful nod, I left Ademar on that lonely Canadian road and climbed into the ambulance at Luke's side. The noise and chaos and blaring alarms comforted me, in a way. I was used to this. I trusted it.

I took Luke's hands and hoped somehow, somewhere, he did,

too.

EPILOGUE:
SIX MONTHS LATER

I liked my hovel, but I wanted a view.

Rearranging my father's office had required months of careful, if not reverent, deliberation. My mother wanted to replace all the furniture, since most of it was older than I was. The sofa and bookcases did eventually go to new homes. Some of her artwork was donated as well—"Your father never cared for art except the little watercolors you brought home from school"—and replaced with the creations of my younger patients. By Christmas, my father's crusty old quarters had experienced a resurgence in color, comfort, and personality. Most importantly, the desk went back over by the window.

I was finishing up my fifty-page report on NWE when all hell broke loose at around 2 P.M.—an expected, welcomed hell. Lea Morceau had a nosebleed. Tommy Hess knocked out another tooth. George Abernathy couldn't remember if he needed to take his water pills once, twice, or three times a day, so he'd decided to stop taking them altogether. Now he couldn't breathe all that well and his shoes didn't fit.

"Poor George," Joe said. "I think he needs a manual."

Joe was a fantastic resident—young and enthusiastic and lovely with patients—but he would be going back to Boston in a month. Then we'd get somebody new, and the cycle repeated itself every eight weeks. I liked how the rural medicine elective had worked out so far.

"I'll talk to him," I said. "How about the nosebleed? Is that under control?"

"I packed it. Just waiting to see if she's comfortable to go home."

"And...who was it? Tommy?"

"Tommy Hess knocked out his front tooth."

"Again?"

"He says somebody punched him."

"Do you believe him?"

"Well, his story is pretty involved—"

"Let me guess. Somebody called his sister a bitch/slut/cow and he stood up for her and got punched."

"I think it was 'whore,' actually."

"He needs a new story."

Joe cracked a smile. It took time to learn these things. I still didn't know everyone's story, but I knew everyone's name. That mattered. Everyone called me Aubrey, but I'd come to accept that. My father would always be Doc. I would always be Aubrey.

We passed the CDC guy in my old office. I kind of missed Sheldon with his nautical ties and irritating chuckle, and I said as much at his funeral. CDC-guy had no sense of humor whatsoever. He toiled over the files like a man in chains.

"Hi, Rod," I said.

"Hello." He went back to the files. *Better get used to it*, the CDC Director had told me the week after it all happened. *He's gonna be there for the long-haul.*

I didn't mind. It brought funding and attention and a subtle sense of security to a town that sorely needed it after a bioterrorism attack. The CDC agreed with my assessment that Callihax had served as a pilot study for a parvo-polyoma-supervirus, which thrived in water and targeted children. Perpetrator unknown, but thought to be associated with a major terrorist network based out of Eastern Europe. Levofloxacin was curative. Even so, NWE was a powerful biological weapon. With the right amount of planning and a shortage of levofloxacin, the virus could cause worldwide devastation.

Hence the CDC-guy, Rod. I wasn't relying on Rod to save the world, but he had a purpose here. I hoped he stayed in that office for a good long while.

"That it?" I asked.

"Not quite. Ophelia Sinclair's in 1, and you've got a follow-up in 4."

"Who's the follow-up?"

"Uh...I didn't get the name."

"Don't worry about it. Why don't you deal with Tommy's anger issues and we'll call it even."

"Deal." Joe gave one of his faux-salutes and disappeared into Room 3. I liked him. Maybe he'd come back to the North Woods someday and beg me for my job.

Eh, probably not. I'd traded my temporary license in for a permanent one, and after moving out of my LA apartment, resigning from a job I'd never worked, and making yet another overnight stop at the Sanderson place, it felt right. I'd turned the mill into my home, with better lighting and a more functional toilet. My mother dropped by occasionally to make hot cocoa and a salty meal. At night, I left the kerosene lamps burning bright. The North Woods didn't scare me so much anymore, but the night always would.

I stopped in Room 1 first. Ophelia bobbed her five-month-old son on her knee. Most new mothers wore exhaustion like a second skin, but not Ophelia. She had taken to motherhood with surprising ease. She gave me one of her stern, I've-been-here-for-over-10-minutes harumphs as I walked in, but she softened up quickly.

"Hi, Ophelia," I said. "How's your little one?"

"Oh, he cries and poops and eats like a friggin' champ."

"Good."

"I think he's getting a little chubby."

I checked his length and weight while Ophelia appraised the numbers. "Nope, he's doing just fine. Perfect, really."

"Well, good. I'm doing my best."

"You're doing great."

"You mean that?"

"I do."

She smiled. "Well, thanks. You did a good job delivering him. I know I'm kinda high-maintenance..." She took a breath. "Anyway, I appreciate it. You're good to me."

"I'm doing my best, Ophelia," I said softly. "Just like you."

She watched while I examined her happy baby boy. Ophelia prattled on as she always did, and this time she talked about her husband's homecoming from overseas next week. She'd bring him by, she said. She wanted him to meet me, and to be honest, I kind of wanted to meet the guy that had snagged Ophelia.

We agreed on a follow-up appointment in two weeks—Ophelia continued to insist on more intense scheduling than necessary, but I'd accepted that—and I wished her a Happy New Year. Next stop was Tommy Hess. No, Joe had that under control. Lea was on her way out the door. George Abnernathy would take hours.

I'd swing by Room 4 and tell whoever it was this really wasn't the time for a walk-in. Maybe tomorrow. Or the next day. Clinic in Callihax was always hit-or-miss, like every ER and Urgent Care clinic in the United States. No rhyme or reason to it.

I knocked twice, then entered.

Fatigue turned to a sultry nervous energy at the sight of Luke Ainsley in my procedure room. He had Lois by the hand and a smirk on his face.

"Hello, Dr. Lane."

"Why, hello."

I bent down to meet Lois at eye-level. Luke had her in more layers than most little girls' bodies could handle, but she took it in stride. "Hi, Lois," I said.

"Hi."

She never said very much, but the words she did say were deliberate and meaningful. The depth of her expression and the intensity of her gaze made them even more so.

"For you." She smiled shyly as she handed me a brown paper-bag.

"Uh oh," I said, feigning alarm. "What's this?"

Her smile widened. My prize was a peanut-butter-and-jelly sandwich, a banana, and shortbread cookies. The cookies were a little misshapen, but the PB&J looked divine.

"Lois made the sandwich," Luke said. "I made the cookies."

"Well, it's a perfect sandwich." I tucked Lois' scarf under her chin. "You're very talented, Lois. Thank you."

"You're welcome."

Luke frowned. "No compliments on the cookies, huh?"

"Is that what they are? I couldn't really tell..."

Lois giggled.

"Harsh," Luke teased.

"It was nice of you to bring me lunch. I wish I had time to eat —"

"Joe's got it covered," Luke said.

"What did you do, pay him?"

"Maybe."

"You're so bad," I teased.

"I know, but we were desperate." He swept Lois off her feet, which made her squeal with delight. "Right, Lo?"

"Yep," she said, still laughing.

"So," he said. "Do we have a date?"

"How could I ever say no to you?"

"You can't."

Lois grabbed the brown bag and ran out the door. "I guess she's hungry," Luke said.

"I guess so," I said.

He eased the door closed. *So much for the patient-doctor relationship.* I let him come a little closer. I *wanted* him closer. He drew the blinds.

"I know what you're thinking," he said.

"That I have professional standards?"

"Well, I'm not technically a patient."

The look in his eyes made me blush. The last six months had changed him, just as it had changed everyone in Callihax. In some ways, he was more vulnerable; in others, stronger. He was more than Lois' uncle; he was her family now, as much her father as any man had ever been.

Some might say that our relationship had changed, too, but I knew better. Luke and I had come full circle, the kind of story that takes its twists and turns until finally, somehow, it simply settles into place. Two lovesick teenagers under a red-green sky; two tentative adults finding their way back to each other. We were the same. We were different. We were simple and complicated and happy.

"I would love to have lunch with you," I said, and kissed him softly; almost chastely, an invitation for more. He snaked his hand behind my back and drew me flush against him, our hearts beating in tandem. His lips found the soft skin under my jaw. "That's a very wise decision," he murmured.

"I've been making more of those these days," I said, breathing harder now. Faster. Inappropriate for a doctor's office, to say the least.

"I love you," he said.

He hadn't said those words to me in twelve years, but it felt just as true. It *was* just as true. I started to say as much, but the door swung open. I backed up, smoothed my white coat. Nothing to be done about the fire in my cheeks.

Lois poked her head in the room. She dangled the brown-bag in the air.

"I'm hungry," she said.

"Me, too," Luke said, all gruff and stern and trying to hide the huskiness in his voice. "Let's go." He gestured toward the door. "After you, Aubrey."

"No," Lois said.

"No?" We both said it at the same time.

Lois patted the giant pockets of my white coat, which had gained some order in the past few months. Fewer papers. Less chaos. The St. Christopher medal was still in there, though.

Lois smiled—a bright, lovely, little-girl smile. Her eyes danced with it.

"This is Dr. Lane."

Author's Note:
Thank you for reading!

I also write under the pen name Claire Kells
(www.clairekellsbooks.com):

National Parks Mystery series
VANISHING EDGE
AN UNFORGIVING PLACE

GIRL UNDERWATER

Made in the USA
Middletown, DE
03 May 2023